The beautiful trop~~i~~ predators, from high ~~...... ~~ ~~bottom~~-dwelling criminals. When the body of an island patrician is found in a warehouse fire, tracking his killers will bring openly gay Honolulu homicide detective Kimo Kanapa'aka into contact with many of those predators, natural and otherwise. Kimo and his detective partner Ray Donne dig deep into the history of Hawai'i as the islands were teetering on the brink of statehood in order to understand the victim, his killer, and their motives.

# MLR PRESS AUTHORS

Featuring a roll call of some of the best writers of gay erotica and mysteries today!

| | | |
|---|---|---|
| Derek Adams | Z. Allora | Maura Anderson |
| Simone Anderson | Victor J. Banis | Laura Baumbach |
| Helen Beattie | Ally Blue | J.P. Bowie |
| Barry Brennessel | Nowell Briscoe | Jade Buchanan |
| James Buchanan | TA Chase | Charlie Cochrane |
| Karenna Colcroft | Michael G. Cornelius | Jamie Craig |
| Ethan Day | Diana DeRicci | Vivien Dean |
| Taylor V. Donovan | S.J. Frost | Kimberly Gardner |
| Kaje Harper | Alex Ironrod | DC Juris |
| Jambrea Jo Jones | AC Katt | Thomas Kearnes |
| Sasha Keegan | Kiernan Kelly | K-lee Klein |
| Geoffrey Knight | Christopher Koehler | Matthew Lang |
| J.L. Langley | Vincent Lardo | Cameron Lawton |
| Anna Lee | Elizabeth Lister | Clare London |
| William Maltese | Z.A. Maxfield | Timothy McGivney |
| Tere Michaels | AKM Miles | Robert Moore |
| Reiko Morgan | Jet Mykles | William Neale |
| N.J. Nielsen | Cherie Noel | Gregory L. Norris |
| Willa Okati | Erica Pike | Neil S. Plakcy |
| Rick R. Reed | A.M. Riley | AJ Rose |
| Rob Rosen | George Seaton | Riley Shane |
| Jardonn Smith | DH Starr | Richard Stevenson |
| Christopher Stone | Liz Strange | Marshall Thornton |
| Lex Valentine | Haley Walsh | Mia Watts |
| Lynley Wayne | Missy Welsh | Ryal Woods |
| Stevie Woods | Lance Zarimba | Mark Zubro |

*Check out titles, both available and forthcoming, at*
*www.mlrpress.com*

# NATURAL

# PREDATORS

*A Mahu Investigation*

## NEIL S. PLAKCY

**mlr**press
*www.mlrpress.com*

Published by
MLR Press, LLC
3052 Gaines Waterport Rd.
Albion, NY 14411

Visit ManLoveRomance Press, LLC on the Internet:
www.mlrpress.com


Editing by Kris Jacen

Print format: ISBN# 978-1-60820-840-1
ebook format also available

Issued 2013

# ACKNOWLEDGEMENTS

A big mahalo nui loa to Cindy Chow, whose advice and comments on life in the Aloha State have inspired me and helped me avoid so many mistakes -- though any remaining errors are my fault, not hers.

I have learned so much from work with the members of my critique group and I am always grateful to Sharon Potts, Christine Kling, Christine Jackson and Miriam Auerbach for their excellent advice.

For their personal support I am grateful to my mother, to Eliot Hess and Lois Whitman, Fred Searcy, Jackie Conrad, Jose Macia, Steve Greenberg, Eileen Matluck, Andrew Schulz, Vicki Hendricks, Elisa Albo, and Lourdes Rodriguez-Florido. Gratitude is due to my other colleagues in the English department at Broward College's South Campus for their encouragement, and to the college's Staff and Professional Development program, which has allowed me to attend conferences and conventions.

For professional advice I want to thank Wayne Gunn as well as my fellow members of Mystery Writers of America.

Mahalo as well to Laura Baumbach, Kris Jacen and the staff at MLR Press for all their help in bringing the Mahu Investigations out in new editions and to all the fans who have written to me to say how much Kimo and his stories have meant to them.

To Marc, once again. I still can't help falling in love with you.

"I know I'm not supposed to feel this way, Kimo," Mike said. "But I can't help it if I do."

We were going around in circles, talking about having a child enter our lives. Neither of us knew what the right answer to the question was, but we both had our own ideas.

"I just don't understand why you feel the way you do," I said.

"Do the math. I'm an only child. I have a couple of cousins on my mom's side back in Korea. Because the only Korean I know is *hello, how are you*, and *where's the bathroom*, and they speak about that much English, I can barely talk to them."

Mike fits the cliché of tall, dark and handsome—he's six-four, with the best features of his Korean mother and his Italian-American father. His black hair is thick, with a stray curl that dangles over his forehead. He got up from the sofa and started pacing. That's never a good sign.

"All I've got on my dad's side is my cousin Daniela and her family back on Long Island. We're Facebook friends and she shares pictures of her kids. But that's not exactly a close connection."

He stopped pacing and looked at me. "After my parents go, all I'll have is you."

"And I don't understand why that's not enough."

I could see the pain in his eyes.

"Because of what we do. The risks we take. Suppose something happens to you. I'll be all alone."

Mike was a fire investigator, and I was a homicide detective. He walked into burning buildings, and I chased bad guys with knives and guns. The danger inherent in our jobs was a big reason why I was reluctant to commit to fatherhood.

I motioned him back to the sofa next to me. "Come over

here. Sit."

He sat, and I put my arm around his shoulders and he leaned against me. "In the first place, if anything happens to me you have my family. My brothers, my nieces and nephews. They're your ohana now, too. They'll look after you."

The technical definition of *ohana* is family, but to Hawaiians it means much more—a sense of community, of mutual caring and responsibility. When my family brought Mike into our ohana it was more than just accepting our relationship; he became as good as a son to my parents, as good as a brother to mine.

"It's not the same as having a kid of our own."

We had been talking about the issue for a week by then, after our friend Sandra Guarino, a lesbian attorney in a long-term partnership, asked if we would consider helping her get pregnant.

"No, it's not. But even if one or both of us donated sperm, and Sandra delivered a baby, there's no knowing whether that kid would be there to love you and take care of you in your old age. And expecting that is a lousy reason to bring a kid into the world."

Which brought us right back where we started. Mike wanted a child and I didn't. That was the bottom line. So far neither of us had been able to change the other's mind.

I wasn't opposed to children. I love my nieces and nephews. But becoming a dad was a huge step, even if Sandra and her partner Cathy were willing to take on the full responsibility for raising the child.

Sandra had mentioned the possibility of one or both of us donating sperm nearly a year before, but she wasn't ready to get pregnant. Things had come to a head about six months before, when Sandra and Cathy invited us to dinner at their house.

They had moved out of their condo in Waikiki to a house a few blocks up Aiea Heights Drive from ours. It was nice having them close, even if we didn't make a baby together; my best friend, Harry Ho, and his wife and family lived in the neighborhood, too.

Sandra not only practiced law for one of the island's most prominent firms, she donated her time to a dozen LGBT causes, including the Hawai'i Gay Marriage Project, which was still struggling to legalize marriage for us. Cathy was a delicate half-Japanese woman who ran the gay teen center in Waikiki. She was the more maternal of the two, but some medical problem kept her from having children.

We moved out to the lanai after dinner. Cathy brought coffee and chocolate cake out for us, and Mike and I sat back in comfortable chairs looking at the dark, wooded slopes of Keaiwa Heiau State Park. "We're getting ready to move forward," Sandra said. "With having a baby."

"Oh," I said.

"We've decided to harvest Cathy's eggs and have them implanted in my womb," Sandra said. "I'll carry the baby, then Cathy's going to quit her job and stay home with him or her."

I looked over at Mike. He was paying close attention to everything Sandra said.

"We have a lot of options for sperm donation," Sandra continued, "but you guys are our first choice. Our doctor can take sperm from either one of you or both of you, if that's what you want."

Cathy leaned forward. "It's called using a directed donor. There are lots of hoops to jump through—the donors have to be tested for all kinds of disease, and the sperm has to be frozen for six months before it can be used. And there's no guarantee that it will even be usable after the freezing process."

"We'll pay all the expenses of the procedures," Sandra continued. "I'll draw up a document outlining the rights and responsibilities of all parties. Cathy will adopt the baby and we'll be his or her legal parents. But we'd like a father to be part of the situation, and we can work out all the details of visitation and so on."

"It's a lot to take in," I said.

"We think you're both smart and strong and handsome, and

either of you would make a great sperm donor, assuming you pass all the tests," Cathy said. "And both of you would be great dads."

"How soon do you need an answer?" Mike asked.

"We recognize we're asking for a lifetime commitment," Cathy said. "And you shouldn't take that lightly. What we were thinking was…"

Sandra stepped in to get pragmatic. "Here's the deal. Let's say you take a couple of months to think about it, and then neither of you pass the health test. We've lost that time. Or say you pass the test, and you donate, but then six months later the sperm can't be used. Or by that time you change your minds. It's a cliché, I know, but I have a biological clock, and the sooner I have this baby the better its chances are for a healthy, safe birth."

"This isn't exactly news, Kimo," Mike said, turning to me. "We talked about this last year."

I nodded. "Give us a couple of days," I said. "Then we'll get back to you."

Mike and I talked about it in the car on the way home. The next morning we continued to talk before work, and that evening over dinner. "I want to start the ball rolling," Mike finally said. "Get tested and see if we pass. At least that much. It's not fair to Cathy and Sandra to keep them hanging if there's something that prevents us from being donors."

"What if one of us passes and the other doesn't?" I asked.

He shrugged. "We'll figure that out if and when it happens."

I wasn't thrilled, but it was clearly something Mike wanted to do, so I went along. He scheduled us for testing at the clinic, and then a week later we had the results. We were both good to go.

Before we called Sandra and Cathy to give them the news, we sat in our living room with Roby, our golden retriever, sprawled at our feet. "What do you want to do?" I asked.

"I want to donate. Let them put the sperm on ice for six months, and during that time we can decide if we want them to use it."

"What if the six months passes, and we decide the answer's no?" I asked. "Wouldn't that be worse than just stalling until we're sure?"

"You heard Sandra. Her clock is ticking."

"Yeah, but it's not all about her. It's about you and me, too. Do we want to be fathers?"

"I do," Mike said.

I looked at him. We had been through a lot together—falling in love, a tortured breakup, getting back together and learning to trust one another. Pile on coming out issues, alcohol problems, sex addiction, family drama and the stress of two demanding jobs. I knew that I loved Mike, and that he loved me, and that between us we could get through anything life threw at us—even dirty diapers and rebellious teenagers.

"Then I do, too," I said.

We called Sandra and Cathy and gave them the news. "But we're taking this one step at a time, right?" I asked. "No commitments until the final squirt of the turkey baster?"

Mike elbowed me. "We've been talking, too," Sandra said. "You're our only choice for directed donors. If you say no today, or in six months, we'll make a withdrawal from the sperm bank. So all we're doing is waiting out the quarantine period, and that gives us some time to think, too."

For the first few days after the donation, I was very aware of the days ticking away. But then life got in the way, and the deadline slipped to the back of my mind. I knew that we'd have to make a decision in March, but back then it seemed far away. By the time of the warehouse fire, I'd almost forgotten that the clock had almost run out.

I was awake first that morning, taking Roby out for his opportunity to sniff the messages left for him by other dogs and respond to them. As I got back to the house, I heard my cell phone ring, almost simultaneously with Mike's.

My best friend since childhood, Harry Ho, is a computer geek, and he taught both of us how to customize our ringtones. The one I'd chosen for the police dispatcher was a snippet of the theme song for *Hawaii Five-O*—the original series. Mike was the only fire department investigator for his district, so he was always on call, and the tone he had chosen for fire department dispatch was a piece of the class Doors song *Light My Fire*. When I heard both phones ringing in tandem, I knew we were in for trouble.

Mike and I both scrambled for our phones. Roby and his leash got tangled between us as we both spoke to our respective departments, reaching for pen and paper to write down what we needed to know. We finished at about the same time.

"Warehouse fire, right?" I asked him.

"Off of Lagoon Drive near the airport?"

I nodded. "I'll feed Roby while you take a shower. Ray and I can't do anything until your guys clear the scene anyway."

Ray Donne was my detective partner. While I poured dry food in a bowl for Roby and topped it with a dollop of canned pumpkin, to keep him regular, I dialed Ray's cell.

He answered groggily.

"Let me guess," I said. "Vinnie kept you up all night."

"You must be a detective," he said. His wife Julie had given birth to a son six months before, and little Vinnie still wasn't sleeping through the night. "You know anything more than I do about this body in the warehouse?"

"Nope. Mike and I both got called at the same time. You want to meet out there in about an hour? They should be finished with the overhaul by then."

"I love it when you throw those fire terms around. Since Julie and I only talk about formula, diapers and baby poop these days, remind me what that is."

"Once they think the fire's out, they send some guys in to search for any remaining cinders, anything that could catch again. Mike supervises that; if they don't do it right, they could remove evidence he needs."

Mike left the house a few minutes later. I ate my breakfast, brushed Roby's teeth and refilled his water bowl. After a quick shower I was on my way down to Lagoon Drive, a long curving street between the airport and Ke'ehi Lagoon.

It was a cool, breezy morning in early March, and I rolled up the flaps on my Jeep for the drive down to the airport. Despite its name, which implied an unspoiled tropical atoll, Lagoon Drive was littered with abandoned warehouses, used car operations and small import-export businesses. A dozen sharp-edged wind turbines roosted along the roof line of a building at the far end of the drive like hungry vultures.

A herd of fire department vehicles clustered ahead of me—three fire engines, a ladder truck, and a couple of SUVs driven by higher brass. The strobing lights were enough to give you an epileptic fit. There were two squad cars as well, the officers directing traffic and securing the area.

I parked my Jeep beside a barbed-wire fence as a plane took off from the reef runway, shaking the air. The ground was barren and sandy; even weeds seemed to have a hard time living in the desolate landscape. And yet, in the other direction I could see a vast expanse of shimmering water and the dark green sentinel of Diamond Head in the distance.

I saw Mike in his yellow fire suit and waved at him. He walked over, shrugging off the oilskin hood. "Two story wood-frame building," he said. "Went up like kindling, especially after the run of dry weather we've had lately."

"Arson?"

"Too early to tell. No obvious incendiary devices. I'll have to analyze the fire load and the spread pattern before I can make a determination. But you know that already."

"It's always nice to hear you explain it one more time. How about the body?"

"How about it?"

"You know what I mean."

"First responders saw a body of an older male on the floor of the building when they entered. He burned to a crisp before they could extinguish the flames, though. I don't know how much you'll get out of the ME."

"What a great start to the morning. Neither of us have much to work with."

"I've got to get back inside. I'll talk to you later."

He turned and walked back toward what remained of the building. The air was heavy with ash, smoke and the distinctive smell of charred human flesh. I pulled out my digital camera and started taking pictures while I waited for Ray to show up.

A couple of abandoned warehouses, wood-framed with sheet metal exteriors, sat in the area around the burned building. One brick warehouse still held the original owner's name and the date 1884 engraved over the lintel, though all its windows were boarded up.

A steady stream of cars passed, going to the few remaining open businesses. Ray pulled up as I was finishing a series of shots, and I related what Mike had told me.

Ray is thirty-four, two years younger than I am, and at five-ten, three inches shorter. His hair is a sandy brown while mine is black, and he's one hundred percent Italian, while my ethnic background is a mix of native Hawaiian, Japanese and *haole*, or white. But even with all those differences, sometimes I felt like he was my brother from another mother. We got each other, and we worked well as a team.

I had a tendency to bull forward when I had an idea or a goal, with a single-minded focus. I was willing to skirt around procedures if I thought the end justified the means.

Ray was patient, mindful of the rules, better able sometimes to see the bigger picture. We argued and sniped at each other, but we also joked around and supported each other through whatever came our way.

The ME's team arrived to take away what remained of the body, collecting bones and shreds of fabric. Ray and I stood nearby, our upper lips coated with VapoRub to dampen the smell. One of the techs held up a piece of metal that looked like some kind of futuristic ray gun—a round ball attached to a curved shaft pierced with holes.

"You may be in luck," he said. "You know what this is?" We both shook our heads. "Looks to me like an artificial hip. See this ball here? That's the joint. The serial number has been damaged in the fire, but I'll bet with some advanced imaging you could get enough out of it to initiate a trace."

Every device implanted into our bodies, like artificial joints, pacemakers and so on, has a serial number, which can be traced to the manufacturer, the doctor who implanted the device, the hospital where it was done, down to the person who received it. If we found a body without any identification and had no missing persons reports to match it to, we could use the appliance to identify the victim.

After the ME's team left, I called dispatch and discovered that the fire had been reported by a pilot on an early morning flight into Honolulu International Airport. So there wasn't some hapless 911 caller to interview.

The smell started to get to us, so Ray and I began canvassing the few businesses in the area. Everyone we spoke to said that they had arrived to work after seven a.m., when the fire department was already on the scene. We ended up back at the fire, as the last engine pulled away. The SUVs and the ladder company were gone, but Mike's truck was still there, as well as a single squad car. The site had been blocked off with crime scene tape.

I pulled up next to Ray. "I'll talk to Mike. Why don't you go back to headquarters and see what you can dig up about the building?"

"Will do." He drove away, and I walked over to where Mike was speaking with the uniformed officer.

"Learn anything more that could be useful?" I asked Mike,

as the uniform walked back to his squad car. He'd be stationed there to watch the site for the rest of his shift, and we'd have to keep coverage at least until we were sure we had retrieved all the available evidence.

Mike looked at his notes. "Found a couple of cigarette butts near the where the victim was. He could have been smoking, and accidentally set the fire."

"What was the fuel?"

Living with Mike, and working cases with him, I'd learned a lot about fire. You need three elements to start a fire—oxygen, heat, and fuel. It was called the fire triangle. There would have been a lot of oxygen inside the big building, and the heat could have come from a cigarette, a match or a lighter.

"Looks like there were boxes of paper files stored inside. Once the fire caught them, the whole place went up fast." Mike's first and primary job was to determine the origin of the fire, which he'd do by tracing patterns made by the flames moving away from the site of ignition. "It looks like as soon as some of those boxes caught, the fire climbed upward to the roof, then spread down the walls."

He promised to call if he found anything interesting, and we kissed goodbye.

Even a year before, that kind of public display of affection would have freaked Mike out. He still felt that his sexual orientation was his own business, not something to parade about, but he'd gotten more comfortable in his own skin the longer he'd been out of the closet.

I took one last walk around the property, hoping for inspiration from the victim's restless spirit. I got nothing, though. The ground was damp and the air stunk of ash and burned flesh. Then, out of the corner of my eye, I saw a flash of movement.

I looked more closely in that direction, toward a row of warehouses, with the old brick one on the end. Nothing.

But I kept staring, and a moment later I saw movement again—a young man with dark hair in a ponytail, wearing a yellow

T-shirt and blue nylon shorts. He looked familiar and I started toward him.

He was walking quickly, darting around the warehouses, and I sped up. I saw him again, in profile, and this time I was sure I knew him. "Dakota!" I called. "Hold on. I want to talk to you."

Dakota was a mainland transplant, a haole kid from somewhere in the flyover states who had moved to Hawai'i with his mother a year before, and started coming to the gay teen youth group I mentored at a church in Waikiki. I had no idea what he was doing in this deserted area so early in the morning, but I wanted to find out.

Dakota picked up his pace, and I ran after him. But he had nearly twenty years on me, a head start, and what appeared to be an intimate knowledge of the warehouse area. I lost sight of him after a few hundred yards. I pulled up, my heart racing, and called one last time. "I just want to talk, Dakota," I called.

A jet took off from Honolulu International and the noise was so loud I couldn't even hear my own footsteps as I walked back to my Jeep. What was he doing out there? Did he have some connection to the warehouse fire, and the death of the artificial hip's owner?

I went over the possibilities as I drove slowly around the warehouse neighborhood, hoping to spot Dakota again. Suppose the victim was a pedophile who had met Dakota for sex out there? The kids from my group were a mixed bag. The lucky few were still living at home, with parents who understood and supported them. Others hid their sexuality from families they knew would disapprove, or who would withdraw financial support.

Still others had run away from home, living on the street or crashing with friends when they could. A few turned tricks for cash. I tried to be whatever they needed—talking to them about safe sex and condom use, about self-defense and emotional empowerment. Our sessions were a free-form mix of basic martial arts, lecture, question and answer, and just talking.

I circled around three times without seeing Dakota. But I

couldn't shake the fear that somehow he had been involved in the arson and the death, and that worried me even more than a case normally did.

I got on Nimitz behind a Toyota SUV with a decal on the back window which read "Future surfer on board." A baby in diapers was hanging ten on a surfboard, his chubby little fingers outstretched in a classic pose.

Ray and I were both stationed at police headquarters downtown as homicide detectives for District 1, which encompassed a big chunk of urban Honolulu, Waikiki, and the airport. It was a very diverse area, from exclusive hotels to flophouses, the glitz of Waikiki to the fading exotic charm of Chinatown, the office towers of downtown to the residential neighborhoods of Makiki and Moiliili. The one thing that linked them was that people committed murders there, and Ray and I tried to bring the bad guys to justice. We didn't always succeed, but we tried, and that was what mattered.

It was close to noon, so on my way in I picked up fast food for myself and Ray. "Thank God for whoever invented the hamburger," he said when I handed his bag to him.

While I ate I checked for messages about our other ongoing cases. When I finished, I turned to Ray.

"I got into the records department online to see who owned the warehouse," he said, talking around his lunch. "The main structure was built in 1950 by a company called F&K Enterprises. It traded hands a few times, and the most recent owner is an offshore company called Inline Imports Ltd. They've been paying taxes on the property but as far as I can tell it hasn't been used for anything for a while."

"Except file storage," I said. "You find anything about this Inline Imports?"

"Not yet. You want to call your guy at the department of business licenses?"

Ricky Koele was a couple of years behind me at Punahou,

the elite private school where my parents sent my brothers and me—which boasted a U. S. president among its alumni as well. I'm sure Barack Obama has given Punahou a lot more to brag about than all three of the Kanapa'aka brothers.

A few years before I had helped Ricky get some justice in the murder of his brother, an addict who had gotten into deep trouble, and since then Ricky had been glad to help me with any research I needed.

"Aloha, brah," I said, when he answered. "Howzit?"

"Pretty good, Kimo. How's life for you?"

"I'd say pretty good, too. Listen, can you do some quick research for me? I'm looking for information on a company called Inline Imports Ltd. They own a warehouse on Lagoon Drive that burned down this morning."

"I heard about that fire on the radio as I was driving to work," he said. "Let me see what I can pull up." He put me on hold so I could listen to KINE 105 FM, the Hawaiian music station. They were playing an oldie by the Brothers Cazimero, the kind of ukulele music I'd grown up listening to, and I remembered school mornings, the radio playing as my mom struggled to get us all ready for school. My brothers, Lui and Haoa, are ten and eight years older than I am, so they were bustling around with the self-importance of teenagers when I was a pesky little brother, getting underfoot as they primped in front of the mirror, lied about homework, and tried to figure out ways to scam my parents out of extra allowance.

Ricky came back on the line as the next song was starting, Keali'i Reichel's sweet tenor. "Can't give you much," he said. "It's an offshore registration in Samoa."

"Samoa? That's weird, isn't it?"

"We're seeing more of them these days. They guarantee confidentiality and don't report income to the U.S. All you need is a local nominee director, shareholder and secretary for the incorporation."

"You have that information?"

"Sorry, you're going to have to request that from the government there."

"Anything else in the file? Local address, banking, anything?"

There was nothing else. Ricky apologized again and I told him it wasn't his fault. "So we've got nothing," Ray said, when I told him.

"There's the serial number from the artificial hip," I said.

"I already called Doc Takayama's office. A couple of the digits are worn down, and it's going to take a while to retrieve them and then trace the number back to the manufacturer."

"I have one more lead." I told Ray about spotting Dakota in the warehouse neighborhood.

"You think he might have had something to do with the arson and the murder?"

"Don't know. But I'm wondering what he was doing out there, and if he saw anything."

"You know where he lives?"

I frowned. It wasn't like we took attendance at those meetings, or had kids sign in with name, phone and email address. It was very casual. I shook my head.

"Last name?" Ray asked.

"Nope."

Ray sighed. "I love a case where you have to work for every lead."

"This may not even be one." I pulled out my phone. "Let me text one of the other kids from the group and see if he knows anything more."

Frankie was one of my long-term regulars. He'd started coming to the group when he was fourteen, a shy chubby boy who liked to wear his hair long and circle his eyes with makeup. He had blossomed over the five years to a full-blown queen who wore plus-size rayon Hawaiian shirts from the fifties, painted his fingernails black, and had multiple, elaborate piercings on his ears and eyebrows.

*U know where I cn find Dakota?* I texted him. He was one of my success stories; he was in his second year at Honolulu Community College, getting his AS in Audio Engineering Technology, with a part-time job processing audio files for computer games.

The answer came back almost immediately. *Dakota n trouble. Cn u meet @ HCC?*

HCC was part of the University of Hawai'i system, with a campus on Dillingham out near the airport. *Sure,* I texted back. *When & where?*

*4:00, outside bldg 13. CU.*

As I put the phone down, our boss came out of the elevator, then crossed the room toward us. Lieutenant Sampson is a big guy, a former minor league baseball player who filled out as he got older. Though he normally favored polo shirts and dark slacks, that morning he was wearing his official uniform.

"My office," he said to us.

Like obedient dogs, we hopped up and followed him across the bullpen to his glassed-in office. He motioned us to the two chairs across from his desk, then sat down. "Meeting with the top brass this morning. We're getting pressure from the Feds to delegate a couple of detectives to the Joint Terrorism Task Force. Your names came up."

The JTTF is a program run by the FBI, where local cops work cases under the auspices of the Bureau. Despite the fancy name, in Honolulu most of the cases involve violent crime and gangs, rather than terrorists.

"Why us?" I asked.

"You've both got a very varied record. You've worked cases that involved Chinese tongs and the Japanese Yakuza, as well as prostitution, illegal immigration, drug smuggling and arson. And Donne has some background with the Feds in Philadelphia."

"Just a couple of cases," Ray said.

"Even so. You guys look like the best candidates."

"You're sending us over there?" I asked.

I wasn't thrilled with the idea. I was happy in District 1, with Sampson as my boss and Ray as my partner. We did good work, bringing bad guys to justice and giving their victims some sense of closure. If we were loaned out to the Bureau, we'd be cogs in the giant Federal machine, learning a whole new set of rules and regulations and working with lots of unknown factors.

"Not yet," Sampson said. "The brass are still negotiating. May be a couple of weeks, may not be for a few months yet. They're going to start with extensive background checks on both of you. Any reason why those shouldn't come out clean?"

"Hold on," Ray said. "So we don't have any choice?"

"This is HPD we're talking about," Sampson said. "You know as well as I do that your assignments are made to accommodate the department's needs, not your own preferences."

When I passed the exam to become a detective, I was assigned to a test project, an effort at community policing that placed homicide detectives at local stations. My partner and I worked out of the Kalakaua Avenue station in Waikiki. At the time, I'd been warned about the job—that it was doomed to failure, and that when it fell apart I'd be screwed because I had no relationship with command.

My life and career went into a tailspin about the same time that project fell apart, and I considered myself damned lucky that Lieutenant Sampson had picked me up for his squad. I had worked for nearly nine months without a partner, until Sampson hired Ray and assigned us to work together. That was three and a half years before. Since then we had become comfortable with each other, complementing each other's skill set, finding the best way to work within the HPD system.

"I'm waiting," Sampson said. "Anything in either of your records the FBI won't like?"

"Every stupid thing I've done is public record," I said. "I went behind my boss's back in Waikiki and shot and killed a man who was later proven guilty of murder. I had sex with a male prostitute, though I didn't know he was being paid, and photos were uploaded to a website. Since taken down, of course. My life has been an open book for the last four and half years."

Sampson nodded, and we both looked at Ray.

"Before I became a cop in Philly, I smoked dope and tried a few other illegal substances. My cousin, who was also my best friend, was killed in a drug deal gone wrong." He looked at Sampson. "Will they investigate Julie, too?"

Sampson nodded. "And Mike."

Ray took a deep breath. "Julie did some dumb things when she was younger, before she met me. But that's all behind her now."

Julie? Dumb things? Ray had never spoken about that to me. I'd always assumed she was a goody-goody, like him. Yeah, I knew he'd dabbled in drugs, back in college, but who hadn't? For the most part, Ray was as honest and upright as … well, it's hard to come up with a good metaphor these days, what with the unmasking of priests, ministers, even Boy Scouts and their leaders.

"I'd rather not talk about them, if that's all right," Ray said. "But if the investigation could hurt her, I don't want to be a part of it."

"Is there a criminal record involved?" Sampson asked.

Ray hesitated.

I spoke up. "A juvenile record that's been sealed?"

Ray nodded.

"That shouldn't be a problem," Sampson said. "Now, tell me about this case you caught this morning."

So as long as our records came up clean, we were going to the FBI. Great.

"There isn't much." I described the warehouse fire, the lack of records for property ownership, and the wait for identification of the serial number on the artificial hip.

"Anything on the arson yet?" Sampson asked.

I shook my head. "Mike's working on it. He'll call when he has something."

"You can get back to work," Sampson said. "Keep me in the loop."

"Weird, huh?" Ray said, as we walked back to our desks.

"Yeah. Sometimes we forget we're just pawns the brass can move around as they like."

"It might be cool," Ray said. "You know, something different. Still protecting and serving, just under a different umbrella."

I wasn't sure how I felt, but I shoved the issue aside to think about later. Ray put together a request to the Samoan government for records on Inline Imports and faxed it over to the Samoan consulate in Waipahu, and we spent the rest of the afternoon catching up on paperwork for old cases.

I resisted my urge to quiz Ray on Julie's juvenile record. It wasn't my business; even though we were partners, we didn't have to share every detail of our personal lives, especially those that were awkward.

Just before four, we hopped in the Jeep to meet Frankie. In Honolulu, we don't use mainland directions like east, west, north and south. Makai is toward the ocean, while mauka means inland, toward the mountains. Diamond Head is in the direction of that extinct volcano, while the opposite is called Ewa, toward a town of the same name.

"You think this kid is involved, don't you?" Ray said, as I drove.

"I hope not. But he's the only lead we have right now, until we get the information from the artificial hip. And if Dakota's in trouble, even if it's not related to the case, I want to see what I can do."

"Dudley Do-Right, that's you."

I had taken a couple of courses at HCC while I was a senior at Punahou, so I knew my way around the campus. The buildings were white concrete, interspersed with kukui and palm trees. The students looked like college kids everywhere—impossibly young, flaunting labels on their clothes like symbols of identity. The only thing to distinguish ours is the polyglot ethnic mix and the fact that nobody wears long pants or long-sleeved shirts.

"Put your eyes back in your head," I said to Ray, as we passed a parade of attractive young women in low-cut blouses and skirts so short it was criminal to charge for the material involved.

"I'm allowed to look," Ray said. "Julie says so. And you wait—your tongue is going to come out as soon as we pass a couple of good-looking guys."

"Don't hold your breath." We passed a couple of cute guys as we parked—but they weren't dressed nearly as provocatively as the girls. They wore oversized T-shirts and shorts that sloped down off their hips. I felt like I was channeling my parents when all I wanted to do was tell them to get belts.

As we neared building 13, we saw Frankie ahead of us, sitting on the steps with his cell phone in his hand, texting someone.

"Hey, brah, howzit?" Ray said to him when he shoved the phone in his pocket.

"I'm doing very well, detective. How are you this fine day?"

I looked at Frankie like he'd dropped in from another planet.

"Hey, he's trying to speak local, so I'm trying to speak haole," Frankie said.

"Everybody on this island is a comedian," Ray said.

"So what's up?" I asked, sitting down next to Frankie. Ray leaned up against a tree. "You know something about Dakota?"

"Just what he told Pua. She was taking Yeet out for a walk around the marina and she saw him."

Pua was a baby dyke who'd been in my gay teen group as long as Frankie. A year before she'd decided she wanted a child, and gotten herself pregnant the old-fashioned way, by a cute boy she knew. She delivered the baby soon after getting her AS degree in diesel mechanics. Now she was working at the Ala Wai Marina, with Yeet in day care.

"What's her baby's name?" Ray asked.

"Yeet," I said. "She heard it on a TV program. It doesn't mean anything, as far as we know." I turned back to Frankie. "So what did he tell Pua?"

"Cops picked up his mom for dealing ice, and they tried to put him in a foster home. But he ran away."

Ice was the smokeable form of crystal meth, the most addictive drug used in the islands. "Why didn't he come to me? I could have helped him."

Frankie shrugged. "You're just one guy, Kimo. Once a kid gets in the system you can't do anything."

"Well, I want to help him now. Where is he?"

"I texted Pua and asked her. She doesn't know. But she thinks he turns tricks in the marina park at night."

I groaned. "When are you kids going to learn?"

Frankie held up his hands. "Don't look at me. I'm not pregnant. I'm not turning tricks. I'm just going to school and working my job."

"I know, Frankie. And I'm so proud of you. I'm not mad at you, but I wish Pua had told me Dakota was in trouble before this."

"He's not like us, Kimo. He's a haole. He hates Hawai'i and he wants to go back to the mainland."

"I know how he feels sometimes," Ray said.

I stood up. "You and Pua both keep a look out. If either of you see him, call or text me right away."

"Is he in trouble?"

"Of course he's in trouble, Frankie. His mom's in jail, he's living on the street, and he's having sex for money."

Ray put his hand on my arm. "What Kimo means is that we want to help Dakota. We don't want to lock him up or put him in a foster home where he's not comfortable."

I nodded. "What Ray said."

Frankie looked at his watch. "I gotta go. I have to get to work. But I'll text Pua."

"We'll stop by the marina on our way back to the office," I said. "Tell her I want to see a picture of Yeet."

Frankie stood up and hugged me. "I wouldn't be here without you." He turned to Ray. "You keep an eye on him and make sure he doesn't get into trouble."

Ray laughed. "I've got a baby myself. And besides, Kimo's got Mike for that."

I drove to the Ala Wai Marina, the place where Gilligan and the skipper left for their three-hour tour so many years ago, and we found Pua at Harbor Marine, working on the engine of a sleek cigarette boat. Motherhood had softened some of her tougher edges, though she still looked butch with her dark hair cut short, denim overalls and a plain white T-shirt.

"Howzit, Pua?" I asked.

She looked up and smiled. "Let me get cleaned up." She washed her hands at the big sink on the workroom floor and said, "Frankie said you're looking for Dakota?"

"Yeah. You saw him?" I said.

"Just really quick. I picked up Yeet from day care last week and it was still light out, so we went for a walk along the water."

She led us back outside, where the smell of motor oil wasn't so strong. "What did he say, exactly?"

"I wasn't taking notes. But it was something like his mom getting arrested, him getting sent to some crummy foster home, and running away."

"He say where he was living?"

She shook her head. "I did ask. I offered him some money, and he said he didn't need it, that he'd been getting by."

"Why didn't you call me, Pua?" I asked. "I could have talked to him, helped him."

"I told him to call you. But he didn't want to. He said he was doing fine on his own. I got the feeling he was crashing with some other kids. Maybe in some abandoned building."

That made sense; there were a lot of those along Lagoon Drive.

"You know his last name, by any chance?"

She didn't, and she didn't have any clue where he might be staying.

"You want to see some pictures?" she asked shyly.

"Hell, yeah," Ray said. "If I can show you mine."

I snickered, but both of them pulled out their cell phones and cooed over the baby pictures. Yeet was a round-faced baby with a thatch of black hair and a wide smile. He was pretty cute, and I wondered if Mike and I had a child, if he'd look like Yeet, the Hawaiian coming through, or more like Vinnie, who was all haole.

"He sleeping through the night yet?" Ray asked.

"Sure," Pua said. "Vinnie isn't?"

Ray shook his head. "We've tried everything. He's just a night owl."

"I read to him," Pua said. "And then as he starts to get drowsy I take him into his crib."

"Great to hear," I said. "But we've got a murder to solve. Gotta motor."

Ray elbowed me. "You wait," he said. "You'll be just like the rest of us."

Pua went back to work, and Ray and I walked to the Jeep. "If you're looking for a kid in the system, you should try Child Welfare," Ray said, as we walked back to the Jeep. "Don't you know somebody there? From when you had that thing with Jimmy Ah Wang?"

Jimmy was another kid from the gay teen group, and when his father kicked him out I'd gotten him placed with my godmother, an elderly Chinese woman I called Aunt Mei-Mei. "Yeah," I said. "Wilma Chow. I suppose I could call her."

I plugged in my Bluetooth headphone and called Child Welfare Services as I turned the Jeep on. Wilma had already left for the day, so I left her a message, telling her I was looking for a kid named Dakota who had entered the system when his mom went to jail. "Sorry, I don't know his last name. But I need to find out what's going on with him."

We had nothing else to go on, so I dropped Ray at headquarters and drove to Aiea Heights. I had finally started thinking of the place as home; it was originally Mike's house, and I had moved in with him about a year and a half before. Roby, as usual, was so excited to see me that he jumped around like a demented kangaroo. I put his leash on and took him for a long walk around the neighborhood.

It was just after six, and people were getting home from work. Down the block, a car pulled into the driveway of a single-family house and a man in a business suit got out. As he did, a little boy burst from the front door calling, "Daddy!"

The man picked him up and twirled him around. "How's my boy?"

I couldn't help smiling, remembering the way I'd done the same thing to my own dad when I was that boy's age. It would be sweet to be greeted that way, I thought, looking at the joy and love the father and son shared. But there was a lot more to parenting than those moments.

Roby caught sight of a dark brown anole lizard and took off, dragging me along, and I remembered I already had one furry child to take care of.

As Roby and I got back to our driveway, my cell phone began singing Cilla Black's "You're My World." I pulled it out of my pocket. "Hey," I said to Mike.

"I'm still working on the report on that fire this morning, but I'm almost done. You want to meet me for dinner and we'll go over it?"

"Sure. I'm walking Roby now. I'll feed him and head out. Where?"

"Barbecue's probably out, given what we have to talk about. How do you feel about a steak?"

We agreed on a steakhouse we liked in nearby Halawa. I returned Roby to the house and fed him, then drove down the hill. Mike was already there, sitting on a bench outside the stone-fronted restaurant, answering a text message on his phone.

"Hey," I said, leaning down to kiss his cheek.

He finished his text, stood up, and we walked inside, where the hostess recognized us and said, "Welcome back." The restaurant was paneled with dark woods and intermittent stone walls, with high skylights and lots of big, comfy booths with tiny pendant lights over them.

She led us to our booth, and we settled in with the menus, though we both knew what we'd order. I had the prime rib, medium, with a loaded baked potato and a Caesar salad. Mike ordered the teriyaki steak, only butter on his baked potato, and a house salad with honey mustard dressing.

"We're turning into an old married couple," I said, after the server had taken our orders. "I can predict what you eat. I even know the way you'll say it."

"We *are* an old married couple," he said. "Have you ever listened to yourself moan and groan when you get up?"

"Me! What about you? You sound like my grandfather when you cough."

"I have pulmonary issues," he said. "You think I can spend my days going through fires without having trouble?"

"Speaking of which. You find anything interesting in the fire I should know about?"

"The arsonist used a very simple device. You put a couple of cigarettes between two layers of matchbooks. Tie them up with string or a rubber band, then light the cigarettes. Once they burn down, they ignite the matches. Because there was a lot of paper in the warehouse, once there was ignition, there was plenty of fuel to feed the fire."

"Why would somebody use that?"

Mike shrugged. "It's simple. You don't need anything that an ordinary smoker doesn't already have on him. And it can be hard to detect, unless the investigator is looking carefully. Just finding a couple of cigarette butts might make the fire look accidental."

"But you can tell this one was deliberate?"

"Because of the composition of the matchbook, it's hard for it to burn up completely. So if you find the residue of a couple of books of matches as well as the cigarette butts, you know you've got arson."

The server brought our salads, and we started to eat. "You identify the victim yet?" Mike asked.

"Waiting for the serial number on the artificial hip. Doc promised he'd get me something tomorrow. Can't do much investigating until we know who the victim was."

"Wish I could tell you more. The pattern doesn't match any of our known firebugs. Could be somebody who did a quick Internet search. Maybe they didn't even plan to burn the building down in advance—just took what they had to work with."

Mike had come to my gay teen group a few times, and he'd met Dakota. I told him that I'd seen the teen near the warehouse, and how I'd begun to track him down. "I wish I could get hold of him. He might have seen something."

"Or he might have been involved," Mike said. "You think he's turning tricks? Maybe he picked up an old guy, took him to the warehouse, then something went wrong. He killed the guy, then set the place on fire to cover it up."

"I'd hate for that to be the story. He seemed like a pretty good kid when he came to our meetings."

"I remember him." Mike finished his salad and pushed the bowl aside. "Good-looking kid, but with a real chip on his shoulder."

"Sounds like his mother was the source of the problems," I said. "She's the one with the ice habit." I picked up my water and drank. "You feel like taking a run over to the marina after dinner, help me look for him?"

He shook his head. "I have an early meeting tomorrow, and I have work to do tonight to get prepared for it. Why don't you call Gunter?"

Mike's growing acceptance of my friend Gunter was another milestone between us. I met Gunter, a tall, skinny blond with a taste for very athletic sex, just as I was coming out of the closet. We became friends with benefits, and I had sex with him off and on until Mike and I met. Gunter didn't like Mike at first, and the feeling was mutual. Gunter thought Mike was a closet case, and Mike thought Gunter was a slut.

They were both right, of course. But both of them mellowed their attitude, and now they got along.

"He doesn't get off work until eleven," I said.

"What, you think hookers have bedtimes? If Dakota is turning tricks in the park that's the best time to look for him."

The server brought our steaks and I waited until we were finished eating to call Gunter. "You at work?" I asked.

"If you can call it that." Gunter was the evening shift concierge at a fancy condo building in Waikiki from three to eleven. He got to wear a uniform, which turned him on, and to snoop into the personal lives of the building residents, which was an additional plus.

I explained the situation. "I'm glad you called," he said. "I've been bored out of my mind lately. I could use a little detective diversion."

I arranged to pick him up at eleven.

When I hung up I looked over at Mike, as he was signaling for the check. "Sampson called me and Ray into his office this afternoon."

"What did you do now?"

"That's what we thought. Turns out the brass are looking for a couple of sacrificial lambs to send over to the FBI for a while."

"I can't see you wearing a coat and tie to work every day."

"May not have a choice. You know the way the department works—they assign you where they need you or want you."

The waiter delivered the check and Mike handed over his credit card; it was his turn to pay. Since we moved in together we'd tried to be careful about sharing expenses. We were determined that money shouldn't be an issue between us.

"How does that work, exactly?" Mike asked, when the waiter had left. "You work out of their office?"

"Uh-huh. Ray and I would still be on the HPD payroll, but we'd work Bureau cases."

"Terrorism?"

"Whatever they put us on. But I'm guessing we'd work organized crime."

"How do you feel about making the move?"

The waiter returned the check and Mike added the tip and scribbled his signature. "I just don't know," I said, when he finished and looked back up at me. "It threw me for a loop." I paused. "Ray seems to like the idea. He and Julie may leave Hawai'i when she finishes her dissertation, if she gets a teaching job somewhere. Having Bureau connections would make it easier for him to move." I looked at him. "What do you think?"

"You don't work well within authority structures, and you've found yourself a niche with Jim Sampson. I think you'd butt a lot of heads at the FBI."

"And you and I do enough of that at home."

"You said it, I didn't." We walked outside together, then kissed goodbye, and he left for home. I drove down into Waikiki and went for a walk, thinking I might run into Dakota, or one of the other kids from the teen group.

The streets were buzzing with pale-faced Japanese tourists, local mokes and titas—tough guys and girls—and Midwestern tourist couples in matching aloha prints, most of them still with their store-bought creases. Strobing store display lights competed with multicolored neons, and from store to store the music spilling out to the street changed. Modern rap and hip hop competed with old-school Hawaiian and hapa-haole tunes, ukuleles dueling with back beats.

I lived in Waikiki for years, and patrolled its streets as a uniformed officer. I'd worked there as a detective, too, and I knew every alley where drug deals took place, every corner where you could find a prostitute, every dark space where pickpockets and muggers lurked. Tourists only saw the sunshine, panoramic views, exotic stores and restaurants, but all it took was one chance encounter to show them the dark side of town as well.

It was my job, and HPD's, to minimize the chances of those encounters, and mitigate their effects. Not just to protect and serve the tourist population, of course, but everyone on the island. I tried to make myself inconspicuous, sticking to the shadowy side of the street, mixing in with crowds, but keeping my eyes open.

I didn't see any of the kids from my teen group, and I figured that was a good thing. They were either at home with their families or lying low and staying out of trouble. Just before eleven, I returned to my Jeep and drove to the building where Gunter worked. I parked in the circular drive and waited until he walked outside.

"Just like old times," he said, as he jumped in beside me. His blond hair was short and fuzzy, and he had a new silver cuff on his left ear. "Haven't we done this kind of thing before?"

"Yeah. Too often."

"How's married life treating you?" he asked, stretching his long legs out and angling the seat back.

"Same old, same old," I said. "You know how it is. Wild, passionate sex with the man you love once or twice a day."

He snorted. "Tell me another fairy tale."

When Mike and I moved in together, Gunter told me to put a dollar in a jar every time Mike and I had sex for the first year. Then after that, take a dollar out each time. The jar would never be empty, he said.

I hadn't tried it. Back when I moved in with Mike, we were both randy as rabbits. Since then, life had intervened. We were tired, or working late. His back hurt, or my shoulder. We were still doing it, and still having fun—but not as frequently as we used to.

I parked in the lot at the marina and Gunter and I strolled over to the park entrance. It was closed, but that doesn't stop anyone who really wants to get in. We both jumped the fence and moved forward, keeping quiet and listening for the sounds of sex.

We rounded a corner and saw a young girl, eighteen if she was that old, leaning against a tree. "I charge extra for two," she said.

"We can do fine without you, honey," Gunter said. "Now scamper."

"Faggots," she said, spitting the word out.

"A faggot with a badge," I said, showing her my shield. "Beat it before I call Vice on you."

She sneered, but then turned and melted into the underbrush. "I always meet the nicest people when I'm with you," Gunter said.

I looked up and saw an owl, outlined against the moon, gliding above us. As I watched, the bird suddenly swooped toward the ground and grabbed a small rodent, and then flapped away.

"Predator," I said to Gunter.

"There's a lot of them around here," he said.

I heard a low sound of male voices, and put my finger to my lips. Gunter and I crept forward, parting the branches to see a young man standing in a small clearing, talking to a much older one. They had matching ponytails, though Dakota's was black and the older man's was gray.

"HPD," I said, stepping into the clearing and holding out my badge. "Hit the road, pal. I need to talk to Dakota here."

The man turned around, his mouth gaping, and then began to run. "Try Craig's List," Gunter called after him. "It's cheaper and safer and legal."

Dakota tried to run the other way, but I chased and then tackled him. The ground was hard, and falling on his skinny body didn't provide much cushioning. I felt my breath go out of my body with a big whoosh.

Gunter appeared beside us.

"I didn't… I wasn't going to…" Dakota stuttered, as I stood up.

"When was the last time you had a good meal?" I asked. "Come on, I'll buy you something to eat, and we're going to talk."

We drove over to the Denny's on Kalakaua, and Dakota ordered the lumberjack slam and a strawberry banana smoothie, with side orders of pancake puppies and cheddar cheese hash browns. I remembered when I was his age I could eat massive quantities of food, and how my parents had always shaken their heads when watching me eat.

Gunter got coffee and the New York cheesecake. I ordered a piece of the caramel apple crisp and the strawberry-mango orange juice. If I had coffee that late, even decaf, I'd be up all night.

In the bright light, I saw that Dakota had a sprinkling of acne around his hair line, but the rest of his face was smooth. There was no dewy-eyed innocence to match it, though. He looked hard, and I tried to remember if he'd been that way when I first met him.

"So, Dakota," I said. "Where are you living these days?"

"With a friend."

"Address?"

"Why?"

"Just wondering," I said. "I saw you this morning, out on Lagoon Drive. You didn't stop when I called you."

"I was in a hurry."

"You see the fire this morning?"

He shifted uneasily in his seat. "Yeah."

"You know anything about it?"

"Jesus, Kimo, give the kid a break," Gunter said. "At least let him eat something before you start the inquisition."

I looked at Gunter, and realized he was right. I sighed. "So, I understand you saw Pua and Yeet the other day. He look cute?"

Dakota smiled. "Yeah, he is. Pua couldn't stop smiling when she was showing him off." Then he frowned. "But she'll probably end up a skank like my mom, and he'll grow up to be a loser."

"What's up with your mom?"

The waitress delivered our beverages and Dakota took a long drink of his smoothie. "She's in the WCCC in Kailua."

The Women's Community Correctional Center was the only women's prison in Hawai'i, housing females before trial and after sentencing. "When did this happen?"

"Couple of months ago. She was dealing ice in Wahiawa and the cops picked her up. She copped a plea and got four years."

"That's tough," I said. "You been out to see her?"

He shook his head. "She's a skank, like I said."

"Somebody must be pretty hungry," the waitress said, approaching us with a loaded tray, most of which was for Dakota.

I gave him a chance to eat, and he wolfed down the pancakes, eggs and sausage. When he stopped to take a breath, I said, "What happened to you when they took your mom in?"

"Foster home. This asshole kid kept picking on me so I left."

I nodded. "It's tough to find the right place."

He looked up at me. "I didn't have anything to do with that fire."

"I didn't think you did," I said. "But if you were around, maybe you saw something."

He finished the last of his hash browns. "You're a real member of the clean plate club," Gunter said. "You want dessert? This pie is choice."

I waved the waitress over. "He wants a piece of pie, and a slice of chocolate cake, too," I said.

"Ala mode?" he asked.

"Hey, go for it."

When the waitress was gone, he said, "It was like ten o'clock last night. I was on my way to the bus, walking past that warehouse. This big black limo pulled up, fast."

"You know what kind of car?"

He shook his head. "Just big and black. Fancy. I stepped back into the shadows because I didn't want anyone to see me."

"Who was in the limo?"

"The driver got out first. Big dude, like a bodybuilder or something. Then another big dude got out of the front seat. Two old people in the back—a man and a woman."

The waitress returned with Dakota's desserts. "Go on," I said, when she was gone.

He shrugged. "That's all I saw. They walked into the warehouse, and I kept going."

"You say this was about ten o'clock?"

"Yeah."

He chowed down, and I sat back in my seat. What had happened to the old woman? Could it be that we'd missed another set of remains in the fire?

Dakota finished eating. "I have to pee," he said.

"I'll come with you." I started to get up.

"I can pee by myself," Dakota said. "Ever since I was about two or three."

"Let him go, Kimo," Gunter said. "You gotta learn to trust people."

"When you come back, you want to come up and stay at my house for a few days?" I asked Dakota. "Get you fed, maybe enrolled back in school, see what we can do for you."

"Whatever." He stood up and walked toward the back of the restaurant.

"He's not a criminal," Gunter said. "You shouldn't treat him like one."

"He's a teenager," I said. "You remember what you were like

at that age? It's called tough love."

"Right."

I signaled for the waitress and got the check. "He's taking a long time just to pee," I said to Gunter.

"Shit, I forgot. There's a back door by the men's room."

"I don't even want to know how you know that," I said, jumping up. I rushed back to the men's room, pushing the door open. It was empty, and the back door was ajar.

Well, at least I fed him, I thought.

I dropped Gunter off at the little house he shared with a roommate, behind Diamond Head Elementary. "It's not your fault he ran away," he said, as he got out. "He was going to slip away sometime."

"I know. I just wish he'd let me help him."

"He has to want the help first."

"When did you get so smart?"

"Years of experience." He leaned over and kissed my cheek. "Any chance of you coming in for a nightcap?"

I knew he wasn't serious. "Go on," I said, pushing his shoulder.

Mike was asleep when I got home. I took Roby out for a quick pee and then slid in bed. The next morning Mike was already gone by the time my alarm went off. I went through the ritual with Roby, then drove in to work.

When Ray came in, I told him what I'd learned from Dakota. "There wasn't another body there," he said. "What do you think they did with the woman?"

"No idea." I checked missing persons for anything about an elderly couple while Ray went through the system to see if we'd heard about any kidnapping or ransom reports. Neither of us came up with anything.

Doc Takayama called and invited us to the morgue to check out the autopsy report. Such a gentleman, that guy.

Though it was clear when we left headquarters, the sky had clouded over by the time we got to the ME's office on Iwilei, in a two-story concrete building just off Nimitz. The paint on the building is peeling and the landscaping is overgrown— after all, the dead don't vote. The building is between the Salvation Army and a homeless center— something I always thought was an ironic comment, but maybe was intended as an object lesson to those less fortunate. You never know what the city fathers are really thinking, after all.

We rolled down the flaps on the Jeep and dashed inside just in time to miss a rain shower. Alice Kanamura, the cheerful receptionist, was sitting at the front desk when we walked in. "If you're here for the autopsy on the burn victim you missed it," she said. "Took Doc about five minutes this morning."

"I'm surprised it took that long, considering how little was left after the fire," Ray said. "Any news on the serial number from the artificial hip?"

"Let me call Doc and see what he's come up with."

Doc Takayama is the Medical Examiner for Honolulu City and County, though he looks barely old enough to have graduated medical school. He was a whiz kid, graduated in record time from UH, and he told me once he went into pathology because he didn't have to worry if the patients would trust him.

"He's in the computer lab," she said, when she hung up. "Down the hall to the right."

We followed her directions, trying to avoid the underlying smell of death that lingered no matter how much air freshener was used. Through the glass windows of the lab we saw Doc standing over a young Chinese-American tech who was manipulating an image on the computer screen.

"Just in time," Doc said, when we walked in. "Fermin managed to enhance the image enough so that we could make out the serial number."

He showed us the image on the screen. We could see a company logo, with a set of numbers, and the copyright mark. "That's the model number," Doc said, pointing at the screen. "The 46 mm refers to the diameter of the ball on the end."

He moved his finger farther down on the shaft. "Here's the serial number. Fermin went into the database to see whose hip we had. I think you'll be interested in the result."

Fermin hit a couple of keys and the screen switched.

"Alexander Fields?" I said.

"One and the same. Note the address in Black Point."

"Someone I should know?" Ray asked.

"Prime mover behind the drive for statehood," I said. "There are schools and overpasses and even a sewage lift station named after him all over the island. Also founding partner of Fields and Yamato."

"The law firm where your ex-girlfriend works?" Ray asked.

"Yes."

Doc looked interested. "I'd forgotten the reputation you used to have. Who's your ex?"

I was conflicted when I was younger, to say the least. I knew that I was attracted to other guys, but I didn't think I could be gay and have the life I wanted. So I dated girls a lot, trying to find the one who could make me believe I was straight.

"Peggy Kaneahe." Peggy predated all that; she and I sat next to each other all through high school based on our alphabetic placement, and we had dated through our junior and senior years. We broke up when we went our separate ways to college, and had only recently started dating again when I was dragged out of the closet.

That second break-up was acrimonious, and it took a long time for Peggy and me to return to a carefully managed friendship. She was an assistant district attorney back then, but as many ADAs do, she switched sides when she had a job offer from Fields and Yamato. We had worked together a couple of times, always with the sense that both of us were walking on eggshells. I didn't relish the thought of having to do that again.

"Pretty woman," Doc said, nodding. "Can't hold a candle to Lidia, obviously. But not bad."

Doc had been dating a beat cop named Lidia Portuondo for a while. I wondered sometimes about their pillow talk. But then again, Mike and I managed to leave most of our jobs at work, and I figured Doc and Lidia did the same.

"You come up with a cause of death?" I asked.

Doc nodded. "Follow me." He walked over to another terminal and sat down. Ray and I stood behind him as he got into the system and called up the records of Fields' autopsy. He brought up a picture on the screen and pointed. "These are the fragments of the skull we were able to retrieve from the scene. This is the frontal bone—what makes up your forehead. Notice the bullet hole through the center."

"Execution style," Ray said.

Doc nodded. "From the angle, I'd say Fields was on his knees, and the shooter pointed the gun right at his forehead and fired. Looks to me like hollow point ammunition, because of the damage to all the interior bones of the skull."

"So he was dead before the fire started," I said.

"If I had the lungs I'd confirm that, but I think you're safe with that assumption."

Doc promised to email over a full report. We thanked him and walked back out to the Jeep. The shower had passed, leaving the air fresh and full of negative ions. "If that's Alexander Fields, who was the woman with him?" Ray asked.

I pulled out my phone and did a quick search. "His wife died five years ago. Maybe a date? We should go over to his house."

"Peggy Kaneahe might know."

"That's true. I'll call her after we finish at the house."

"You sure? You're going to have to call Peggy sooner or later. Might as well make it sooner."

"You're not going to be one of those helicopter parents, always hovering over Vinnie and telling him what to do, are you?"

Ray shook his head. "Not while I have you to hover around."

Ray gave up on getting me to call Peggy, and we focused on lunch. "There's a great fish taco truck over by the Pier 19 terminal," he said, as we walked back to my Jeep.

"I thought I was supposed to be the one who knows everything about Honolulu," I said. "You're just the mainland transplant."

"Hey, I've been here three years. And despite what I said to Frankie yesterday, this place feels more like home every day."

"What are you going to do when Julie finishes her dissertation?" I asked. It was a question I'd been wondering about but hadn't been able to bring up before. "She going to look for a teaching job somewhere?"

By somewhere, I meant, 'back on the mainland,' which would mean Ray picking up and following her, as he'd done when they moved to Honolulu so she could attend UH.

"We've been talking about that, now that she's getting close to finishing. And we just don't know. There aren't a whole hell of a lot of teaching jobs these days so we may have to go wherever she gets an offer. And if we go back to the mainland it'll be easier for Vinnie to grow up knowing his grandparents and the rest of the family."

We climbed into the Jeep. "Moving over to the FBI might be a good deal for you," I said. "Once you're in with them, you could transfer to a field office wherever Julie gets a job."

"It's not that easy. Remember, if we're in the JTTF we're still working for HPD. We wouldn't be agents."

"I know. But if you like the work you could go to Quantico and get the training, then make a jump."

Ray shook his head. "I'm not thinking about any of that now. I just want to see what happens with Julie."

"You're a great husband. I don't know that I'd be willing to follow Mike all around the country."

"You do what you have to do," he said.

Losing Ray as a partner wasn't a happy thought; I spent more time with him than with Mike most days, and it was tough to find someone you could get along with as well as he and I did. I pushed the idea to the back of my mind as I made a couple of complicated turns and then pulled up in a warehouse neighborhood similar to the one off Lagoon Drive.

The sky was striated with thin cirrus clouds, the sun peeking back and forth like a kid playing hide and seek, and a fresh salty breeze blew in from the ocean. We waited in a short line at the taco truck, and when it was my turn, I stepped up and ordered my platter, and when Ray and I both had our food we walked over to a bench overlooking the water. A family with two little kids was sitting nearby, and once again I went back to the conversations Mike and I had been having about kids. I couldn't see why the ohana we had built wasn't enough for him. "Did you feel something different when you first saw Vinnie?" I asked Ray.

"Different how?"

"Different from looking at other babies. Because he was yours."

"I guess so. I mean, it's like there's something in the blood—I look at his little face, and I feel this overwhelming urge to protect him and nurture him." He looked over at me. "You and Mike still haven't made up your minds?"

I told Ray about Sandy's offer soon after she made it. "I think it's the other way around. We've both made up our minds. It's just that we don't agree."

"It's because Mike's an only child," he said. "I guarantee you, once he sees a baby who's related to him, that'll all change."

"It's not Mike who needs to change," I said. "It's me."

He put the remains of his taco down on his plate. "You don't want to have a kid? But I've seen you with your nieces and nephews. You're great with them."

"And I think that's enough. Mike doesn't." I turned to face him. "Seriously, Ray. The kind of work we do. Don't you worry about not being there for Vinnie? I mean, how can you make a commitment like that? You've been shot. If that bullet had a slightly different trajectory, you'd be dead. And that could happen to either of us any day."

"You're a regular Mary Sunshine, aren't you?" Ray picked up his taco and took another bite. When he finished chewing he said, "If I really thought about all the dangers out there I'd never leave the house, and I'd never let Julie or Vinnie go out either. But you can't think that way. Otherwise you end up living for seventy or eighty years and never taking any chances."

I finished the last of my taco and crumpled up the plate. "We'd better get over to Fields' house."

As I drove, I plugged in the Bluetooth again and called Peggy Kaneahe. Fortunately for me, she was in a meeting, and I was shuttled to her paralegal, a sweet Australian woman named Sarah Byrne. "Tell her I need to talk to her about Alexander Fields. As soon as possible, please."

"Mr. Fields? He hasn't been active with the firm for years."

"This is in confidence, Sarah. But did you see the reports of that warehouse fire yesterday morning out by the airport?"

"Yes. I saw the smoke on my way in to work."

"A man was killed in the fire. Preliminary medical identification leads us to Alexander Fields. I wanted to give Peggy a heads up and see what she knows about him."

"I'll have her call you as soon as she gets out of her meeting. Poor Mr. Fields. I only met him a few times but he was always very gracious."

Fields lived in a waterfront property off Kahala, just on the other side of Diamond Head from downtown Honolulu. It was an old house in the colonial style, with a hipped roof, big windows, and a broad portico. A wrought-iron gate closed off the driveway from the street, and Ray had to ring the bell and announce himself to the woman who answered.

We drove down the macadam driveway and parked in the semi-circle in front of the portico. A diminutive twenty-something Filipina wearing a maid's uniform answered the door. "Mr. Fields not home," she said.

"We know," I said. We showed her our badges and introduced ourselves. Her name was Marikit, she said, and she was Mr. Fields' aide. "But he go out last night and not come back. I don't know where he go."

"Did he have a car?" I asked, as she led us into the living room, where a bank of French doors looked out on the ocean. The furniture was simple but elegant, a koa wood settee upholstered in a tropical print, with matching armchairs and a low coffee table with a couple of architecture books there.

She nodded. "Yes, but I drive him. Car still here, in back."

"You live here?" Ray asked, as the three of us sat down.

"Yes, in small cottage in back. Mr. Fields like privacy. After I fix dinner and clean up, I go back there. If he need me, he call on cell phone."

"When was the last time you saw him?" I asked.

"Last night, six-thirty. He like to finish dinner by *Wheel of Fortune*." She pointed to the big-screen TV. "I leave him here, watching. I go back to my cottage."

"You didn't hear anyone come in or go out?"

She shook her head. "Mr. Fields, he still pretty sharp. He talk on telephone, he take care of himself. And he have cord around his neck, in case he fall, with a button he push to get help."

"Alexander Fields was seen going into a warehouse near the airport with an elderly woman and two younger men. Any idea who that could be?"

She shook her head. "Widows very interested in Mr. Fields, but he not. No women come here."

"When did you come into the house this morning?" Ray asked.

"Eight o'clock, like usual. I put on coffee and go up to Mr. Fields' room. He not there."

"Bed slept in?"

"No. And he always make himself cup of hot cocoa before bed, and leave mug in sink. Not there today."

"He often go out at night and not come back?"

"No, not at all."

"Then why didn't you call the police?" I asked.

"Like I say, Mr. Fields very private. He not want other people know what he doing."

There was something fishy about that statement, but I let it go. "Mr. Fields passed away last night," I said, choosing my words carefully.

Her lip quivered and she began to cry. "Poor man. I hope he finish book. It matter so much to him."

"Book?" Ray asked. "He was reading one? Or writing one?"

"He have man come to house, and he talk and Mr. Greg, he write down. They going to make big book."

"Mr. Greg?" I asked. "You know his full name?"

"He leave card." She stood up and went across to an antique roll top desk. She slid the tambour cover up and pulled out a business card. "Here," she said, handing it to me.

The card belonged to Greg Oshiro, a local newspaper reporter I knew well. I'd have to call him—but I wanted to wait until I knew more, because anything I said to him was likely to end up in the *Star-Advertiser*, the result of the merger of the *Star-Bulletin* and the *Advertiser*, papers I had grown up reading around the kitchen table with my parents. I handed it back to her and said, "We're going to have to look around."

It was obvious to me from the way Marikit wouldn't meet my eyes that she was hiding something. But whatever it was, we'd find it.

"Do you know how to reach Mr. Fields' next of kin?" Ray

asked.

"Yes, yes." She went back to the desk and brought us a folder. We asked her to stay in the kitchen while we looked around, and she went in there and turned on the radio.

Alexander Fields had prepared well for his eventual demise; the folder had the contact information for his children, both of whom were on the mainland, as well as his attorney (Winston Yamato, his ex-partner, of course), and his investment broker. As a veteran, he was entitled to burial in the National Memorial Cemetery of the Pacific, commonly called Punchbowl, and he had a plot reserved next to his wife.

"I keep telling Julie we have to do this," Ray said, looking over everything. "Just in case. My brother agreed to take Vinnie if anything happens to both of us, but we've got to have the papers drawn up."

My cell phone rang; the display read Fields and Yamato. "Kanapa'aka," I said.

"It's Peggy. Sarah told me Alexander Fields is dead?"

"Yup. We're going to need to talk to Winston Yamato and anyone else in the firm who dealt with Fields regularly."

"It was a homicide?"

"They don't call the cops out when people die of natural causes, Peggy. You know that. When can Ray and I come over?"

"I'll need to organize things and check calendars. I'll get back to you."

She hung up. "Aloha to you, too," I said to the phone.

"You were pretty snippy with her," Ray said. "Why can't you just be nice to the woman?"

"It's called history." We walked to the kitchen. It was a warm, comfortable room, lined with oak cabinets and appliances that looked like they'd been in service for years. Marikit was sitting in a cushioned chair at the plain oak table. "Have you cleaned the house yet today?" I asked.

She shook her head, and I called for a crime scene tech to come out and take fingerprints. It was unlikely that a visitor would have worn gloves, so there was a chance we could pull a print from somewhere. There were no signs of a struggle, so it appeared that if someone had taken Fields to the warehouse on Lagoon Drive, he had left his home under his own power.

The house was sufficiently back from the street that you couldn't see the parking area from the street. The gate system didn't track calls, so we had no idea when the car had arrived for him.

Ray and I both put on gloves and started going through the house. There was no datebook with a mysterious meeting penciled in and no used coffee cup or wine glass to provide us with a DNA sample. Either Fields or Marikit was obsessively neat; everything was orderly.

While Ray worked his way through the bedrooms upstairs, I sat down at the polished dining room table, under a crystal chandelier. The wood breakfront behind me was tastefully stocked with Chinese export porcelain; a Hawaiian quilt, in shades of bright blue and white that matched the china, was framed under glass across from me. I opened the folder Fields had left for his children. His most recent investment statement was there, along with the deed to the house and various other legal documents.

About two thirds of the way through I hit pay dirt: the incorporation records from Samoa for Inline Imports. Fields was the sole owner of the corporation, which had been set up in 1992. There was no information, though, about what kind of material was imported.

A few pages later, I found a list of all the property Fields owned, either directly or through various corporate shells. Halfway down the page was the address of the warehouse on Lagoon Drive, which had been purchased soon after the corporation was set up.

I sat back in my high-backed wooden chair and looked out at the ocean through the French doors that led to the lanai. Was Inline Imports a dummy corporation? There wasn't anything else in the folder that referenced the company or any business it might have done. So it looked to me like Fields had set it up specifically to purchase the warehouse.

Mike had noted in his report that there had been a lot of paper stored there, in cardboard boxes. Fields had been in practice for decades, and he had many business interests. Were those boxes filled with old paper records? Or something more?

I pushed back the chair, picked up the file, and walked through the living room to the polished wood staircase, which turned on itself as I climbed to the second floor.

Ray was in Fields' spacious bedroom, which looked out at the ocean. Through another set of french doors I saw a small balcony where a table faced the water, with a single chair. No recliner for Alexander Fields; it looked like he might sit out at the table and read the newspaper, or whatever else he did, with the waves as his companions. A nice life, if you can get it.

Ray stood next to a long, low bureau. A sitting Buddha anchored one end; the other end held a jewelry box full of expensive watches, gold cufflinks and pinky rings set with star sapphires, tiger's eye and other precious stones. "Not a robbery," he said, pointing at it. "And I found a couple of grand in hundred-dollar bills in the bottom drawer."

"I made some progress downstairs. We won't need those records from the Samoan Consulate after all. Turns out Alexander Fields owned Inline Imports." I held the paper up to show Ray.

"You think he was taken there to retrieve some old records?" Ray asked. "Or something else?"

"No way of knowing yet," I said. "Guess it's time for us to call his kids. You want the son or the daughter?"

"I'll take the daughter. Weeping women are more my specialty than yours."

I took my cell phone out to the lanai overlooking the ocean and sat in a white wooden rocking chair with a hunter green cushion that matched the foliage around the house. It was a beautiful place, and I was sorry Alexander Fields had to leave it in such a terrible way.

I reached Shepard Fields at his office in Cupertino, in the heart of Silicon Valley. I introduced myself and said, "I have some bad news, Mr. Fields. Your father was killed Tuesday night in a fire at a warehouse he owned near the airport."

"And you want my alibi?"

That was an interestingly cold response from a man who's just learned his father is dead. "That wasn't the reason for the call, but if you've got one I'd be happy to hear it."

"My partner and I were at a charity event in the Castro that night. We left the party around ten and returned home. I had an eight A.M. meeting yesterday morning. And as I'm sure you know there's no way I could have left San Francisco after the party, flown to Honolulu, set a fire and then made it back here to my office that early."

"I take it you and your father weren't on good terms?"

He laughed. "You could say that. My father was a bastard, detective. My mother was a saint to put up with him for as long as she did."

So much for Sarah Byrne's observation that the man had always been gracious. "Do you know anything about a company he owned called Inline Imports?"

"Not at all. I spoke to my father every couple of weeks or so. We had a whole list of forbidden topics, from politics to the economy to my sexual orientation. So mostly we talked about the weather in Honolulu, with the occasional detour into my father's disappointment that I hadn't given him a grandchild."

"How about your sister? Was she on better terms with him?"

"My sister is a money-grubbing slut. I'm sure she kept close dibs on Daddy and her eventual inheritance. Be sure to ask her about her alibi, detective. I'm sure you'll find out about her history of drug abuse and petty theft, and the way Daddy always bought her out of trouble."

"Is she in trouble now?"

"I wouldn't be surprised. I haven't spoken to her in at least ten years. Last I heard she was married and living in Oregon, but she's probably been through at least two husbands since then. They can marry, you know. Straight people. They do it all the time."

"I'm aware of that. Did your father ever say anything about any threats against him?"

"My father had a strict policy against talking about work with his family. Growing up we had to learn about his cases from the newspaper. So no, he never told me anything."

"According to paperwork we found in the house, you and your sister are joint executors of your father's estate. You'll want to contact Winston Yamato. I'm sure he can help you expedite the release of your father's remains from the Medical Examiner's office as well."

"Good old Winston. Of course he's got his fingers in this."

I offered my condolences, though I was pretty sure they weren't necessary, and said that I might be back in touch if I had further questions. He told me he'd make arrangements to come to Honolulu and deal with his father's remains in the next few days, and gave me his cell phone number.

After I hung up I looked out at the restless ocean and reminded myself how lucky I was to come from a functional family. I loved my parents, my brothers and sisters-in-law, and my nieces and nephews. Hell, I even loved almost all my cousins. When my father died, and I knew that day was approaching, I would be a lot more upset than Shepard Fields.

I was staring at the sails of a catamaran tacking toward Diamond Head when I heard a baby crying. I looked around, then followed the sound, around the corner of the house to the small cottage alongside it. It was a miniature of the bigger house, with the same hipped roof and front porch, though it was small enough to fit into Fields' living room. I peered in the window and saw one room, with a single bed, a plain dresser, and a crib with a folding table beside it.

I was about to walk in when Marikit came out of the big house behind me. "No, is all right," she said. "I take care."

"Your baby?" I asked, as she opened the door.

The little one was squalling his lungs out, and a quick sniff told me he needed to be changed. She crossed the room, picked him up and put him on the towel on top of the table.

"This what you were hiding, Marikit?" I asked.

She nodded as she began changing the little boy. "Mr. Fields not know about my son. He not hire me if he knew."

"Why not?"

"He no like little kids. Too noisy, he say."

And yet he was harassing his son about giving him a grandchild. People can be so contradictory, which is tough when you're trying to unravel a murder.

"I careful to keep my baby hidden," Marikit said, disposing of the dirty diaper in a garbage pail.

"He never heard the baby crying?"

She shook her head, then expertly wrapped the baby in a fresh diaper. "Mr. Fields have bad hearing. He no like to wear his hearing aids, either."

"What's going to happen to you now?" I asked.

"I work for agency. I call them and they tell me wait here until they talk to family."

I felt sorry for Marikit; her loss was just collateral damage to whoever had killed Alexander Fields.

Ray appeared in the cottage doorway. "Spoke to the sister," he said. "She's a piece of work."

"Just like her brother, I'll bet." We left Marikit to finish with the baby and walked down to the water's edge.

"I feel like I need to take a bath after talking to her," Ray said. "All she wanted to know was how soon she could get her money."

I told him about my conversation with Shepard Fields. "Her brother says she's a money-grubbing slut, which seems to match your impression. She have an alibi?"

"Yeah, she jumped right on that. People watch too many cop shows on TV, you know?"

"Her brother was the same way. I'm starting to think those two have a lot more in common than they'd like to admit."

Ray pulled out his note pad. "Stephanie Elizabeth Fields Potter Cornell. Currently divorced from husband number two, but living with a boyfriend. Her alibi is that she was working out at the gym Monday afternoon near her house outside Seattle. Then dinner with the boyfriend and a romantic evening of TV and sex."

"She told you about the sex part?"

"In detail. I'm telling you, the woman has a loose screw."

"Or she got screwed."

Ray frowned. "Save me from the bad jokes. She talked to her father every Sunday afternoon, but he never mentioned any threats. She was planning to come out here next month to spend some time with him."

"She have children?" I asked.

"No, she said she's got some problem with her period or her eggs. I tuned that part out." He looked at me. "The brother say anything about Fields being sick?"

"Nope."

"Well, Stephanie said her father had end-stage pancreatic

cancer. Just a few months left to live. That's why she was coming out to see him."

"I wonder if Shepard knew. Not that it matters, since both of them have alibis."

"Which doesn't rule out a third party acting for either of them."

I nodded. "True that." I shook my head. "How sharper than a serpent's tooth it is to have a thankless child."

"Thank you William Shakespeare," he said. "Just my luck to get an English major as a partner."

My cell rang, a government number I didn't recognize. It was Wilma Chow, the social worker. "You're in luck, detective," she said. "I handle Dakota Gianelli's case. What do you need from him?"

"It's complicated. Can I come over and talk to you?"

"I'm in my office for the next hour. Then I have a custody hearing."

"I'll be there in about twenty minutes."

As I hung up, Ray said, "If you drop me at headquarters, I'll put together the subpoenas for Fields' bank and phone records. I'm warning you, though, if this kid doesn't want to be in a foster home there's not much you can do about it."

"I know. But I have to try."

We walked back to the Jeep, talking through the case. "Someone comes to visit Fields last night," Ray said. "After six-thirty, when Marikit has gone back to her cottage."

"Could be the old woman was the visitor, or maybe she was an additional hostage."

Ray nodded. "The two guys, or the two guys and the old woman, take Fields, willingly or unwillingly, to the warehouse on Lagoon Drive."

"If he didn't go willingly, there might be a sign," I said.

We looked carefully around the front porch. "What's this?"

Ray asked, pushing aside a branch from a hibiscus hedge. He put his glove back on and picked up a rectangular white plastic object with a red button in the center. "Looks like his medical call button."

A few feet away I found a black cord with a broken clasp. "No reason for him to pull off his call button himself," I said. "So I'm guessing Fields left the house unwillingly."

"But Marikit didn't hear anything. No shouting. He didn't press this button either."

"If somebody had a gun to his head he couldn't have raised an alarm."

We put the broken cord and the alert button in evidence bags and got back into the Jeep. On the way downtown, I said, "There must have been something at the warehouse the killer wanted. Otherwise why not just kill Fields at his house?"

"And why burn down the warehouse? To cover the murder?"

"Maybe the killers were worried there was more evidence in the warehouse. They didn't want to take the chance that we'd find it."

"Mike can figure out how much paper was in the warehouse, can't he?"

"Yeah. He has to calculate the fire load, which is based on the amount of combustible material in the square footage of the burn site. Why?"

"I'm wondering if there were a lot of files there, or just a few. A lot of files makes it more likely they burned the building because they didn't have time to go through everything."

"They could have been after something other than paper," I said. "Maybe smuggled artifacts, for example. Once they got what they wanted, they burned the place just to cover their tracks."

"All good theories," Ray said.

I dropped him at headquarters and drove a couple of blocks to Wilma Chow's office. She was a pleasant, heavyset woman, wearing a shapeless white cardigan over a light blue silk blouse with a Chinese collar.

"I called the foster home where Dakota had been placed, and I learned he ran away three weeks ago," she said, after I was seated across from her.

"You didn't already know?"

She shook her head. "We've been having problems with this foster mother. She has six children in her care and she doesn't always give us full reports." She sighed. "We have so many children who need care, especially ones like Dakota whose parents have drug problems, and it's tough to manage. Ninety-nine percent of foster parents are loving, caring people who devote themselves to the kids in their care. But the one percent cause us the most problems."

"What can you do to find Dakota and get him placed somewhere else?" I asked.

"I can't do anything until I know where he is. This office just doesn't have the resources to track down missing kids. That's a job for HPD."

"What can you tell me about his mother? Maybe she has some idea where he'd go if he was in trouble."

She looked through her file. "Angelina Gianelli is at the WCCC. Her last known address was in Wahiawa, so it's possible Dakota went back there, to a friend or a neighbor."

I wrote down the Wahiawa address, and thanked Wilma for her help. "If I find him, what should I do? Call you?"

"That's a good start. I'll find him someplace temporary, and then we'll look into longer-term placement. Dakota is almost fifteen, and Angelina's going to be in jail for at least four years, so that means we need to look after him until he turns eighteen."

"And after that?"

"After that he's on his own," Wilma said. "We hope that by the time a child ages out of the system, he or she has made enough connections, either with the foster family, or with friends and members of the biological family, to be able to manage. Of course, that's not always the case, but we have limited resources and we have to focus on the children who aren't old enough to help themselves."

I had met a couple of foster kids through my work with the gay teen group, and I knew that often they didn't develop those resources, and fell through the cracks. I hoped Dakota wouldn't be one of those.

I wanted to know what kind of book Greg Oshiro was working on with Alexander Fields, and if anything that had come up might have bearing on Fields' murder. But I called Mike first, using the Bluetooth as I drove back to headquarters.

"I need to talk to Greg, and I was thinking of seeing if he was free for dinner. How do you feel about that?"

I'd gotten in trouble with Mike before when I'd made plans without consulting him. It was one of those little things about being part of a couple I was learning how to handle. It was hard, because my natural temperament is to act first and think second.

"I wouldn't mind seeing his girls," Mike said. "Maybe we can meet up at their house."

Greg had donated sperm to a lesbian couple a few years before, and become the father of twin girls. After the birth mother's death, he and the other mom, an artist named Anna Yang, had moved in together to look after Sarah and Emily. It was an odd situation, as far as I was concerned. What if Greg met a guy? Or Anna met a woman? How could both of them settle for a relationship like the one they had, linked only by the two girls?

I hung up and called Greg. He covered the police beat for the *Star-Advertiser*, and I'd known him for years. We got along fine until I came out of the closet, and then he turned into an asshole. I thought he was a homophobe until Ray pointed out, some years later, that Greg was as gay as I was, but angry that I could be out and he was closeted.

Once we got over that hurdle, we'd become friends again. "Hey, Kimo," he said. "Got a scoop for me?"

Since he didn't immediately assume I was calling about Alexander Fields, I figured he didn't know. So I decided to be cagey. "Yeah. But it's something I want to talk to you about face to face. You free for dinner tonight?"

"That depends. Big story or little one?"

"Big one."

"You've got my attention. You want to meet somewhere?"

"Mike wants to see the *keikis*. Can we come over to your house around seven? How about if we bring takeout?"

"Two large from Piece A Pizza, one meat lovers with a thin and crispy crust, one veggie with the stuffed crust. And a dozen garlic rolls."

"That just for you?"

Greg was a big guy, with an appetite to match.

"If you're nice, Anna will share the veggie with you. The meat lovers is all for me."

I was tempted to ask if there was anything else he needed, but I held my tongue. "See you at seven."

When I got back to my desk I told Ray about meeting with Greg. "Be careful what you tell him," Ray said. "You don't want everything spilled out in the paper tomorrow."

"I do have some experience working with the members of the fourth estate. Get those subpoenas?"

"Had Judge Yamanaka sign off on both of them and faxed them over. We should have the records tomorrow morning. And I called the agency Marikit works for. They said she never gave Fields or the agency any trouble. I'm still running her information, just to be sure, though."

It was close to the end of our shift, so we walked over to Lieutenant Sampson's office, and Ray rapped on the door frame.

Sampson looked up from his paperwork. "Have a suspect in the arson homicide?"

"Not yet. But we do know who the victim is."

He nodded toward the chairs, and we walked in and sat down. "Alexander Fields?" he asked, once we told him how we'd identified the victim. "That's going to get hot fast. He had a lot of very powerful friends in town."

We spelled out how we were proceeding, and he said, "Let me know if you need any juice on this. I'm sure Winston Yamato's going to start pulling strings soon. It won't look right if he doesn't press this when Fields was his partner."

"We're hoping to talk to Yamato tomorrow," I said. "Peggy Kaneahe is pulling the records on all Fields' cases, in case any of those might lead us to a motive or a suspect."

"Only in Hawai'i," Sampson said. "There's only one or two degrees of separation between every person on this island. Your ex-girlfriend works for the victim's law firm. And that's just the start."

"There's Greg Oshiro, too," I said. "The housekeeper said Greg was working on a book with Fields. I'm having dinner with him tonight."

"I'm sure there will be more. Just be careful."

We stood up and went back to our desks, and a half hour later I was on my way home. I thought about detouring past the Women's Community Correctional Center to see Dakota's mom, but I didn't have the time to make it up there and back before dinner. Instead I walked and fed Roby, then took a shower before Mike got home.

I was sitting in the living room, wearing only a pair of nylon running shorts, with the fan blowing cool air at me, when he walked in. "Hey, handsome," he said, as Roby came running toward him.

"Hey yourself," I said.

He looked sexy, with a loosened tie hanging askew over his white shirt. He didn't often dress up, but I figured that his morning meeting had been with someone high up.

"I was talking to the dog."

I threw one of the decorative sofa pillows at him. "Asshole."

He laughed and caught the pillow, then tossed it back at me.

"That how you're going to dinner?"

"Depends. Maybe I'll get the information I need from Greg if I put out."

Mike shrugged. "Usually works for me. You put out, and I give in."

"Really?" I stood up, and dropped my shorts to the ground. I was proud of my body. Though I was thirty-seven, I still ran and biked and surfed, and watched what I ate. I wasn't going to win a body-building competition, but I had muscles in the right places, and though I didn't have a six-pack, I didn't have a pot belly either.

"You feel like giving in now?" I asked.

"That depends on what you want from me." He pulled off his tie and tossed it on the sofa, then began unbuttoning his shirt.

"Whatever you want to give." I crossed the room to him and wrapped my arms around him, and he leaned his head down to kiss me, bridging the distance in our heights.

Roby nosed around my legs and I nudged him away. "Go lie down," I said.

"Good idea," Mike said.

"I was talking to the dog. But you can obey, too, if you want." I turned toward the bedroom, looping my hand in his belt and tugging him behind me.

We were both naked soon, rolling around in our king-sized bed, and by the time we were finished we both needed a quick shower before we could go over to Greg's house.

I called Piece A Pizza with our order, with a large ham and pineapple for Mike and me to share, and by the time we had taken the H3 through the center of the island to Kaneohe, on the windward coast, the pizzas were ready. It was just a few blocks to Greg and Anna's townhouse, in a development just off Haiku Road.

Greg had owned the place for years, and moved Anna and the girls in soon after the death of their birth mother, an accountant named Zoë Greenfield. He converted the first-floor den to a bedroom for himself, and turned the master bedroom and the smaller bedroom upstairs over to Anna and the girls.

Greg let us in, taking the pizzas from me. Three-year-old Sarah and Emily were playing with magnetic dress-up dolls in the center of the living room when we walked in. They wore matching white shorts but different tops, one red and one blue, and they jumped up and ran over to us as Mike knelt down to hug them.

Anna waved hello from the kitchen where she was setting the table. She was barely five feet tall, and her glossy black hair was cut on a sharp angle. She wore a sleeveless white blouse speckled with blue paint or blueberry baby food—hard to tell at that distance.

Greg carried the pizzas to the kitchen, and I joined Mike on the floor for hugs and kisses and baby play, laughing as the girls tried to climb all over us. They were identical and I had no idea which was Emily and which was Sarah, but it didn't matter.

The twin in the blue shirt sat down on the floor and yawned. Anna picked her up. "All right, ready for bed," she said. She was mainland Chinese, and still had a heavy accent. Mike picked up the other twin and followed Anna upstairs, the two of them talking about kiddie sleeping habits.

I sat down across from Greg and we popped open the pizzas. "So what's this case?" Greg asked, taking a slice of the meat lovers' pizza.

"Arson homicide." I watched his face carefully. "The victim was an attorney named Alexander Fields."

I was satisfied to see that Greg nearly choked on his pizza. I know, it's mean. But the police and the press are natural enemies, and Greg had pulled a bunch of stunts on me in the years that I'd known him.

"But…" he said. "I was working with him."

"I know. That's why I came to you."

He put the pizza down. "I should get my pad."

I was impressed that he was willing to postpone dinner for his story. "No, let's eat," I said. "I'll give you all the details later."

Greg looked like he might burst, but Anna and Mike returned from tucking the girls in and Anna said, "Yes, please. Let's eat first. You can talk about murder later."

Anna was a very talented artist, and she had painted murals all around the living and dining room, and we talked about them, and about some new commissions she had gotten. She and Greg had married a year before, to solidify her citizenship status as well as provide stability for the girls, and she was building her freelance art business.

They both looked happy with their arrangement, and I gave them credit for that. Anna smiled a lot, and so did Greg. I'd seen many heterosexual married couples who got along worse.

After we had demolished the pizzas and the garlic rolls, accompanied by big draughts of root beer and water, Anna and Mike retired to the living room, and Greg got out his notebook. He and I sat at the kitchen table and I said, "Tell me about the book you were working on with Fields."

He frowned. I knew he wanted to get the details of the murder first, so he could work on his story, but I'd played that game with him a few times. I had to get my information first or he'd never tell me anything.

"Vanity biography, basically," he said. "Alexander Fields, pioneer of Hawaiian statehood, that kind of thing."

"He digging up any old scandals?"

"Not that he told me. Everything we've gone over so far is puffery."

"You have a publishing contract for this?"

"No, he was going to self-publish—e-book with Amazon and so on, put out his own paperback with one of the services."

"Tell me some of it," I said. "I'm looking for a motive for his murder and I can use any background I can get."

"Born in San Francisco in 1921; graduated from Stanford in '42, then went right into the Navy for two years in the Pacific theater. He met his wife, Yuki, when he was stationed in Yokohama."

I pulled out my netbook and started taking notes. I had finally become a member of the computer generation, thanks to Harry's help and the need to keep a lot of information together. I used my netbook to take notes, take pictures of crime scenes, and keep track of data like autopsy reports, websites, and so on.

"Fields went back to Stanford for law school, and once he had his degree he moved to Honolulu and began working with import-export firms who needed U.S. legal expertise," Greg said.

"Good time for a smart guy to move to the islands," I said. "Must have been a lot going on then."

Greg nodded. "He chaired a public interest group that advocated statehood, and then in 1959 he and a couple of other lawyers formed a partnership. Handled mostly civil cases like business disputes. When Winston Yamato retired from the state Senate in 1980, he and Fields got together. In 1995, Fields retired, though he stayed "of counsel" to the firm for another ten years."

"He ever mention any specific cases that got ugly? Any threats?"

Greg shook his head. "If there were cases like that he was covering them up. Although…"

"Although what?"

"He did say he had a few things he was saving up to tell me. More explosive. But the guy was such a bullshitter I didn't know whether to believe him or not."

"He never said what those things were?"

"No. But he did say he had a lot of records from the past that would substantiate everything he said."

"He probably kept those in the warehouse on Lagoon Road. Mike says that a lot of paper went up in flames there."

Now it was Greg's turn to start taking notes. "Any idea why

he was killed there?"

"Hold on, cowboy. We don't know that he was killed there. He could have been killed somewhere else, then brought to the warehouse."

That wasn't true; Dakota said he saw Fields alive, going into the warehouse. But I needed to be careful what I told Greg, because whatever I said would end up in the *Star-Advertiser*.

"Let's step back," I said. "We know that Alexander Fields left his home on Monday evening, after six-thirty, when the housekeeper left him watching *Wheel of Fortune*. We know his body was found in the ashes of the warehouse fire. The warehouse was owned by a company called Inline Imports, which in turn was owned by Fields."

Greg scribbled quickly. "You could have called me earlier today," he said, when he finished. "I'll never make tomorrow's edition."

"Too bad. But think what a great story you can put together for Saturday's paper. If it's a slow news day, you could even get a couple of inches on the front page."

"Anyone else know about this?"

I shook my head. "We haven't released any more information. I came to you because you were working with Fields and I was hoping you could give us some information, maybe even a motive."

"The only motive I can suggest is that he was an asshole," Greg said. "On the surface he was this very courtly gentleman, but underneath he was a money-grubbing bastard who trampled over people whenever he had to."

"That's the impression I got from his kids," I said. "But you don't know anyone he trampled on who'd have a reason to kill him now?"

"You'd have to go back and look at his old cases. He was never a criminal attorney, but some of his cases did end up putting people in jail. He did some union-busting back in the fifties, for example."

"The fifties? You mean before statehood?"

Greg nodded.

"Come on, Greg. The movers and shakers from that time must be in their eighties by now. Or dead."

"Fields was alive. Until Tuesday night."

He had a point there. And he had last been seen in the company of an elderly woman—perhaps someone who had been around in the fifties in Honolulu, too.

I knew someone else who'd been around during that time, and I was surprised that I hadn't thought to ask him what he might know.

My father.

We left Kaneohe a half-hour later. "You mind if we stop at my parents' house on the way home?" I asked. "I want to talk to my dad."

"It's all about you," he said. "I'm just along for the ride."

I called my mother and told her we wanted to stop by. "Your father's already asleep," she said. "I don't want to wake him. But if you come over for dinner tomorrow you can have coconut cake for dessert."

My mother was famous for that dessert, coconut milk infusing the white cake, with a rich cream cheese icing, dusted with shaved fresh coconut. I turned to Mike. "Dinner at my parents tomorrow? Coconut cake for dessert."

"It's a date. But only if I get two pieces."

My mother heard him. "If there's that much left by tomorrow. Lui's boys came over this afternoon and ate half the cake."

"You'll just have to make another one," I said.

"Drive carefully," she said, and hung up.

When we got home, I pulled together everything I had on Fields' murder, creating folders on my netbook for the arson, the homicide, his family background and so on. It helped me feel like I was making progress when I did stuff like that, and it was easier to find things when I need them.

Mike watched TV, and I ended up on the couch with him for a while, Roby sprawled on the floor next to us. Mike scratched behind Roby's ears, and I rubbed the dog's stomach. He was one spoiled golden retriever.

As I was driving to work on Friday morning, Peggy Kaneahe called me. "I have some material for you. Can you be here at nine?"

"Yes, ma'am," I said. "Should we bring the coffee?"

I thought I was being sarcastic; lately everyone had been expecting me to be their errand boy. But Peggy took me seriously. "I'll have a Caramel Brule Latte, and Sarah likes the Macadamia Mocha. Mr. Yamato will want a bold coffee—he'll put his own milk and sugar in here. Better make all three of them Longboard sized. It's going to take a while."

She hung up before I could complain. I had to repeat her order like a mantra until I got off the H1 and I could pull over and write it all down.

I had just enough time to get up to my desk, check for phone messages—none—and email—nothing important, just general department crap sprinkled in with the occasional piece of spam that somehow slipped past the filtering system. Then Ray and I had to scoot to stop past the Kope Bean, the local-grown Hawaiian chain.

Ray laughed when I told him about the pizza the night before, and the coffee we had to stop and pick up. "Hey, if I'd known you were taking orders I'd have started placing them a long time ago."

"Ha frigging ha ha."

"You get anything from Greg last night?"

"Just vague speculation and general bullshit. I'm sure I gave better than I got."

"That's what I hear Mike say all the time."

"You like this neighborhood?" I asked. We were driving through a scummy corner of downtown, taking a shortcut to the offices of Fields and Yamato. Bums and bag ladies regularly strolled the streets, pushing shopping carts laden with soda cans and unnecessary sweaters. Half the buildings were shuttered and scrawled with graffiti.

"Just saying." Ray laughed as I pulled into the drive-through lane for the Kope Bean. Instead of small, medium and large, or the tall, grande and venti of Starbucks, they served up shortboard, funboard, and longboard sizes. We waited behind an old man so short his head was blocked by the headrest on his seat. I saw they were debuting a new, even bigger size, the twenty-ounce paddleboard. I decided that if we were going to be in a long meeting we'd better try those out.

My drink is the raspberry mocha. Ray is a coffee snob; he maintains it's worthless to drink expensive coffee if you can't taste the quality of the beans. He'll only drink pure Kona, which the Kope Bean charges extra for, with extra foam. I felt like a true yuppie when I placed my order through the hula dancer's mouth.

The tab was nearly twenty-five bucks, which would have shocked my father, who had never paid more than a dollar or two for a cup of coffee. But I handed over my credit card without a whimper. I drove to the office tower where Fields and Yamato have most of a floor, and Ray and I carried the two trays of coffee up in the elevator.

Sarah Byrne met us at the reception desk. "You're my savior!" she said. "I was just wondering how we were going to make it through this meeting without massive doses of caffeine."

"I love coffee, I love tea," Ray sang, surprising me. "I love the Java Jive and it loves me."

Sarah got it right away, picking up the next stanza from the Manhattan Transfer song, "I love java sweet and hot, Whoops Mr. Moto I'm a coffee pot."

I hadn't known Ray could sing until the last time we'd been on a case that involved Sarah, when he had sung along with her. This time, they both broke into laughter, which carried us down the hall until we reached the conference room, where Peggy Kaneahe was speaking in low tones to Winston Yamato.

Every time I see Peggy I'm reminded of the girl she was in high school, though she's twenty years older and there are the occasional gray streaks in her close-cropped dark hair. She's just as slim as she was then, and she dresses the way we did when we had to pose for formal portraits. She wore a high-necked ivory silk blouse with a single strand of pearls, and a navy blazer and matching skirt. Only the few lines around her eyes and on her forehead showed her age.

Winston Yamato had to be in his sixties, with a mane of white hair and a tanned face. He was still a competitive sailor, and often participated in races on his own boat. Peggy looked up from their conversation and said, "Good, you're here. We can get started."

Ray and I had met Yamato in the past, but Peggy introduced us again as Sarah slid into a chair and opened her laptop. Peggy had a stack of file folders in front of her. "These are from the firm's archives," she said, as we sat down at the oval conference table, in front of big windows that looked out at Honolulu Harbor. "More recent cases are all digital."

"These all involved Alexander Fields?" I asked.

Peggy nodded. "And they're all cases that ended badly for Mr. Fields' opposition, and which might provide a motive in his murder."

"How many cases?" Ray asked, his mouth slightly open in surprise.

"Twenty-four that we've found. The most recent was ten years ago, but the cases go all the way back to the fifties, when Alexander Fields was a sole proprietor."

"You really think there's a motive in cases that old?" Ray asked.

I remembered what Greg Oshiro had said, that Fields had some kind of bombshell to drop about something in the past, and that he had been seen with a woman of about his age as he went to his death.

"I can see a motive," I said. "If anything, I can see way too many motives."

"Sadly, detective," Yamato said, "I have to agree with you." He sighed. "I don't know if it's relevant, but Alex Fields was a very sick man. Another few months and..."

"That's what his daughter indicated," Ray said. "Cancer?"

"Of the pancreas," Winston said. "I don't know why we're

hearing so much about that particular type right now, but apparently it's very deadly."

"As is murder," Peggy said, her years as an assistant district attorney coming out. "Shall we work backwards, in chronological order?"

"You're running the show, counselor," I said. "We're just the audience."

The last case Fields had been actively involved in took place in 2005, during his final year "of counsel" to the firm. "Alexander took the case as a favor to an old friend," Yamato said. "Eleanor Keli'i Poe was a close friend of Yuki Fields, who was still alive then. Eleanor's nephew on the mainland alleged that she was losing her faculties and wanted to establish a conservatorship over her assets. Alex defended her."

"And?" I asked.

"He won. Alex usually did. Eleanor died a few months later, leaving her estate to her houseboy, a young drifter named Kasuo Yamamato. The nephew, Lee Poe, alleged that Alex was deficient in his responsibility to Eleanor and her original heirs, and complained to the Bar."

"Li Po?" I asked. "Like the Chinese poet?"

Everyone in the room looked at me and it was Peggy who finally said, "Your education is showing, Kimo." She spelled the name for me.

"Was Fields deficient in Poe's grandmother's case, do you think?" I asked.

Yamato shook his head. "I knew Eleanor Poe myself. She wasn't the smartest woman in the world, but she knew what she wanted, and she wanted that boy. It was her money, after all. Lee Poe continued to send threatening letters to Alex for several years. They're all in the file."

"Where is Lee Poe now?" Ray asked.

"He lives in Oregon."

That rang a bell. Stephanie Cornell lived in Oregon, too. I

wondered if they happened to know each other.

"Next?" I asked.

Fields had specialized in representing big corporations in disputes, often against much smaller, less powerful adversaries. Peggy took the lead, and with the occasional reminiscence from Winston and additional research from Sarah, we went through a mind-numbing list of cases, starting with a farmer in the Kalama Valley who believed that a nearby factory had polluted his land and destroyed his crops. Fields hired high-priced consultants to argue that there were other factors at work, and the farmer got nothing.

In the next case, a woman alleged that a hotel owner had been negligent in not cordoning off a part of the building under reconstruction. She fell and broke both hips, and sued for her medical bills and damages. Fields brought up her membership in Alcoholics Anonymous and argued that she had fallen off the wagon, gotten drunk, and ignored the warning signs. She ended up settling out of court for a pittance.

And so it went, back decade by decade. In the 1980s Fields represented a Japanese company that was on a land-buying spree in the islands, when the yen was strong and natives of the Land of the Rising Sun were investing in U.S. real estate like they weren't making any more of it. Several small landowners had refused to sell, and been strong-armed into doing so.

In the early seventies, when the islands were a staging ground for the Vietnam War, and many GIs came to Waikiki for R&R, Fields defended a club owner accused of gouging patrons. Then in the sixties, he had represented numerous corporations in suits brought by unions over working conditions. Back in the late '50s he had defended a developer named Emile Gardiner against a lawsuit by native Hawaiians over development of their ancestral property in the Kalama Valley.

In each case there was someone with a vendetta against Alexander Fields and a record of credible threats.

"But what I don't see is why now," Ray said, when we finished going through the folders. It was nearly lunch time, and my stomach was grumbling from the excess of caffeine and the lack of nutrition to balance it out. "Why would someone who wanted to kill Fields way back when wait until now?"

"That's your job to figure out, isn't it?" Peggy asked. "We're just giving you the information you need."

"Can we get a copy of Fields' will?" I asked Winston Yamato.

He nodded. "It's already in the file for you."

Sarah left the conference room to make copies of the documents we needed. Yamato stood up. "Please let me know if you need me to open any doors or grease any wheels for you. Alex was my friend as well as my partner. I want to see justice done for him."

"We'll keep that in mind," I said.

When he was gone, Peggy turned to me. "Of course if you find any connection between the death of Alexander Fields and this firm, you'll let me know."

"Peggy, you know the rules as well as I do. You're not an ADA anymore. We don't have to share anything with you or your firm."

She glared at me, and once again Ray had to step in as mediator. "If any of the firm's cases end up being connected to the murder, of course we'll come back to you. And please let Mr. Yamato know that we'll do everything in our power to solve this case."

She nodded curtly and stood up. She led us out to the lobby where we waited for Sarah to finish the copying. "Sometimes you can be a real ass," Ray muttered to me. "You need to stop letting your past get in the way of your future."

"That something else you learned in your college sociology classes?"

Fortunately Sarah arrived then with a banker's box of paperwork, as well as a jump drive filled with data. I volunteered to carry the box as a small gesture of apology to Ray for being a jerk.

"How are we going to get through all this?" Ray asked, as we rode down in the elevator, my implicit apology accepted wordlessly. "It's going to take weeks to sort through all this stuff, and to track down the people, if they're even still alive. Sampson's never going to let us work on this that long."

My stomach rumbled, as if in agreement. We stopped at a Zippy's on the way back to headquarters for lunch and brainstorming.

"Say we start working backwards, chronologically, just the way Peggy laid it all out for us," I said. "I like the coincidence that Stephanie Cornell and Lee Poe both live in Oregon."

"It's a big state, you know," Ray said, digging into his chili.

"Yeah, but you want to bet they both live in the same city?"

"Loser pays for this morning's coffee," Ray said.

"I already did."

He held two fingers up to his forehead in the shape of an L, and I kicked him under the table.

Back at headquarters, though, a quick search told us that Ray was the real loser. "Fork over the cash, pal," I said, turning my monitor to face him. "They not only live in the same state, same city. They live in the same damn house."

Sure enough, the address we found for Lee Poe matched the one for Stephanie Cornell. "And he's her alibi, isn't he?" I asked.

"Looks like we've got a pair of prime suspects," Ray said.

Ray called Stephanie Cornell, on the pretense of giving her an update on her father's case. He discovered that she and her boyfriend, Lee Poe, would be coming to Honolulu over the weekend, to attend her father's funeral on Monday. Ray made arrangements to speak to her after the interment.

For such a rich man, Alexander Fields had a very simple will. He made a few specific bequests to charities, but the bulk of his estate was divided equally between Shepard and Stephanie. His bank and phone records came in, and we looked through them. There was no pattern of large cash withdrawals, no payments other than the ones necessary to keep his lifestyle going. And Marikit's record was clean, too; she had no major debts and no association with known criminals.

We ordered credit reports on both Stephanie and Shepard, and then spent the rest of the afternoon going through the materials we had gotten from Fields & Yamato, organizing and prioritizing. Even though we had some good suspects in Stephanie and Lee, we couldn't ignore the other possibilities. There was still the question of the elderly woman who'd been with Fields; who was she and where did she fit into the case? Were the two bodybuilders hired thugs, or did they have some other connection?

Late in the afternoon, we sat down with Lieutenant Sampson to go over our progress. "Convenient," he said, when we were finished. "I don't have to pay you overtime this weekend, and you get a couple of days off. I like the way this case is working out."

Ray admitted that he could use the chance to catch up on sleep, and I planned to get some surfing in. Since our prime suspects weren't going to be in town until Sunday, that meant we could put the case aside without guilt. "You can come back to your other suspects on Monday morning, and plan to attend Fields' funeral. Talk to the brother and the sister and anyone else who has something to say."

I drove home and walked Roby. I didn't feed him; he was going with us to my parents' house and I knew my father would slip him table scraps. Mike got home as I was getting out of the shower, and after he cleaned up we drove over to St. Louis Heights.

My parents still live in the house where I grew up, along a twisting road that abuts Wa'ahila Ridge State Park. I always have this sense of déjà vu as I drive up their street, remembering the flat place where my father taught me to ride a two-wheeler, the hilly slope where I used to hide as a teenager when I needed to escape, the homes of neighbor kids, and the corner where I waited for the school bus.

Mine was a pretty good childhood. My father worked too much, and let his temper loose on us kids too often, but I always had a roof over my head and food in my stomach and the deep sense that I was loved.

Looking back now, I wonder how they managed. My father's business rose and fell with economic cycles. When times were good he had plenty of work, building houses and stores and warehouses. When the economy tanked he did small remodeling jobs and managed the investment properties he had begun to assemble.

My mom kept the house and supervised the three of us. I imagine she was just able to catch her breath with both my older brothers in school and then she turned up pregnant with me. My parents always insisted that I wasn't an accident, even though Lui and Haoa kidded me I had to be. But I never knew what had convinced my parents to have a third child, if it was a conscious decision.

My father is one of six children, four of whom lived to adulthood. He was born just short of a year after the death of his oldest brother, also named Albert, after Queen Victoria's husband. My grandparents had clearly decided to have another kid in the wake of the death of Albert the first, as we called him. There was one girl after my father, a baby who died in infancy. By then, I imagined my grandparents were done.

As we pulled up in the driveway, Roby started going crazy, jumping around in the back seat and trying to climb up front with us. He loved his tutus, and they spoiled him even more than we did. They always said that was their right as grandparents.

My niece Ashley, Haoa's eldest, came out of the house as we walked up the driveway. "Aloha, Uncles." She no longer had to get up on her tiptoes to kiss my cheek; she was almost as tall as I was. She still had to stretch a bit to kiss Mike, though.

She got more breathtakingly beautiful each time I saw her. The genetic soup she inherited from her parents had resulted in ash blonde hair, a lean, willowy frame, and a heart-shaped face with just a trace of her Japanese great-grandfather around her eyes. She was about to graduate from Punahou, and was going to try her hand at the surfing circuit, postponing college for at least a year.

She was carrying a plastic container. "You're not taking all the coconut cake, are you?" I asked, reaching for it.

She kept it away from me. "Just enough for me, Ailina, and Apikela," she said. Those were her sisters. "Alec can come get his own cake if he wants some."

Alec was her brother, and there was the same kind of rivalry between him and Ashley as I'd had with Lui and Haoa.

"Aloha!" she said, waving her hand and hurrying down the driveway.

"Can you just imagine what Haoa must go through every time she goes out on a date?" Mike asked, watching her walk away.

"Ashley can take care of herself," I said. "She's got her mother's beauty but her father's personality. Not that Haoa and Tatiana don't worry."

The front door opened again, and I saw my mother in the frame. She looked smaller and more frail than the last time I'd seen her, though I'm sure that was just my imagination. She was a petite China doll, and even in her late sixties she still looked lovely. She wore an orange silk blouse with a Mandarin collar and fine white embroidery.

After a flurry of hugging and kissing we followed her into the kitchen, where my father was already sitting at the kitchen table. His hair seemed sparser, his face a little less full, than the last time I'd seen him. He was as handsome as my mother was beautiful; I'd gotten great genes from both of them.

"I was wondering when you were going to get here," he grumbled. "I'm hungry."

"You don't look like you're starving," my mother said.

His jet-black hair started to go gray about five years before, and he looked quite distinguished. He had just a few forehead lines; the rest of his face was smooth. The older I get, the more I look like him.

We sat down and my mother began dishing out the food. Because of my father's heart disease and high blood pressure, she had begun grilling meat and fish, serving more vegetables, and using a light hand with rich sauces. He grumbled about the low fat content and the skimpy portions of rice, but the food was delicious.

Roby stationed himself next to my father, who dropped him tidbits of chicken. I didn't realize dogs liked broccoli; it's not a vegetable you'd ever find in our house. But Roby gobbled up whatever his tutu gave him.

Over coconut cake, I brought up the reason for our visit. "I'm working a case right now, and the victim is Alexander Fields," I said.

"The attorney?" my father asked.

"Yeah. Did you know him?"

He shrugged. "I ran across him a few times over the years. I wouldn't say I knew him."

"I knew his wife," my mother said. "Yuki. She was in the PTA at Punahou with me and Evelyn Clark. Her oldest boy was in Haoa's class."

"You ever hear anything about him?" I asked. "People who didn't like him or had a grudge against him?"

"He was a tough businessman," my father said. "When you're like that there are always people who don't like you." He sat back in his chair. "You remember I used to work for old Judge Fong when I was a teenager, taking care of his yard?"

I had met the ancient, wizened judge a few times when I was a kid. He had been a mentor to my dad, convincing him to go to UH instead of just getting a job after high school. "Fields used to come over to the judge's house all the time back then. Even I could tell he was going to be an important man."

"When was this?" I asked.

"Middle of the 1950s," he said. "I graduated high school in what, 1956? I kept on working for the judge my first couple of years at UH."

"That must have been such an interesting time," Mike said. "Just before statehood."

My father snorted. "Interesting is one word for it. For most of us, it wasn't an issue at all. The businessmen, they had a lot at stake. We were paying federal tax—more than some of the states—and we had no voice in setting tax rates, and we were never sure of getting our fair share back in federal services and money for improvements. People said that only statehood could guarantee us our rights."

He took a long drink of water. "But other people wanted Hawai'i to remain a territory, because they hoped that someday we could be an independent people again."

"How about you?" I asked. "What did you think?"

"I was just a teenager. I didn't know what to think. But I listened to the judge, and he said that there were over half a million people in Hawai'i, more than some states, and nine out of ten of them were born on U.S. soil. They shouldn't be denied the rights of citizenship."

Roby got up and walked over to Mike, nuzzling against his

knee. "I remember learning something in high school social studies class about the opposition to statehood," Mike said. "Didn't most of it come from the mainland?"

"The haoles on the mainland were worried about us mixed-race people. This one Senator even came to Honolulu for an investigation." He laughed. "Turned out he was investigating the prostitutes in Chinatown instead. Somebody killed him and the police hushed it up. Didn't want it to look like we were all savages."

"I wonder where Alexander Fields stood," I said.

"Fields was always on the side of big business," my father said. "I remember one case, a friend of mine. He wanted to get some work on the Pali Tunnel. This must have been what, right after statehood? Fields represented a big company that wanted the work, and they shut my friend out. That was the kind of man he was."

"Things were very difficult back then," my mother said. "My father went on strike a couple of times in the sugar cane fields." My mother's father had been recruited from his native Tokushima Prefecture, on Japan's Shikoku Island, to work chopping and weeding sugar cane on a huge plantation. The workday was long, the labor exhausting, and, the workers' lives were strictly controlled by the plantation owners.

"I never heard that," I said.

She nodded. "During the strikes, my father was out of work and we had to live with my mother's family for a while." She looked at Mike. "They were native Hawaiians and they didn't have much money, either. My father had to learn to fish to help out."

She put her hands on the table in front of her. "Statehood was good for us. We got money from the government for food, and I was able to stay in school and graduate. I got a job in the Amfac office, and met Al."

"You two worked together?" Mike asked. Roby gave up on being petted and sprawled on the floor on his side.

"I was a construction superintendent by then," my father said. "I heard they had hired this beautiful wahine in the office and so I made it my business to go over there." He reached out and took my mother's hand. "As soon as I saw Lokelani I knew she was the one for me."

"Love at first sight," Mike said. He looked at me. The first time I saw him, I was carrying a dead chicken and I smelled of blood and feathers. When I saw him again a few days later, and I realized he was gay, too, I felt an electric current surge through my body. I wondered if that's what my parents had felt when they met.

"You tell your parents about your situation at work?" Mike asked me.

"What?" my father asked. "Someone making trouble for you, talking stink?"

I shook my head and smiled. My father was always quick to jump to my defense, and I'd often relied on his strength. "Nothing like that. HPD may send me and Ray on assignment to the FBI."

"I like that," my mother said. "That's office work, isn't it? Much safer for you than what you do now. Maybe I can relax some."

"Mom. My job isn't that dangerous."

"Every night I say prayers for all my boys and their families. I say a special one for you, to keep you safe." She looked at Mike. "You, too. Running into fires."

We both laughed. "Thanks, Mom." My family had never been big on organized religion; we had too many races and traditions all jumbled together. But my parents had both always been spiritual, and it didn't surprise me that my mom still said her prayers every night.

We convinced Roby to get up, and took a big hunk of coconut cake home with us.

Saturday morning I woke up early. While Mike was still sleeping I put my longboard in the back of the Jeep and drove down to Makapu'u Point. It's one of the best breaks on the south shore of O'ahu and one of my favorites. I snagged a parking spot in the lot, put on my rash guard, grabbed the board, and started down toward the water.

The park area is studded with abandoned structures from World War II, and I remembered all the buildings around the Inline Imports warehouse on Lagoon Drive. Was Dakota living in one of them? Was that why he'd been able to see Fields being taken into the warehouse in the middle of the night?

I stepped into the water. It was cool but it felt good, and I got onto my board and paddled out, duck-diving through the breakers. In the distance I saw a whale surface, and then I focused on the waves, the wind, and the position of the other surfers around me.

For years, surfing was my escape from everything I saw as a cop—the myriad ways in which people mistreated each other, committing violence on strangers and loved ones alike. The waves revived and cleansed me, and my whole identity was built around not only being a cop but being a surfer, too.

Then my relationship with Mike grew more and more important, and I moved away from Waikiki, where I was only steps away from a decent surf break, to Aiea Heights, miles inland. Life with him became my safety valve and I didn't get to surf much anymore. But I still felt that pull of salt water, stirring something deep inside me that went back to my Polynesian ancestors who lived at the ocean's mercy.

I sat on my board until I felt a wave building beneath me, and as it surged I stepped up, balanced myself, and rode the wave, doing an inside turn, then catching the curl and riding the lip of the wave parallel to the beach.

When the wave died I jumped off into the cold water, then paddled back out and did it all over again. I wiped my brain clear of arson and murder and runaway teenagers and the pressing issue of whether Mike and I would become fathers. I just surfed.

But once I was out of the water and on my way home, everything came back to me and I knew that I had to go see Angelina Gianelli, Dakota's mother. It was easier to go there on my way home, so I continued along the Kalanaiana'ole Highway, which hugged the windward coast, until I came to the Women's Community Correctional Center. It's a low-slung white complex in the shadow of the Ko'olau mountains in Kailua, and I'd been there a few times in the past to talk to suspects and witnesses.

I parked next to an old Kia sedan with a row of round-faced Japanese dolls on the back ledge, wondering if it belonged to someone who worked at the place or someone visiting an inmate. I hoped it was an employee, because that row of dolls looked so sad.

I showed my HPD ID to the guard at the front gate and then again when I got inside. I was directed to a visitation room that overlooked a small playground. Through a window I saw a couple of mothers playing with little children on slides and staircases. It could have been any playground in Honolulu, except for the barbed wire fence and the moms in matching prison uniforms.

Angelina was brought in a few minutes later. Hers was a pretty name for a woman who once had been very attractive. But the ravages of her addiction to smoking crystal meth showed in the paleness of her skin and her gaunt figure.

I introduced myself and we sat down across from each other. "I came up to ask you about your son, Dakota," I began.

"He ain't got nothing to do with my situation," she said. "I have a problem. I know. But I wasn't selling drugs. That was something the police put up on me. They don't like white people here in these islands. They call us howlers."

"Haole," I said. "And it's not derogatory. It's just a way of classifying people."

"As soon as I get out of here I'm getting my boy and going back to New Jersey. I have family there. They'll take care of us."

"When is that going to be?"

She frowned. "I got ten to fifteen, but they say I'll be out of here in five."

"How old will Dakota be then?"

She closed her lips tight as if she was thinking. "Eighteen or nineteen."

"What's going to happen to him in the meantime, Angelina? You know where he is now?"

"He's in some foster home. That's what they told me."

I shook my head. "He ran away from there. I saw him Tuesday night at Ala Moana Park. I bought him dinner, but he slipped out after he ate."

"How do you know Dakota anyway?"

I wasn't sure if Angelina knew that Dakota was gay, and if she didn't I wasn't going to out him. "He came to a youth group I volunteer with on Waikiki sometimes," I said. "One of the other kids saw him and heard he'd run away, so she told me."

I thought by slipping the feminine pronoun in, I might be fooling Angelina, but she was more savvy than I thought. "Not that faggot group?" she asked. "I told him to stay away from that. He's just confused, is all. I should never have brought him here."

She leaned close toward me. "You're not one of them, are you? There's always these men leering around him."

"I'm not interested in Dakota for sex," I said. "I just want to make sure he's living in a safe place and not doing anything stupid. Do you have any idea where he might be staying?"

She shook her head.

"Any friends he had in Wahiawa, who he might have turned to? Neighbors?"

"We kept to ourselves."

I leaned forward. "You even care about what happens to Dakota? You don't know where he is or what he's doing. You didn't even know he ran away from the foster home."

She stood up. "I got my own problems. Dakota, he's almost a grown man. He's just gonna have to take care of himself."

She walked over to the door of the room, and the guard opened it and took her away. I sat there for a couple of minutes. That was what ice did to you, I thought. You got so all you cared about was the next fix. I hoped Dakota wouldn't end up the way his mother had. And I knew that if I could do anything to help him, I would.

I drove through the mountains back to Aiea Heights, grateful that my parents had cared for me better than Angelina Gianelli had for her boy.

That afternoon, Mike and I drove down to Lagoon Drive. The neighborhood was deserted and all the businesses closed, but we cruised around, looking for any signs of life. If Dakota was holed up in one of the abandoned warehouses, by himself or with others, there had to be some evidence.

We parked and I pulled a flashlight out of my glove compartment. Then we started combing the area on foot, looking for broken windows or doors that had been forced. As we approached a two-story brick building, its windows boarded up, Mike sniffed the air. "Fried chicken," he said. "I'd know that smell anywhere."

We followed his nose around the building. "There," I said, pointing. One of the boards covering a window had come loose. When we examined it, I saw it could be pried open just enough for a person to slip through.

"What do you want to do?" Mike asked. "Call for backup?"

"For what? A kid, or a couple of kids, hiding out? I'm going in."

"Kimo. You don't know what's in there."

"I can handle teenagers." Even so, I pulled my gun out of its thumb holster, and kept it in one hand, my flashlight in the other. As Mike held the wood back, I leaned inside and shone the light.

"Anybody in here?" I called.

There was no answer but the smell of fried chicken was a lot stronger. I hoisted one leg over the windowsill, scraping my nuts on it as I tried to slither inside. My entrance was somewhat less than gracious, accompanied by a couple of curse words my parents would be displeased to discover I had first learned on the playing fields at Punahou.

"You all right?" Mike asked from outside.

"Fine. I'm going to look around."

I shone the light in a slow arc around the inside of the building. The ceiling was two stories up, while ahead of me I saw a row of four offices, and a staircase to a level above them. The floor was littered with debris and I walked carefully ahead, shining the light down so I wouldn't trip.

Each office held one or more sleeping bags, along with piles of clothes and other personal effects. The remains of a bucket of fried chicken were in the last one. There was a tiny bathroom at the far end; the power didn't work but the water still did.

I turned around and walked back to where Mike waited, climbing carefully out of the window. "Someone's been staying here," I said. "At least four or five people. From the clothes I'd say they're teenagers or young adults."

"What do we do? Call Child Welfare?"

"I don't know." I looked at him. "First of all, we don't know who's living here—they could be kids, or they could be over eighteen. They're trespassing for sure, which is a crime. But for the moment they're not hurting anyone and they're not in danger."

My instincts were warring. As a cop, I knew I should report the squatters and protect the property owners' rights. If there were underage kids staying there, they should be in the system, so they could be placed in foster care, given regular meals and the chance to get an education.

But if Dakota was staying there, at least he was safe. He had run away from one foster home; chances were good he'd run away from another. And then he might end up somewhere much worse than a secure old warehouse with running water.

"I think I should talk to Terri," I said.

Ever since junior high, I'd depended on the insight of my best female friend, Terri Clark Gonsalves, when it came to emotional questions. She had helped me understand the psychology of victims and villains in other cases, and I trusted her instincts.

We walked back to where I'd parked the Jeep and I called Terri. "Why don't you come over for dinner?" she asked, when I told her that I needed to talk. "Levi's barbecuing and Danny's got a couple of friends coming over."

She had been dating a divorced guy named Levi Hirsch for a while, and he seemed to get along really well with her son, Danny. I looked over at Mike. "Fine with me," he said. "We can bring the beer."

I told Terri we'd be there at six and hung up.

We were driving back up the Nimitz Highway toward home when Mike said, "We could do that kind of thing too, you know, if we had kids."

"What kind of thing?"

"Barbecue. Have a bunch of keikis running around."

"We could do that without having kids of our own," I said. "You want to have a party sometime? Invite everyone?"

"You just don't get it." Mike turned toward the door.

I gave up. I was tired of having the same argument and it was clear to me that neither of us was going to change his mind.

"I'll take Roby," Mike said, as I pulled into the driveway. He hooked the dog and they trotted down the street as I went inside. I opened up my netbook and looked up the address of the warehouse where I'd seen the fried chicken and the sleeping bags. The last owner had gone bankrupt, and the bank had foreclosed on the mortgage. Like a lot of property, it sat abandoned, waiting for some economic revival that might never arrive.

Mike came back with Roby, and we left for Terri's soon after. Neither of us spoke much on the drive, but Mike broke out in a huge smile when Terri's son Danny came rushing out of the house to meet us. He was about to turn ten in a few weeks, and he still couldn't decide if he wanted to be a fireman when he grew up, like Mike, or a cop, like me and his late father.

"I saw a fire last week!" he crowed. "It wasn't very big, not like a house or anything, but the flames were a really light color, like almost white, not like when we burn wood in the fireplace in Colorado."

Levi had introduced Danny to skiing at a condo in Vail the year before, and they were due to spend another spring break there soon.

"White flame means there was gasoline in the fire," Mike said. "Now the stuff in your fireplace, that's wood, so that burns red."

Terri came out the front door. "Danny, let your uncles get in the house, please."

Danny grabbed Mike's hand. "Come on, I want to show you something."

Mike followed him to the backyard, and Terri and I went inside. She looked great, in a tight white polo with plaid shorts and a white fabric belt. For a long time after her husband died, it was like some of the life had leached out of her, too. But since meeting Levi, she had returned to the girl I knew.

"Can we talk?" I asked. "Before we go outside?"

"Sure. What's up?"

I sat on the floral-print sofa. Terri's living room represented her personality—a combination of easy-going tropical with an understated elegance. I thought I was going to tell her about Dakota, but instead I said, "Mike and I keep going around and around about having kids."

She nodded. "It's been six months, hasn't it? Is Sandra ready?"

"Yeah. I just don't think I am."

She laughed. "You're never ready. Especially as you get older and you know more about being a parent."

"You and Levi thinking of having more kids?"

"No. He has his girls, and I have Danny. Neither of us want to start over again." She smiled. "He moved in last week, though."

"Really? That's good." Levi had been keeping a condo in Waikiki even though he was spending more and more time at Terri's house.

"Yeah, it is." She shifted in her seat. "So where are you on the issue? Who wants what?"

"Mike wants to be a dad. I can see it every time he looks at or talks to a kid."

"And you don't?"

"It's such a huge responsibility, you know? Even if Sandra and Cathy are going to be the primary parents. And I think Mike wants a baby for the wrong reasons."

"He's not some teenage girl who wants someone to love him," Terri said. "He's a grown man and he knows what he wants and why he wants it." She looked at me. "Do you think this is something that would break you guys up?"

I crossed my arms and rubbed my biceps. "I hope not."

"It should be a joint decision between the both of you. But what if Mike decides to go forward with Sandra. How would you feel about that?"

"Like what we have together isn't enough for him."

I didn't mean to say that; it just blurted out. But then, that's me. Speak first and think later.

"Do you think you'd resent the baby, or the time Mike wanted to spend with him or her?"

"How can I predict that? People say that once you see a kid who belongs to you, everything changes. I don't believe that." I leaned forward. "I went to see this woman today, at WCCC. Her son has been coming to my gay teen group, and when I confronted her about him and his whereabouts, she didn't seem to care."

"You can't base your decision on what some woman in prison says," Terri said. "I've seen you with Danny, and with your nieces and nephews. You're great with kids."

"But then I can send them home," I said.

"And how is that going to be different if Sandra and Cathy are raising this as yet conjectural baby?"

"Won't it be different, if it's my baby, or Mike's?"

"You're the only one who can say that."

I sighed. "You haven't been particularly helpful, you know that?"

Danny came running in. "Levi says to tell you that the burgers are ready." We followed him outside, where his friends clustered around the grill as Levi dished out the food.

Terri and I loaded up our plates with Levi's burgers and strips of red and green pepper from the grill, along with Terri's homemade potato salad and Waialua root beer, and we sat at the picnic table with Mike. Levi joined us when he'd given out all the food. The kids sat on the ground beneath Danny's ranger tower.

Mike speared a blackened pepper strip and asked, "So, Terri, what do you think we should do about Dakota?"

Terri looked at him. "Dakota?"

"Isn't that what Kimo was talking to you about?" He looked

at me.

"I never actually said his name." I turned to Terri. "The kid I was telling you about, whose mom is in prison?"

"Oh, yeah."

"He's fourteen, and he ran away from the foster home where he was sent."

The kids under the ranger tower started jumping around, and Levi got up to look after them.

"Mike and I found an abandoned warehouse out by Hickam Air Force Base, and it looks like Dakota might be staying there, maybe with some other kids," I said.

"Did you call Child Welfare Services?"

"See, that's what I said," Mike said. "But Kimo didn't want to. We think the kid might be turning tricks to survive. And who knows who else is staying with him at that warehouse."

"But if Child Welfare picks him up they're just going to ship him to another foster home," I said. "Suppose he runs away from there, too?"

"Kimo, you can't think like that," Terri said. She took a deep breath. "Did I ever tell you that I went through the process to become a foster parent myself?"

I shook my head. "When was this?"

"Two years ago. Just before I met Levi. I knew that I needed something else in my life and I wasn't sure what it was." She leaned forward. "If you find this kid, I can ask to have him placed with me, at least temporarily. Then you'll know he's safe."

"You don't even know him," I said.

"I know you both. And if you think he's worth worrying about then I'll take the risk on him."

"Don't you have to clear that with Danny and Levi?" I asked. I pointed at Mike. "I can't even make dinner plans without asking Mr. Large and In Charge over there."

"Danny would love an older brother, even if it's only for a

little while. And you know Levi. He has a huge heart."

"Still, I'd feel better if you talked to them first," I said.

She laughed. "I must be having some effect on you, after all these years." She stood up. "I'll be right back."

Terri returned a couple of minutes later. "Come on, let's get moving."

"What?" I asked.

"We're going out to that warehouse and see if we can find this kid, and then we'll bring him back here. On Monday I can start the official paperwork."

Terri called a neighbor, who agreed Danny could spend the night at her house. Then we took off toward Lagoon Drive, Mike and me in my Jeep, Terri and Levi following in her SUV.

Mike and I didn't talk until I was getting onto the H1 freeway. "What did Terri say about us having kids?" he asked.

"How do you know I asked her advice?"

"Because I know you and how you operate. What did she tell you to do?"

"She's like a therapist. She just asks a lot of questions." I looked over at him. "The biggest one she asked was how I would feel if you went ahead and donated sperm on your own. Would I be jealous or resentful."

Mike didn't say anything.

I took a deep breath. I knew that what I was about to say would change everything between us, forever.

Then my cell phone rang. It was a number I didn't recognize, and I was tempted to let it go to voice mail. But old habits die hard, and so I answered.

"Kimo? This is Dakota."

I tilted the phone so that Mike could hear. "Hey, Dakota, howzit?"

"I saw one of those guys," he said. "Those bodybuilders, the ones who brought that old man and old woman to the warehouse that burned."

"You did? Where? When?"

"A couple of minutes ago. On this little street in Waikiki called Tusitala. You know where that is?"

"I used to live right near there. I'm in my Jeep right now and I'm not far from Waikiki. Can I meet you there and have you show me where the guy is?"

He hesitated.

"I'd really appreciate it, Dakota. I can buy you another dinner, if you want."

I looked over at Mike. He nodded.

"All right. I'll be waiting outside the ABC Store at the corner of Kuhio and Liliu'okalani."

I hung up and dialed Terri. "Change of plans." I explained what I knew. "Why don't we all park near my old apartment, and then Mike and I will get Dakota?"

We got there first, and I parked just a block from where we were to meet Dakota. Mike and I walked quickly to the ABC Store—but he wasn't there. "Shit," Mike said.

I saw a pay phone, one of the few left in town, and checked out the number posted on the dial. It matched the one that had come through on my cell. "At least we know he was here," I said. "Let's split up and see if we can find him. Maybe the bodybuilder took off and Dakota's following him."

"Or he got cold feet and took off."

"Ever the optimist," I said. "You go a couple of blocks Diamond Head and I'll go the other way, and we'll circle back and meet here."

I had lived on Liliu'okalani Street for years, and I knew the sidewalks, storefronts and alleys of that part of town by heart. I prowled along, keeping in the shadows, looking for Dakota's distinctive long ponytail.

"Kimo!"

I turned at the sound of the whisper. Dakota was standing between two buildings. "He's in that Chinese restaurant over there," he said, pointing across the street.

As we watched, a black limousine turned off Kuhio Avenue and glided down the street. "That's the car!" Dakota said.

"You can't be sure," I said. "There must be dozens of those on the island."

"But still." Dakota shifted into the light and I got a good look at him. He was a handsome kid, about five-seven, with his dark hair pulled straight back from his forehead and knotted into a ponytail. He had a slim, aquiline nose and just the faintest trace of a mustache on his upper lip. He was wearing a ratty T-shirt, baggy board shorts and dark green rubber slippers.

I held up my index finger as the restaurant door opened and a muscle-bound guy stepped out, carrying a takeout bag. I pulled out my cell phone and flipped to the camera app. He walked across the sidewalk and I took a couple of quick shots of him. I got a good one of his face under the street light.

Then I hurried out into the street as the car pulled away, taking a picture of the license plate. It was one of the special ones in support of the Bishop Museum, and I pulled out my wallet and scribbled the number down, just in case I'd jiggled the phone and the number didn't come through clearly.

"Why didn't you stop him?" Dakota demanded.

"On what grounds? Illegal restaurant take-out? I've got his picture and I've got his license plate number. Now I can track him down and see who he is and what kind of connection he has to this case."

Mike rounded the corner and I waved at him.

"I gotta go," Dakota said.

He turned away from me but I grabbed his arm. "Hold on, Dakota. What about that dinner I promised you?"

"I already ate."

"How about a coffee or something? A Frappucino? We just

want to talk to you."

Mike came up to us then. "Hey, Dakota. What's going on?"

Dakota shrugged. "Nothing much. Just hanging."

"Well, then, come hang with us," Mike said. "We're meeting a couple of friends. Just relaxing and chilling."

Dakota looked from Mike to me, and I smiled.

"You're not mad, are you?" he asked. "That I ran out of Denny's?"

I shrugged. "I'm glad you got a good meal. And that you know you can call me if you need anything."

"Can I have a mocha coconut Frappucino?" he asked. "They're my favorite."

"Mine, too," Mike said. They walked a few feet ahead of me, and I called Terri and told her to meet us at the Starbucks on Kuhio, just a couple of blocks away.

They joined us as we reached the restaurant, and I introduced them to Dakota. "Terri and I have been friends since we were your age," I said.

"Kimo," Terri said. "Never say anything to a teenager that has 'when I was your age' in it." She smiled and reached for Dakota's hand. "Besides, maybe I don't want Dakota to know that I'm as old as you are."

"You look a lot younger than my mom," Dakota said. "And she's old, like thirty-five."

I didn't want to tell Dakota that we were all older than that, at least by a couple of years.

"See, he's a gentleman," Terri said. "You could learn some manners from him, Kimo."

We walked inside and got in line, behind a posse of Japanese tourists and a drag queen in six-inch stilettos. "I don't see how you can walk in those, Helen," I said.

Helen Wheels was an occasional emcee at drag nights at the Rod and Reel Club, a gay bar on Waikiki that had been my regular hangout before I moved in with Mike.

"It's all about the balance." She looked the five of us up and down. "Aren't you a mixed bag tonight?"

I introduced Helen to Mike, Terri, Levi and Dakota. "You're a cutie pie," she said to him. "Isn't it past your bedtime, though?"

"Isn't it past your sell-by date?" he asked her.

We howled with laughter, and the Japanese tourists all turned around to stare. "This one's got spunk," she said, then she turned on an imitation of Ed Asner in the Mary Tyler Moore show. "I hate spunk."

Dakota looked confused as the rest of us laughed. "It's an old-folks joke," I said to him.

Helen stepped up and ordered her drink, then Levi said, "Put it all on one tab."

She turned to him. "Where have you been all my life, handsome?"

"Obviously hanging out in all the wrong places," Levi said.

We continued to banter as we waited for our drinks. Then Helen teetered off to a gig, and the five of us settled in a group of comfy chairs in the back corner.

"You strike me as a pretty smart kid, Dakota," I said.

"I know how to take care of myself."

"Yeah, but you're also smart enough to see you can't stay in that warehouse on Lagoon Drive forever. You need a stable place to live, food on the table, a chance to go to school and have fun, just like any other teenager. Without having to worry about the cops or criminals or people who prey on kids."

He shifted uncomfortably in his chair and it looked like he was trying to see a way out of the coffee shop.

"What Kimo's saying is that you need to go back into foster care," Terri said, leaning toward him.

"No."

"It doesn't have to be bad," Terri said. "Levi and I were thinking you might come stay with us for a few days, just to see how we all get along. I've already been approved as a foster mother. Levi and I live in a house in Wailupe, just outside Honolulu, with my son Danny, who's almost ten."

"I don't want to," Dakota said, looking down.

"You've probably had adults disappoint you," Levi said. "I know how that is. My dad died suddenly when I was twelve. My mom didn't know how to pay a bill or fix anything around the house. She was completely lost, and my older sisters and I felt like we'd been abandoned."

I didn't know much about Levi's life before he had become a corporate mogul, then ditched it all to gunkhole around the islands in his sailboat. He'd come into our lives when he met Terri, and though I'd been introduced to his two daughters and learned about his business career, he'd never talked before about his youth.

"I never had a dad," Dakota said. "I think he was just some one-night stand of my mom's. She would never tell me anything about him."

"That's tough," Levi said. "At least I have memories of my dad, and of my mom when things were good. After he died my mom started dating this real jerk, and he and I butted heads for a long time."

He leaned forward. "The thing is, you have to let people help you. As soon as they could, my sisters moved out of the house, and they helped me get a scholarship to a boarding school. The teachers there really cared about helping me succeed. Without all of them, I don't know where I'd be."

"I don't need any help," Dakota said.

I thought maybe Dakota needed some tough love. "That's stupid," I said. "And you know it. You're just scared. Right?" I shook my head. "I never thought you were a wimp, Dakota. I thought you had balls."

"Kimo!" Terri said.

Mike glared at me.

Dakota sat up straighter. "I'm not scared. But I'm not going anywhere with a stranger. Can I come stay with you and Mike?"

"We aren't—" I started to say, but Mike interrupted me.

"Of course. We've got a spare bedroom where you can stay. But it's not a hotel. You'll have to help out with walking the dog, keep your room clean, that kind of thing."

Dakota nodded. "All right. I can do that."

That wasn't the way I was expecting things to work out. "I think that's a great idea," Terri said.

Everyone looked at me. What was I going to say? That we weren't foster parents? That we weren't ready to look after a troubled teenager? That I was scared things would change between Mike and me if we opened our home and our lives to a kid?

"I agree," I said. "We'll keep things between us for a few days and see how things work out. And then if we need to, Mike and I will go through the process to be official foster parents."

"I can help with that," Terri said. "Since I've been through it already."

I looked at Dakota. "You have stuff somewhere? Back at that warehouse?"

"Some clothes. But I don't want to go back there tonight."

"There's a twenty-four hour Walmart near Ala Moana Center," Mike said. "We can swing by there on the way home and get you whatever you need to hold you for a couple of days."

We stood up. "If you need anything, call me, Kimo," Terri said.

"I will. You can count on it."

We all hugged and kissed goodbye, and Dakota shook hands shyly with Terri and Levi. "Thank you for being interested in me," he said.

"Kimo and Mike will take good care of you," Levi said. He opened his wallet and pulled out a business card and a couple of bills. "In case there's something you want at the Walmart that they won't buy for you. And feel free to call us any time."

Dakota took the money and the card and stuffed them into the pocket of his board shorts. We split up a block later as Terri and Levi headed to her SUV, and Mike, Dakota and I walked along without saying anything.

The Walmart was bright and busy, even late on a Saturday night. I got a shopping cart and followed Mike and Dakota over to the clothing section, where Mike started loading up the cart with underwear, shorts and T-shirts. "He's going to need something to wear to school," I said. "Get him a couple of collared shirts and long pants."

"I don't want to go to school," Dakota said. "You guys can home school me. I know kids who do that."

"Yeah, right," I said. "In our spare time. Mike and I both went to high school here in Honolulu and you will too. What grade are you in, anyway?"

"Eighth."

"That's Aiea Intermediate," Mike said. "I went there."

"How come you didn't go to Aiea High?" I asked, as I followed them to the grocery section, pushing the shopping cart.

"Got into a special science magnet at Farrington," Mike said. He turned to Dakota. "Geez, if you're in eighth grade already we'll have to start looking at high schools, see where the best one is for you."

"Don't go overboard, bud," I said. "Let's get Dakota settled first."

Dakota got to pick out a couple of snacks he liked, and we stocked up on food supplies. By the time we hit the register the cart was piled high with stuff. Dakota pulled the cash Levi had given him out of his pocket and tried to hand it to me.

"Hold on to that," I said. "Every kid needs a little money of his own."

We drove home, and Dakota met Roby. It was love at first sight. He got down on the ground and Roby jumped all over him, licking his face as Dakota giggled and scratched the dog's stomach. By the time we had everything unloaded and put away, and got Dakota set up in the guest room, it was after midnight, and I was grateful to crawl into bed.

"You're not mad, are you?" Mike asked, sliding in next to me. "About Dakota coming to stay with us?"

"We don't know that it's permanent." I yawned. "It just means no more sex in the living room for a while."

"You think he can hear us in here?"

"Yup. Go to sleep." I leaned over and kissed his cheek, and then we spooned together and drifted off.

I half expected Dakota's bed to be empty the next morning. I wasn't sure he'd stick around, even though he'd seemed happy the night before. But he was still asleep when I looked in on him, his hair spread around him on the pillow, tiny snores coming out of his mouth.

I went downstairs, walked Roby, then started fixing breakfast. By the time the bacon was fried and the eggs scrambled, both Mike and Dakota had come down to the kitchen.

"Can you get the orange juice?" I asked Dakota. "Glasses in the cabinet above the dishwasher."

The three of us sat down to breakfast, Roby sprawled behind Mike's chair waiting for some bacon bits.

"This is cool," Dakota said. "Back home we used to go to my uncle's house sometimes for breakfast. Then he and my mom had a fight and after that she picked us up and moved here."

We talked for a while about growing up, and then Dakota asked, "Are you going to be able to find that guy?"

"What guy?"

"The one from the car last night."

"Oh, yeah. Him. I'll have to run a trace on that license plate. And I'll send the picture to a guy I know at the FBI, and ask him to run it through their facial recognition software." I looked at him. "But I can't do that until tomorrow. In the meantime, you ever been surfing?"

He shook his head. "I can't swim."

I nodded. "Well, that's something we can work on today. Your first swimming lesson."

Dakota went up to his room to put on the bathing suit we had bought the night before, and I said to Mike, "What are we going to do with him tomorrow? We can't enroll him in school because he's not legally supposed to be living with us."

"We don't even know if he's at an eighth-grade level. They probably have placement tests online somewhere."

I nodded. "That's a good idea. We can find him a placement test online, and then if he's behind in some area, we can get him a book or something and have him study. Then in a couple of days we'll know where we are."

Dakota wasn't thrilled about taking an online test, but Mike convinced him while I surfed around and found a good site. "It's going to take you half an hour," I said. "And then we'll go swimming, all right?"

He grudgingly sat down at the laptop and started taking the test. Looking over his shoulder I saw that there were questions in science, math, social studies, and English, along with some optional sections on computer science, foreign language and health.

He was adept at using the computer, and I was hopeful that meant he'd gotten some good schooling somewhere. When he finished the test, Mike and I looked at the results with him. His reading comprehension was pretty strong, as was his knowledge of grammar and punctuation. But he was way behind his grade level in math and science.

"I'm sorry," he said. "I tried, I did. But some of the stuff I just never heard of."

"No problem," I said. "We'll get you some books to study over the next couple of days and see if we can get you up to speed. Mike's Mr. Science Guy anyway—he can help you with that stuff."

We decided to drive out to Maunalua Bay Beach Park, in Hawaii Kai, because it was so shallow and calm that Dakota could learn to enjoy the water without surf or fear of drowning. As we pulled into the parking lot, he was as excited as I'd ever seen him. We parked next to a huge minivan with a line of little decals on the back window: father, mother, ballerina daughter, soccer player son, baby in diapers, and a cat licking its paw.

We hauled our stuff down to the sand and set up an umbrella and a couple of towels, and we had a lot of fun hanging out, laughing with Dakota as he figured out how to move his arms and legs under the water, and marveled over all the fish and the scenery.

"This is so cool," he said. "I never even knew there were places like this."

He made friends with two girls, tourists, and impressed them with his knowledge of Hawai'i. As we left the park, he was smiling and happy, which carried through our dinner at the Boston Style Pizza parlor in Hawai'i Kai, where we ordered the three-pound special. Mike insisted on ham and pineapple, his favorites; Dakota got to add black olives and mushrooms. It was heart-warming and sad at the same time to see how much he enjoyed small things I'd always taken for granted, like the chance to choose his own pizza toppings.

We stopped at a big chain bookstore on the way home and bought him a self-study book for science and one for math. I was tempted to buy one of those "parenting for dummies" guides. Mike and I needed to study up just as much as Dakota did. But I figured our best lessons would be the ones he taught us. And maybe, just maybe, if things worked out, I'd feel better about having a kid, and Mike and I would have a better idea what we were getting ourselves into.

Later that evening I was relaxing on the sofa with Mike, reading a gay mystery novel by Mark Richard Zubro. Dakota was sprawled on the floor with Roby, reading the first chapter of his science text, when my cell phone started to ring with Cyndi Lauper's "True Colors."

I followed the ringing sound to the kitchen table, where I grabbed the phone just before it went to voice mail. "Hey,

Gunter, what's up?"

"I kind of need a favor," he said. "Could you bail me out of jail?"

Mike heard that and looked up. I said, "Gunter. What did you do now?"

"Nothing, really. Just a harmless prank."

I skipped the details for the moment, and asked where he was. "The main police station downtown. My bail is $250. I'll pay you back, I promise. We can go to an ATM as soon as you get me out of here."

"I'm on my way," I said.

I stood up. "I can't believe you're going to bail him out," Mike said.

"He's my friend." I looked over at Dakota. "I take care of my friends."

Mike humphed and went back to what he was reading. I called a guy I knew at a bail bond company while I was on the road, and he looked up Gunter's sheet. "Two-fifty cash bond," he said.

A cash bond is one posted by friends or family of the defendant. They require the full bail amount and are not financed through a bail bondsman, but you still have to go to one to get the right paperwork. I told him to get the papers ready for Gunter, and I stopped at an ATM to get the cash.

The bail bondsman's office was a single-story building, the front windows plastered with signs and special offers. A bumper stick affixed to the glass door read "CSI: Christ Saves Individuals."

Once I had the bond, I parked in the headquarters garage and walked across to the holding cells. I saw my friend Rory Yang and asked him, "What's the story with Gunter Franz?"

He turned to the computer and pulled up Gunter's sheet. "Three counts of disorderly conduct," he said, looking up at me. "He and a bunch of other guys were driving a pink convertible down Kalakaua, shouting derogatory comments and spraying water guns at a Boy Scout march."

I groaned. "How come he didn't get pretrial release?" Usually the court allowed defendants in misdemeanor cases who had no prior criminal record, and evidence of strong ties in the community, to get out without paying for a bond.

"The way I heard it from the bailiff, Judge Burns was an Eagle Scout and he was very upset that all the little scouts were getting soaked and being called bad names."

I showed him the bond, and he went to get Gunter. When he appeared he was wearing a pink T-shirt that read "MAHU NATION" and matching pink rubber slippers. His white shorts were so tiny and tight I could tell he wasn't carrying a wallet, just a single house key.

I thanked Rory and waved Gunter toward the door. He started to explain, but I said, "Not here. Wait 'til we're outside."

He pressed his fingers together and pulled them across his lips as if he was zipping them shut. I resisted the urge to punch him.

We walked outside. The sun was finally going down and the air had cooled. "What the hell did you think you were doing?" I asked.

"It's called civil disobedience."

"No, it's called three misdemeanors." I turned to face him. "You were calling Boy Scouts dirty names?"

"Not the scouts," he said. "There was this march today, down Kalakaua. My friend Nick called me this morning and asked me if I wanted to help out with a protest. You know me, I'm always up for a party."

I led him to my Jeep in the parking garage. "Go on."

"Nick bought this used pink convertible, and he thought we could drive real slow down their route, telling them exactly what we thought of their rule against openly gay scout masters."

"I heard there were water guns involved."

"Just in fun," he said. "Come on, Kimo, where's your sense of humor? We rode along, calling out things like 'Boy Scouts are prejudiced,' and 'If they're the masters, are you the slaves?' We had a couple of those super soakers, and the boys looked hot, so we thought we'd cool them down."

"Gunter. They're kids. You can't go around yelling things at little kids and spraying them with water guns."

"I wanted to be a Cub Scout when I was a kid, back in Jersey," he said. "They wouldn't let me in. They said I was too girly." He smiled. "Payback's a bitch, isn't it?"

I waited for a break in traffic on South Beretania to pull out of the garage. "If you want to go back to New Jersey and look up those boys who called you names, or even the Scoutmaster who let them, more power to you. Go for it. But these boys didn't do anything to you."

"But they're still doing it to other boys," he said. "And what kind of example does it set for the kids if a scoutmaster can't be gay?"

"I can't argue with your principles. But you broke the law, Gunter. You harassed a bunch of innocent little kids. If I'd known what you did before I came down here I might not have come at all."

"Fine. Be that way." He turned toward the window and sulked.

When I pulled into his driveway I said, "I'm not going to lecture you, Gunter. You're an adult. You know that what you do has consequences."

"Mike is going to give you shit for bailing me out, isn't he?"

"Yeah. But I'll survive. You're my friend. And like I told him, I take care of my friends."

He leaned over and kissed my cheek. "Thanks." Then he scampered out of the car and up his driveway, like some kind of big blond fairy. Oh, wait, that's exactly what he was.

By the time I got home Mike and Dakota were in the living room together with Mike's laptop on the coffee table. "I took

Dakota next door to meet my folks," Mike said.

We lived in one half of a duplex; Mike had grown up on the other side, and his parents still lived there. He had bought the house where we lived before I met him, in what I thought was a colossally stupid move for a gay man who hadn't come out to his family. My interaction with Dominic and Soon-O Riccardi hadn't been positive at the start. Though they had no problems with him being gay, Dominic in particular thought I was bad news, that I'd broken his son's heart and driven him to drink. It had taken a long time for our relationship to overcome those obstacles, and though we all got along, I was glad Mike had taken care of introducing Dakota.

"Then we came back here and found a YouTube video somebody uploaded. You've got to see this." He swiveled his laptop screen around so he, Dakota and I could watch together. Roby was interested, too; he came over and squeezed between Mike and me so we could both pet him at the same time.

It looked like someone had taken the video with a cell phone camera. Gunter was very visible, his lanky frame sticking up from the back seat of the convertible. Along with a third guy in the front passenger seat, Gunter and a friend with a Mohawk used industrial strength water guns to spray the Scouts as they drove past, yelling the things he'd told me.

I had to admit it was funny watching the kids scramble as the water hit them, even though as a cop I knew it was wrong.

The scoutmasters in their quasi-military uniforms yelled back at Gunter and his friends. A police siren began to wail, and the driver gunned the convertible out of the cameraman's vision.

"What an asshole," Mike said, when the video was finished.

"It's just Gunter's idea of a prank." I looked at Dakota. "Don't get any ideas."

Mike wouldn't let it go. "Kimo, those are kids."

"I know. I already yelled at him."

"Not very strongly, I'll bet." Mike stood up. "Come on,

Dakota, let's take Roby out for his late night walk."

I was upstairs getting ready for bed when Mike came in to the bedroom. "Gunter's your id, you know? You like it when he acts out."

My grasp of psychology was pretty basic, a result of lectures and reading on criminal behavior. I had a vague idea that the id was the part of your psyche that looks for pleasure. "I have my own id, thank you very much."

He began to undress. "Watching him is a safe way for you to vent your frustrations and exercise your fantasies."

"Since when did you become a psychiatrist?"

"I was really into psychology when I was a teenager. I made the mistake of telling my father I wanted to be a psychologist. Of course he had to take over and tell me all the reasons why the only valid practice was psychiatry, because it required you to go to medical school. The rest was all mumbo jumbo."

"Sounds like Dominic. So let me guess—you ran away from that idea as fast as your little legs would carry you."

"They weren't so little by that time. But you're right. I wasn't going to do anything my father said."

I finished stripping down and tossed my dirty clothes in the hamper. Mike was down to his white briefs, and once again I noticed how damn sexy he was. "And you want to have kids," I said. "Just so they can do the opposite of whatever you say?"

"That's not the reason, and you know it."

"It's certainly part of it, isn't it? You want to have your own kid so you can try to correct the mistakes your parents made with you." I slid into bed.

"Like your parents never made mistakes." He tugged down his briefs and his half-hard dick swung free. He faked a jump shot and tossed the briefs into the hamper, then joined me in bed.

"Of course they did. But I'm not obsessed with fixing the past. I've got enough to do just keeping up with the present."

"I'm not obsessed with the past. But you've got to admit you'd love to have the chance to mold a kid. You do that already with the teen group."

"Yeah, but somebody else has already changed their diapers. And at the end of the meeting I send them home."

"Sandra and Cathy would be the moms," Mike said. "They'd do all that stuff."

I turned on my side to face him. "Are you really that naïve? This isn't about just jerking off in a cup and letting the women do all the work. It's a lifetime commitment to a child. Despite what you may think about your father, he's always going to be there for you. And even after he's gone, he's going to be in your head. It's a huge responsibility that goes beyond whose turn it is to babysit."

"And you're not interested in that."

I thought about the way my parents had loved me unconditionally through my childhood hijinks, my failed attempt to become a professional surfer, and my coming out. What an amazing gift they had given me.

With Mike's help, I could give that gift to someone else—our child.

I took a deep breath. "I think you'd be an awesome dad. Me, I'll have to work at it more. But I'm willing to give it a try if you are."

Mike reached over and took my hand. "For real?"

I leaned over and kissed him lightly on the lips. "For real. For now and for always."

The next morning neither of us brought up what we'd talked about the night before. I think we were both were getting accustomed to the idea before we jumped into all the specifics.

We left Dakota at the house with strict instructions. He was to look after Roby, taking him out for a walk in the middle of the day, and he was to study at least one chapter of science and one of math. He could watch anything he wanted on TV.

Both Mike and I worked on laptops which we carried to work with us, so there was no computer for him to waste time with. We trusted him; there wasn't much in the house worth stealing, and besides, Dakota knew that if we'd tracked him down once we could do it again.

As I pulled into the garage next to headquarters, I got a call from Lieutenant Sampson. "I'm on my way in," I said.

"Cancel that. There's some kind of disturbance between members of the Fields family at the Kawaiaha'o Church. You and Donne need to get over there pronto."

The Kawaiaha'o Church is the oldest on O'ahu, dating back over 250 years. Built of slabs of coral rock, it has seen the baptisms, weddings and funerals of Honolulu's elite since then. It wasn't a surprise that the services for Alexander Fields would be held there. But it was only seven-thirty in the morning. What had dragged them all out so early?

We'd been planning to attend the funeral at eleven, and Ray had already made arrangements to talk to Stephanie Cornell after the service. I figured I'd catch Shepard Fields on the fly.

I made a U-turn in the garage, and while I waited for the exit gate I called Ray. "Yeah, I spoke to Sampson. I'm just a few blocks away from there now."

"He say what kind of disturbance?"

"No idea. Maybe Fields has risen from his coffin like a

vampire."

"Well, he was an attorney."

It took me a few minutes to find a parking spot in a garage on South King Street and hurry over to the church. A squad car was parked in front, its blue lights flashing, and a uniformed officer stood in the doorway of the church.

Ray was just inside the sanctuary, talking quietly to a short, middle-aged woman with pronounced Japanese features, wearing a severe black suit and sensible black pumps. Two Japanese men and an older haole woman stood just to the side.

The royal pews were on either side of where they stood, marked with four feather staffs, called *kahili*, symbols of royal rank. Hawaiian kings and queens once sat there; now the church was a mainstay of a different kind of royalty, the economic elite of the islands.

My first visit to the church was on an elementary school field trip decades before, when we learned about the history of the building, and the portraits of the *Ali'i*, or Hawaiian royalty, that lined the walls of the upper level. Since then I'd been back for Terri Clark's wedding, her husband's funeral, and a few other ceremonies.

Ray saw me and nodded toward a tall, patrician man with sandy blond hair who looked a great deal like the portraits of Fields I'd seen, with just a touch of his Japanese mother. He was standing on the other side of the sanctuary with a group of other men.

I crossed the floor to him. "You must be Shepard Fields," I said, sticking my hand out to "I'm Detective Kanapa'aka."

"I hope you're here to arrest my sister."

I nodded my head toward the other group. "I take it that's her?"

"Shepard and his sister don't get along," the man with Fields said. He offered his hand. "I'm Tim O'Donnell, Shepard's partner."

O'Donnell was short and dark-haired, some kind of an ethnic mix like me and Fields, with smooth skin and an epicanthic fold over his eyes.

"What happened this morning?" I asked him, after I shook his hand.

"My bitch sister—" Shepard began.

Tim interrupted him. "I'll explain. You take another Valium."

Shepard glared at him, but turned aside and pulled a pill bottle from his jacket pocket.

"The funeral director arranged a private viewing for us this morning," Tim said. "What he neglected to mention was that he had also arranged for Stephanie to see her father at the same time. She and Shepard started to argue."

"And the police?"

"The funeral director got worried and called 911. But nothing would have happened."

I looked over to where Ray stood with Stephanie. She was glaring in her brother's direction, and he was returning her scowl.

"Anything in particular they were arguing about?"

Tim shrugged. "The same things they've been arguing about since they were kids. Who got special treatment, which one was the most spoiled. That kind of thing."

I lowered my voice. "Any accusations of murder?"

Tim wouldn't meet my gaze. "They're both very upset."

A portly man in a dark suit approached us. "If you'd like to finish your visitation?" he asked.

"Yes, let's," Tim said. He took Shepard's hand, and they followed the funeral director.

I stepped over to two men who had been hovering behind Shepard and Tim. One looked about Shepard Fields' age, fifty-three, while the other was fifteen or twenty years older. I introduced myself. "Friends of Shepard's?"

"Longtime," the younger man said. He was well-fed and prosperous, the kind of man who exemplifies the business elite of Honolulu. "From when we were keikis." He held out his hand. "Eliseo Gomez."

I knew the name; he was a defense attorney in Honolulu, specializing in personal injury. He advertised his services on taxicabs and bus benches.

"What happened this morning?" I asked.

"Shepard and Stephanie," Gomez said. "Like oil and vinegar."

"More like dynamite and a fuse," the older man said. His name was Andy Gardiner, and he had the red-veined nose and flushed complexion of a man who drank too much. He was a hapa-haole, like so many people in the case, though it looked like he had some Tahitian in him. "Shep and Sluttany haven't gotten along since they were kids."

"Sluttany?"

"His nickname for her. She was pretty easy with her virtue, even for the times."

"She looks good now, though," Gomez said. "And isn't that Lee Poe with her?"

I looked back at Stephanie and her boyfriend. Lee Poe looked the most Hawaiian of anyone in the room, with dark hair and broad shoulders that reminded me of my brother Haoa.

But Ray was handling Stephanie and Lee. I turned back to Gomez and Gardiner. "What did Shepard think of his father?" I asked.

"Idolized him," Eliseo said. "But wouldn't admit it."

"His father didn't approve of Shep's 'lifestyle,'" Andy said, wagging his fingers. "He was always his mother's favorite when he was a kid, and Stephanie was always able to wind the old man around her little finger. That used to drive Shep crazy."

"Crazy enough to do something?" I asked.

Both of them looked at me. "You think Shep killed his

father?" Andy asked. "He wasn't even here."

"You grow up rich, you get accustomed to hiring people to do things for you," I said.

"Of course," Andy drawled. "I have an upstairs maid, a downstairs maid, and a third one just to wipe my ass for me."

"Shut up, Andy," Eliseo said. "Shep isn't like that. He's a nice guy. He just has a blind spot about his sister." His cell phone buzzed and he stepped away to take the call, and Andy turned away from me.

I walked back across the sanctuary to where Ray stood with Stephanie Cornell and Lee Poe. Ray introduced me.

"I see you've been talking to the cabal," she said. She nodded across the way toward her brother's friends. "Do they share my brother's opinion, that I had Daddy killed to satisfy my lust for money and power?"

"I didn't talk to them about you," I said. "But is that what they would have said?"

"Shep and Eliseo have been thick as thieves since they were teenagers," she said. "They covered up for each other no matter what happened. Andy Gardiner may be a senior citizen by now, but he's just as juvenile as they are. If you're looking for suspects, I'd check them out."

Lee put his hand on her arm. "Let's not start accusing anybody. That's how things got out of hand this morning."

The portly funeral director returned. "Your brother and his partner have left the chapel," he said. "If you'd like to go back there you can."

"Thank you. I'd like that," Stephanie said. She took Lee's hand, and the clutch of people with them followed as they walked toward the front of the church.

"Distant relatives," Ray said as they walked away. "Seems like the family is siding with her."

I shook my head. "I got lucky with my brothers. We fought like crazy when I was a kid, and the two of them picked on me something fierce. But now? We'd do anything for each other."

"My family's like that, too," Ray said. "All except for my brother Paul. He gave up on the rest of us years ago."

"Really? Why?"

Ray shrugged. "Who knows? We're a big, rowdy, Italian family. We yell at each other and get our feelings out, and then we hug and kiss and drink wine. Paul took every little slight to heart, and as soon as he could get out of the house he took off and never looked back."

"Where is he now?"

"Nobody knows. Someday we'll have to track him down, when Mom or Pop goes. But for now we just leave him alone."

"What kind of vibe did you get from Stephanie? You think she could be behind this?"

He shook his head. "She seemed pretty broken up."

"Shepard's friends said she was Daddy's little girl, and that the mother favored him. I don't see how parents can do that."

"Just look at them," Ray said. "Stephanie takes after her mother, and Shepard after his father. Of course the parent is going to go for the kid who looks like the person they fell in love with."

"You think?"

He shrugged. "That's what my college professors would say. Some kind of transference, I think."

My oldest brother Lui looks the most Japanese of the three of us; Haoa is the most Hawaiian, and I inherited the most haole genes. But our parents hadn't favored one of us over the other, and certainly not in the way that Mr. and Mrs. Fields had. Bad parenting was never an excuse for murder. But I couldn't help feeling that family dynamics had something do with Fields' death.

During the funeral service, Shepard Fields described his father's distinguished career, from his efforts on behalf of statehood to the many constructions projects he had been involved with as an attorney. "Alexander Fields shaped the landscape of this state," he concluded. "His legacy can be found in the projects he championed and the laws he influenced."

Stephanie, on the other hand, spoke about her father as a man. "His public persona was only one part of him," she said. "He was passionate and driven in business and civic life, but when he came home, he was just Daddy. He loved my mother, and he was never too busy to ask me about my day. He was determined to give my brother and me everything we needed to succeed in life."

I thought I heard Shepard Fields snort.

"In his last years, my father changed," she continued. "He began to look back on his life and consider his legacy, and he wanted to make amends for some of the hurts he had caused. Those of us who were lucky enough to still be close to him saw a different side of him."

She pulled a tissue from her pocket and dabbed at her eyes. "Goodbye, Daddy. Rest in peace."

The church was full; Winston Yamato, Peggy Kaneahe and Sarah Byrne sat among a group of mourners from Fields and Yamato. Other figures I recognized from civic life were scattered around the church. I scanned the crowd for elderly women, wondering if one of them had been with Fields when he was driven to his death.

There were two separate limousines for the family—one for Shepard and Tim, and another for Stephanie, Lee, and the distant cousins. I left my Jeep in the garage and rode with Ray at the end of the long funeral procession.

"So what do you think?" I asked, as we followed the limos and the hearse up Punchbowl Street toward the National Memorial Cemetery of the Pacific. "They're both willing to point the finger at each other. There's something screwy going on, but I don't see either of them as behind this."

"I'm inclined to agree with you." Ray waved at the motorcycle cop managing the back end of the procession as we passed him. "I suppose we'll have to go back to those case files Peggy gave us."

"That reminds me," I said. "I didn't tell you what Mike and I did this weekend."

I ran through the details as we circled around the back of the cemetery on Puowaina Drive. "I need to run the license plate when we get in."

"What did you do with the kid?"

"He's staying with Mike and me for a couple of days."

Ray turned to look at me. "You think that's a good idea?"

"He didn't want to go to Terri's. And if we put him into the system I thought he'd just run away again."

"But he can't stay with you forever."

"Why not? Mike and I could sign up as foster parents."

"You mean instead of having a kid of your own?"

I hadn't seen it like that. "Two different things. Dakota's almost an adult. He'll be on his own in a couple of years." I paused. "And, well, we decided we're going forward with Cathy and Sandra. We're going to be dads."

"For real? That's great. Congratulations!" Ray pulled up beside the oval grass lawn at the front of the cemetery. In the distance I could see the skyline of downtown Honolulu; a single American flag waved in the light breeze. "I always get a lump in my throat when I come to a place like this," he said, as we got out of the Highlander. "All the sacrifice."

"I know what you mean." We were silent through the interment, then waited until the other cars had left the cemetery before we did. We knew that both Stephanie and Shepard were staying in Honolulu for a few days; if any questions came up we knew how to get hold of them.

We stopped at a Zippy's for takeout burgers, and Ray dropped me at the church to pick up my car. When I got back to headquarters, I emailed the photo I'd taken of the bodybuilder on Saturday night to Francisco Salinas, an FBI agent we'd worked with on several cases, and asked if he could put it through their facial recognition software.

The credit reports we had ordered came in, and after we finished eating, we looked them over. Shepard Fields was wealthy in his own right; he had invested in a couple of small software companies in Silicon Valley that had gone public, and despite the downturn in the market for tech stocks he was still doing very well.

Surprisingly, so was his sister. Each of her divorces had ended with a substantial cash settlement, which she had invested carefully. She owned the home where she lived with Lee Poe.

"I wish we'd requested a credit report on Lee," I said, turning to Ray.

"Why?"

"Suppose he's broke, and living off Stephanie. He might be greedy and want to get his hands on her daddy's money, too."

"But she knew he had terminal cancer," Ray said. "Why take the risk? Why not just wait for him to go on his own?"

"People get greedy," I said. My email beeped with a response from Francisco Salinas. "If you'd come over to work with us you could do this yourself," he wrote. "But in the interest of inter-agency cooperation I'll run the picture for you."

I looked over at Ray. "So Salinas knows. You think our moving over to the Bureau is already a done deal?"

Ray shrugged. "We're just cogs in a wheel. If the brass wants us to work for the Feds, yeah, it's a done deal."

"Even if we don't want to?"

Ray looked at me. "You don't want to?"

"I don't know. I like what I do. Homicide is the top of the heap when it comes to detective work. Do you want to give that up to go chase paperwork for the Bureau?"

"Look at it this way," Ray said, leaning back in his chair. "We work within a very narrow range here. The crime has to occur in District 1, it has to be assigned to us, and it has to be something serious. Not always homicide. We can investigate robbery, assault, sexual assault, domestic violence, child abuse, financial fraud and forgery, auto theft, and white collar crimes."

He leaned forward again. "But those are all small potatoes when it comes to the big picture. Individual cases, individual victims."

"That's important," I said. "We bring justice for those victims."

"I'm not saying it's not important. But the Bureau, they handle bigger cases. Things that affect more people, maybe even the whole country. I think it would be cool to be a part of that."

"The Bureau isn't going to look into homicides," I said. "Think about all the specialized skills we've got that we wouldn't be able to use."

"Think of all we can learn," he said. "Isn't that cool? Not just the toys they have—the weapons and the databases. But stretching to investigate in different ways."

"What are you, some kind of recruiter?"

"No. But I talked about it with Julie over the weekend." He took a deep breath. "I'm up for the change. Even if you're not."

I nodded. "I haven't made up my mind yet. But it's good to know where you stand."

We were both quiet for a minute. I remembered what it had been like for me as a detective before Ray became my partner. Things had improved a lot since then. But which mattered more to me—being a cop, protecting and serving the people of Honolulu with aloha? Or working that larger canvas like Ray suggested, continuing our partnership?

I took a deep breath. "We still have to track the license plate for the limo." I ran the check; it led me to a company called Royal Rides.

I found the company's website and called the phone number. "Royal Rides, this is Chris. How can I help you?"

I identified myself and asked how I could track the use of the limo. "Last Tuesday night," I said.

"Our drivers are independent operators. We don't withhold taxes or give them any benefits. We book some clients for them, but they also have their own customers. Hold on and let me check the records for last Tuesday."

Instead of music, their system played an endless stream of ads for the company, repeating their tag line, "Royal Rides, where we treat our customers like kings and queens," until I felt it was ingrained in my brain.

"I have nothing on the books for last Tuesday night," Chris said, when he returned to the line. "The driver's name is Pika Campbell. You want his phone number?"

"Sure." I wrote down the name and number. "You have an address for him?"

"Let me see. Here it is. 364 South King Street, Apartment 12."

I turned to my computer and typed in the address. "Can't be, brah," I said. "That's the Iolani Palace."

"Maybe it's a typo. But that's what I've got."

I thanked him and hung up. Then I dialed the number he'd given me. "Aloha, this is Pika," a deep male voice said. "I'm busy right now, showing off our beautiful island in my luxury limousine. But if you leave a message I'll get back to you as soon as I can."

"This is Detective Kanapaka'aka with HPD. Please call me." I left both my desk and cell numbers.

"There's something fishy going on," I said. "Why would this guy give a fake address to the dispatcher? And why didn't they ever check it?"

"Great questions. Let me know when you get some answers." Ray picked up the folder Peggy had given us. "We might as well get back to our paperwork."

While we waited for Pika Campbell to call us back, or for Francisco Salinas to generate a match to the photo of the bodybuilder, we began the slow, tedious process of tracking down people involved in the cases Peggy had pulled for us.

"Let's start with Lee Poe," I said. "I don't think it's a coincidence that he's living with the daughter of the man he thought cheated him out of his aunt's estate."

Ray called Stephanie's cell phone, and discovered she and Lee were at their hotel, the Moana Surfrider, on Kalakaua in Waikiki. He arranged to meet them there.

The Moana Surfrider has been called the First Lady of Waikiki. Its history dates back to 1901, when it was the height of elegance, with the first electric elevator in the islands. Even today it's one of O'ahu's most luxurious.

Stephanie and Lee were sharing a junior suite with a balcony that overlooked the curving beach, with Diamond Head looming in the distance. She sat with Ray in the living room, and I asked Lee if he'd come out to the balcony with me.

"How did you and Stephanie meet?" I asked him.

"We knew each other growing up. I was living in Portland and I ran into her there."

"Kind of a coincidence, isn't it?" I asked.

He shrugged. "There are a lot of Hawaiians in Oregon," he said. "I went to Lewis and Clark, and I liked it and stayed. Stephanie had friends who went to the U of O, and she came to visit them and met her ex."

"So no connection to the fact that you sued Alexander Fields over the disposition of your aunt's estate?"

"That was years before Stephanie and I got together."

"But it would be safe to say you held a grudge against her father?"

"I got into Buddhism after my aunt died." He held up his wrist to show me a red string bracelet, which I knew was connected with the Tibetan branch of the religion. "I learned to leave behind old problems and disappointments."

"What do you do for a living now?"

"I'm between jobs at the moment. Stephanie was really upset by her dad's diagnosis, and I've been looking after her."

I wanted to say 'sponging off her,' but I held back. Maybe I am maturing as I get older. "Must be a nice change for you to get back to Honolulu. You both probably have lots of old friends here."

Lee Poe was no fool. "You mean old friends who we could recruit to murder Alexander Fields? Neither of us has that kind of friends."

"The thought never crossed my mind," I said.

Lee turned around and went into the living room, and I followed. Ray stood up. "Thank you very much. I'm sure we'll be back in touch to let you know what kind of progress we're making."

"That went nowhere," I said to Ray, as we walked out through the hotel's grand lobby, passing across the porch, where tourists sat in comfy rocking chairs. "Lee has a history with Fields, but he knew the man was dying. And there's no financial motive since Stephanie already has money. Plus, how would he even know about the warehouse?"

"Stephanie seems genuinely broken up by her father's death," Ray said. "Unless there's something we haven't found yet, I don't think she had a motive."

It was quitting time, so I dropped Ray back at headquarters and drove home. I'd completely forgotten about Dakota during the day and as I drove up the hill toward our house I started to worry about what I might find.

When I approached the house I saw Dakota on the front lawn, throwing a stick for Roby to fetch. I pulled carefully into the driveway, and Roby came bounding over to me.

"I found a chicken in your freezer and put it in the oven," Dakota said. "I hope that's okay."

"You know how to cook?"

He shrugged. "I had to learn, living with my mom."

"How'd the studying go?" I asked, as we all walked inside.

"You want to know the difference between potential energy, biological energy and kinetic energy?" he asked.

"No, but thanks for the offer. I take it you read that?"

"Yeah. It was boring but not too hard."

Mike got home a few minutes later, and we all sat down to eat together. "This is great, Dakota," he said, after he tasted the chicken. "What else can you cook?"

Dakota shrugged. "Mostly stuff with pasta and rice. That's usually what we had around, if my mom ever went shopping."

I felt a sharpness in my chest. I hated to hear about any kid who didn't get proper care, and it always reminded me how lucky I was to have grown up the way I did.

My cell rang after dinner. "How's Dakota doing?" Terri asked.

I took the phone and stepped out into the back yard. "So far, so good. He studied like he was supposed to, and he cooked dinner."

"You're going to have to get him into the system sooner or later, you know."

"I know. But let's give him a couple of days to get settled with us."

"What are you going to do about the other kids in that warehouse?"

"I don't know. I ought to talk to Dakota about who's there, exactly."

"Well, you're the detective. Go detect."

"Thank you, Lieutenant Gonsalves. If non-profit administration doesn't work out for you, you can always come join the force. We're pretty non-profit ourselves."

"I've got enough on my plate as it is. Call me if you need anything."

I thanked her and walked back inside. Mike and Dakota were cleaning up, and I sat down at the table. When they finished, I said, "Let's talk about the place you were staying, Dakota." I pointed to the chair next to me.

He looked shifty as he sat down. "What about it?"

Mike leaned up against the refrigerator.

"Who else was staying there with you?" I asked.

"Different people. It's not like we signed leases or anything."

"What kind of people? Kids?"

"Sometimes."

"Dakota. If there are kids staying there, we need to get them someplace safe, where they can get food and clothes and get to go to school. Like you."

"There was a girl," Dakota said. "She was staying at the foster home where I was. She told me about the warehouse, and she and I ran away together."

"Is she still there?" Mike asked.

Dakota shook his head. "One day she picked up her stuff and left. She wouldn't tell me where she was going." He looked up at us. "The only other people there right now were these two homeless guys."

"You have anything there you want to go pick up?" Mike asked.

"I guess. But I don't want to go back there at night. It's creepy."

"I can take you there tomorrow morning," I said.

"Cool. Can we watch TV now? That's the thing I missed the

most."

In that moment, Dakota looked like any other teenaged kid. And that was a pretty good thing.

Mike and I both hated the reality crap he wanted to watch, so we retreated to our bedroom. I could see Mike was hesitating to say something about our conversation the night before, so I jumped in, the way I always do.

"I haven't changed my mind, even though I'm scared shitless at the thought of being responsible for a child. You're still in, aren't you?"

He nodded.

"Then let's get this train rolling." I picked up my phone and dialed Sandra Guarino's cell phone.

"Kimo," she said. "No legal emergency, I hope. I saw the video of Gunter's stunt at the Boy Scout march yesterday."

"No, nothing legal. Mike and I have been talking and… we're in, if you are."

I heard her relay the news to Cathy. Then she was back on the phone. "I'll call the clinic tomorrow and have them start the test on the frozen sperm." She paused. "What do you want to know?"

"What do you mean?"

"Suppose one of you passes the test and the other doesn't."

I looked at Mike. "We're both in this together," I said, and he nodded. Then he reached out and took my hand.

The next morning I called Ray as I was on my way down to Lagoon Drive with Dakota. "I'm taking Dakota past the warehouse for a look around," I said.

"I'll start checking the landowners who felt like they got ripped off," Ray said. "See you when I see you."

I pulled up in front of the warehouse where Dakota had been staying. "There's a flashlight in the glove compartment," I said to him.

"There's pretty good light inside during the day," Dakota said.

I opened the door. "If you say so." The wind was blowing off the ocean, a fresh, salty smell that lay over the fading aroma of the burned building a block away.

"I can go in by myself," he said, hopping out. "You can wait here."

I shook my head. "You don't know who's in there. I'm not letting you go in alone."

"Kimo. I lived there and I survived."

"Yeah, but now you're my responsibility." I held up my hand. "No argument."

I pulled the plank aside and Dakota slipped in the window, and I followed him. He was right; there was a lot of light inside. "It's me," he called into the big, echoing room. There was no answer.

I sniffed the air. The fried chicken smell was gone, and there was nothing fresh or new to replace it. Just a musty mildew smell. Dakota led me to the office where the fried chicken had been. It was gone, and so was the sleeping bag he'd been using. "Mother fuckers," he said.

He collected the couple of pieces of clothing he had left there, along with a book with a couple of old pictures inside, of him and his mom. "That's it," he said. "Let's roll."

We went back out the window. "I want you to show me where you were when you saw the limousine pull up," I said.

He shrugged. "Sure." We walked around the corner of the warehouse and he stopped. "I was here when the limo turned the corner and the headlights swept around. I hung back until I was sure no one could see me."

"Think back. Tell me again what you saw."

"I already did."

"People often remember things later," I said.

He described again how the two bodybuilders had gotten out of the front of the limo. "I thought at first the one guy was helping the old man, but then I realized he was pushing the old man along."

"How about the woman? Was she being pushed, too?"

He shook his head. "She was really short and she had these high heels, but she walked on her own. Didn't even stumble once."

"You remember anything about what they were wearing?" I asked. "The old lady with the high heels—was she dressed up, like she was going out?"

He closed his eyes and concentrated. "Kind of. Not in a ball gown or anything. But just, you know, fancy. This really colorful jacket and black pants. I think maybe she was Chinese or something—I can't say exactly, but she had this black hair piled up on her head and there was just something about the way she walked."

He opened his eyes and looked at me. "Sorry I can't remember anything more."

"No, you've been real helpful," I said, and we walked back toward the Jeep.

"Do you think you could drop me at HCC?" Dakota asked. "I could study in the library there, maybe hook up with Frankie."

"Sure. But you know, we need to get you a phone." Back on Nimitz, I pulled into an office supply store and got him a prepaid cell. "For starters," I said. "Once we have all the paperwork settled we'll look into something more permanent."

"This is so cool," he said. "I really wanted a phone but there was just no way I was getting one."

I gave him Frankie's number, and Pua's, and Mike's and mine, and wrote down his. Then I gave him a twenty-dollar bill. "So you can get some lunch," I said. "I'll call you when I'm leaving work and then I'll pick you up."

I left him outside the HCC library and drove to headquarters.

"Find anything out at the site?" Ray asked, when I slid into my desk.

"Dakota remembered a few more details about the old woman who was with Fields and the two bodybuilders. He thinks maybe she was Chinese. But since he's pretty much a *malihini*, I don't know that he could tell Chinese from Korean from Filipina." A malihini was a newcomer to the islands; it took a long time to become a *kama'aina*, a long-time resident. After nearly four years, I'd begun to think of Ray that way. "How are you coming?"

"Nothing good. Those land deals went down so long ago that nobody is around who knows anything about the people who got cheated."

"I think that's going to be the trouble the farther back we go." We worked through the afternoon; one of the secretaries went out for lunch and brought us sandwiches on her way back.

We delved farther and farther back in Fields' case histories, and came up blank every time. The farmer who had sued the factory owner had sold his property to a developer a few years later, and died a wealthy man. The recovering alcoholic woman who broke her hips at the hotel owned by Fields' client died in the hospital and left no heirs behind to continue her suit or hold a grudge against Fields. The native Hawaiians who had sued Emile Gardiner over development rights in the Kalama Valley had all died out or moved away.

I tried Pika Campbell again, and got the same voice mail recording. I opened the department database, and found that Pika had a couple of misdemeanor arrests—drunk and disorderly, possession of a small amount of marijuana, and so on. He'd never gone to trial, and the address in the system was the same one he'd given the limo company, the Iolani Palace. There was no information about any known associates, and nothing that would help us find him.

I called my old friend Karen Gold at Social Security and asked her to run his report. "You have his number?" she asked.

"Just the name."

"Hold on." She put me on hold, but at least this time I got some jazzy background music instead of incessant advertising. When she returned she said, "You're in luck. There's only one Pika Campbell in the system. I saved his file as a PDF and emailed it to you."

I thanked her and I switched over to email, drumming my fingertips on the desktop as I waited for the file to sail through cyberspace. When it did arrive, there wasn't much in it. Campbell was twenty-four and had a spotty work record. His last known employment had been with Rascals Gym, a low-end spot favored by those who were serious about working out, not checking out the rest of the clientele. And once again, he'd put down the Iolani Palace as his address.

"How come nobody ever noticed that?" I grumbled. "I mean, if I put 1600 Pennsylvania Avenue down as my address somewhere on the mainland, you'd think someone would catch it."

"This isn't the mainland," Ray said. "And I've never heard anybody here refer to the Palace by its street address, the way people do with the White House."

We decided to check out the gym. It was a gorgeous, sunny day, with only a few scraps of cirrus clouds overhead, and hardly a whisper of a breeze. It was a day to be lounging at the beach, sun tanning or surfing, and there were thousands of tourists out there doing just that. Ray drove, and we put the windows down and enjoyed the late afternoon.

Rascals Gym was at one end of a run-down shopping center, the kind my father could have bought in his heyday, spruced up, and made successful. But my father was retired by then, and whoever owned that center didn't care much about it. The grass in the strip between parking lanes was dead, and crumpled coffee cups and empty power bar wrappers littered the lot.

There was no fancy reception desk, no inspirational posters on the walls or gleaming mirrors. Just a series of different machines in rows, and what looked like the door to a locker room along the far wall.

A muscular haole in an orange Y-back tank top let go of the lat-pull down machine he was working out with and stood up. "Help you?" he asked.

We showed our IDs. "You are?" Ray asked.

"Randall Buck. I own the gym."

"We're looking for Pika Campbell," Ray said. "You know where we could find him?"

"What's this about?"

"Police business," I said.

Mr. Muscles looked from Ray to me. "Don't know."

"He used to work here?" Ray asked.

"Yeah. But he got fired about a year ago. He was juicing, and I don't put up with that."

"Just using steroids?" Ray asked. "Or selling them, too?"

"I run a clean gym. And unless you've got some grounds I think you should leave. Right now." Buck squared his shoulders in some kind of imitation of a muscle-man pose, as if his tattooed delts and biceps were going to scare us away.

Instead of laughing I looked over his shoulder to a series of photos on the wall, from a celebration of the gym's tenth anniversary. I saw Gunter's smiling face, and beside him a guy with a Mohawk who looked familiar as well. Why waste time with Buck, when we could talk to the most gossipy queen on the island?

"Let's go," I said to Ray. "We're done here."

"I'm not." He turned back to Buck. "You have an address for Campbell?"

"Had one. Tried to send him his tax forms at the end of the year and they came back. Turns out he gave me the address of the Iolani Palace."

I could smell the testosterone rising between Ray and the bodybuilder. "We've got an appointment," I said. "Come on, we'll be late."

Ray and Buck glared at each other, but Ray turned and walked out. I followed him.

"What was that all about?" I asked when we got outside.

"What?"

"You nearly bit that guy's head off."

Ray's shoulders eased, and he beeped the Highlander open. "I hate that kind of guy. Those muscle-bound jerks were the kind who picked on Joey."

Joey was Ray's cousin, and his childhood best friend. He was gay, and got himself killed doing something stupid.

"Well, we got something from our visit," I said. "Gunter's picture is up on that wall. It's almost three, and he'll be starting his shift in a couple of minutes. Let's go over to Waikiki and talk to him, see if he knew Pika Campbell."

Ray lucked into a metered spot a block away from the Kuhio Regent and we walked over there, climbing up the curving driveway to the two-story marble and glass lobby.

Gunter was behind the concierge desk talking on the phone. He wore his standard pseudo-military uniform, a white shirt with epaulets and button-flap pockets, a puka shell necklace and dark slacks.

"Don't tell me I missed some bail appointment," he said, when he got off the phone.

"Nope. Something different. You know anything about Rascals Gym?"

He wouldn't meet my eyes. "What about it?"

"We're looking for a guy named Pika Campbell, who used to work there."

Gunter relaxed. "Oh, him. I don't know him that well, just met him a couple of times."

"You know where he lives?" I asked.

"Nope. Cinco might, but…" He stopped.

"Cinco?" I asked.

"A guy I know. He works out there. That's how I met Pika."

"You know Cinco's last name? Or he just a random visitor?"

"Fuck you, Kimo."

"I thought you already had," Ray said.

Gunter swiveled his head toward Ray, but my partner appeared immune to the death-ray queen stare. I laughed. "My bad. I shouldn't have said that," Ray said.

"For your information, I know a lot more about him than just his last name," Gunter said, regally. "His real name is Eddie DiMaio, but everybody calls him Cinco, after the holiday. He and I have been dating since New Year's. Monogamously."

I didn't think Gunter knew the meaning of that word, but I wasn't going to antagonize him any further. "You want to give him a call, then?" I asked. "Make an introduction, see when we could talk to him?"

"He's working now," Gunter said. "But I can try."

He picked up his cell phone and turned away from us. While he spoke I looked at Ray. "We're both on edge today. I'm stressing over the baby thing with Mike. You?"

"Lack of sleep. Vinnie's got a pair of lungs on him like some operatic soprano. I swear he could break glass. It hurts my ears just to hear him."

Gunter turned back to us. "He can meet you at the Hawksbill Bar near the Aloha Bowl at four."

"How will we recognize him?" I asked.

"He's got a Mohawk," Gunter said.

The penny dropped. "He was in the convertible with you, water gunning those Boy Scouts."

Ray looked at me, and I realized I hadn't told him about Gunter's escapade. "That was you?" he said, turning to Gunter. "Somebody sent me the YouTube video. You're a bad boy." He wagged his index finger at Gunter.

"Ray was a Boy Scout," I said to Gunter.

Ray laughed. "Even so, I got a hoot out of seeing that. Those kids were falling over like dominoes."

Gunter laughed with him. "Don't encourage him," I said. "I had to bail him out." I turned to Gunter. "Which reminds me. You owe me two hundred fifty bucks."

"Won't you get it back when I show up for my hearing?"

"I'm not waiting that long."

"Fine." Gunter dug in his pocket. "I've had it for you. I was just waiting to see you."

As Gunter handed me the cash, I said to Ray, "Get a picture of this, will you? If Cinco won't talk to us we can make it sound like Gunter's paying me for sex."

"As if," Gunter said, but his desk phone rang and he answered with his other hand. "Kuhio Regent Concierge desk, this is Gunter. How may I help you?" The message he was sending with his eyes was much less welcoming, though. I took the money and gave him a shaka, extending my thumb and pinkie while keeping my other fingers curled down, a traditional island greeting.

He replied with another kind of greeting, the one with only one finger extended, as Ray and I laughed again and walked out the door.

The Hawskbill Bar chain is a local one, decorated in what my father calls "Early Fishnet," with colorful Japanese glass fishing floats nestled in old rope nets, pieces of driftwood serving as restroom signs, and other faux nautical décor. I directed Ray to the branch on Salt Lake Boulevard near the Aloha Stadium. Mike and I had been there many times, often taking advantage of their happy hour specials.

We parked next to a pickup truck decorated with the bar's signature Hawksbill turtle, along with lots of slogans and bumper stickers, then walked inside. A guy with a Mohawk was up on a ladder, replacing a light bulb, and we waited until he was finished. "You Cinco?" I asked.

He turned around. "Oh, hey, you're Kimo. I've seen your picture around Gunter's. Nice to finally meet you."

He pointed at the ladder. "Gunter called and said you were coming over. Let me just clean up my crap and we can talk. You want a beer? It's on me."

"Sorry, we're still on duty," I said.

"We've got Waialua root beer on tap," he said.

I looked at Ray, and he nodded. "We could take two of those."

We sat down at a table near the door, and the waitress, a petite, busty Filipina in a Daisy Duke top and hot pants, brought us our drinks. Cinco joined us a couple of minutes later, carrying a mug of the real stuff.

"You work here?" I asked, as he sat down.

"I work for the chain. I go around taking care of maintenance stuff. That's how I met Gunter. He was sitting at the bar over in Waikiki and I had to ask him to move so I could get access to a hatch." He smiled. "He's been moving for me ever since."

I was still thinking over the idea that Gunter could be

monogamous with someone, and then wondering why he hadn't told me about Cinco. We'd been friends with benefits for a few years, before I settled down with Mike, and Gunter usually loved to dish on his sexual conquests to me, trying to tease me about all I was missing by confining myself to one guy's dick, ass and mouth.

Now he was doing the same thing, and bashful about revealing it. Interesting.

"You know a guy named Pika Campbell?" Ray asked.

Cinco nodded. "He used to work at the gym where I work out."

"Any idea where we can find him? We've already ruled out the Iolani Palace."

Cinco laughed. "Pika got a kick out of using that address. But yeah, I know where he lives. Or at least where he used to—last time I was there was about six months ago. He got plastered and I drove him home."

"He gay?" I asked.

"Pika? No way. Hundred percent straight. Though he does have a bromance going on."

I looked at Ray. There had been two guys in the limo with Fields and the elderly woman, and there'd been someone driving the limo when I saw Campbell on Saturday night in Waikiki.

"First things first," Ray said. "You remember his address?"

"Couldn't tell you the house number, but I'd recognize it if I saw it again. Run-down place, like a trailer without wheels. He was crashing there with these stoner cousins of his."

"Not Leroy and Larry Campbell?" I asked. We'd run across them in a previous investigation, when they had come up as suspects in the murder of a woman who had complained about their drug-dealing activities.

"Yeah, I think that was them. Pair of fat Hawaiian types. One of them bald, the other with dreadlocks."

"We know where to find them," Ray said. "But about this bromance. You know the guy?"

Cinco shook his head. "Just met him a couple of times. Mainland haole from LA. They call him Tacky—short for something foreign, I think."

We finished our root beers and thanked Cinco. "Try to keep Gunter out of trouble, will you?" I asked, as I stood up. "No more police involvement, at least."

"Will do," Cinco said.

As we walked out to the Highlander, I called the number for the prepaid cell I'd bought Dakota that morning. There was no answer, and he hadn't set up the voice mail. "Fuck," I said. "You mind if we swing by HCC on our way back in? I left Dakota there this morning."

"My ride is your ride," Ray said.

I called Frankie's cell, and though he didn't pick up at least he had voice mail. "I'm looking for Dakota," I said. "If you see him call me." I repeated the message in a text.

I hung up the phone. "Fuck, fuck, fuck. I never should have left him on his own."

"If you love someone, set him free. If he comes back, he's yours," Ray said. "If he doesn't, he never was."

"Please, spare me the Rod McKuen sentimentality."

"I'm serious. You have to trust the kid. If you try and keep him in a cage he'll just escape again."

"He's only fourteen, Ray. He needs a permanent home and a structure, not some pair of guys who are too busy to look after him."

I started calling anyone I thought Dakota might get in touch with, saving Mike for last. "What do you mean he's missing?" he asked.

"Well, not missing exactly," I said. "I dropped him at HCC this morning. He was going to hang out with Frankie and do some studying. I thought it would be good for him. I even got him a cell phone so we could stay in touch."

"Did you talk to Frankie?"

"Left him a voice mail and texted him. Ray and I are on our way to HCC now."

"You want me to meet you there?"

"Hold off. If Ray and I can't find him between us, then he's not there, and there's no use your making the trip."

I hung up and stared out the window as Ray pulled into the HCC campus, scanning the kids I saw talking in small groups, sitting under the trees, or walking to their cars. Dakota wasn't among them.

"What exactly did he say to you this morning?" Ray asked, as he pulled into a parking space.

I thought back to our conversation. I was in a hurry to get to work and wasn't paying full attention. "I think he said he was going to do some studying in the library."

"Then let's go over there."

We walked in the library. Dakota wasn't at any of the computers, or in the comfy lounge chairs. We started striding up and down between the stacks.

I was moving fast, darting around students who were trying to pick books off the shelves. "Stay cool, Kimo," Ray said.

"Haven't they ever heard of the Internet?" I said. "Who uses real books for research anymore?"

"Julie does. Sure, there's a ton of new stuff online, but sometimes you need something from the past. Now slow down and calm down."

I took a deep breath and rounded a corner. There, ahead of me, was Dakota, sitting at a carrel, reading a book.

I walked up behind him. "What's the point of my getting you a phone if you don't answer it?"

He looked up. "Hey, Kimo. I put it on vibrate because of the library and all. Sorry. You tried to call me?"

I didn't know whether to hug him or smack him. I did neither; I just took a deep breath. Dakota hadn't done anything except what he'd said.

Ray came up behind me. "I'm Ray," he said. "Kimo's partner."

Dakota looked from Ray to me and his mouth opened.

"Detective partner," I said. "We work together."

"Oh." Dakota nodded his head.

"Come on, let's get out of here," I said. "You feel like pizza?"

Ray dropped Dakota and me outside the headquarters building. "I need to go upstairs for a few minutes," I said to Dakota. "You want to see where I work?"

"Cool."

I took him to our desks and sat him at Ray's while I checked my email. Francisco Salinas at the FBI had been able to match the photo I took in Waikiki to Pika Campbell. They had no more information on him than we did, though.

I was scribbling a couple of notes when Lieutenant Sampson appeared with his stepdaughter, Kitty, a uniformed officer, and I introduced them to Dakota.

"Kitty, why don't you keep Dakota entertained for a few minutes while I talk to Kimo in my office," Sampson said.

"Sure. You want to look at some mug shots?" Kitty asked him.

"That would be neat."

I followed Sampson to his office. "You and Donne thought more about the FBI offer?" he asked.

"Do we have a choice?"

He sat down behind his desk and motioned me to sit across from him. "I don't want to lose either of you, and I've made it clear that this would only be a temporary assignment, and that you'd both come back here at some point."

He fiddled with the miniature cannon on his desk, rocking it back and forth on its base. "But if you're dead set against the move, I'll do my best to keep it from happening."

"I'll be honest with you, Lieutenant," I said. "I haven't made up my mind yet." I looked at him. "You went out on a limb for me when I had to leave Waikiki, and I'll always appreciate that. You've always gone to bat for Ray and me with the brass, and I hate to leave that kind of support."

I took a deep breath. "But Ray has made some good points about the work we could do with the Bureau, and I know he wants to make the jump. My parents are in favor of the move because they think I'll be safer over there, even though I've told them I'd still be working cases."

"What does Mike say?"

That was one of the things I loved about working with Sampson. He treated Mike just the way he would Julie Donne. "He has some doubts about my ability to work within a more structured environment," I said. "If I'm being honest I have to agree with him."

"I didn't just assign Donne to be your partner because you were solo at the time," Sampson said, leaning back in his chair. "I could have juggled assignments if I wanted to. But I could see he was the kind of solid, methodical cop who would work well with you. You have a tremendous sense of determination and I've seen you push forward against odds that would have knocked another cop for a loop. But you sidestep the rules now and then. I won't say I approve, but I tolerate that behavior because you get results."

He fiddled with the cannon again. "This might not be the right move for you," he said. "I know the Special Agent in Charge, and he won't let you get away with anything. But at the same time I think it's a move that would be good for you. You're what—thirty-seven?"

"Thirty-eight in a couple of months."

He nodded. "Then it's time you got your impulsive side under control. Working with the Bureau can do that for you."

He looked up behind me. "Seems like Kitty and Dakota are getting along. He's one of the teens from your group?"

"Yeah. His mom's at the HCCC and he ran away from his last foster home. He was camping out at an abandoned building on Lagoon Drive, and he witnessed Alexander Fields being taken into the warehouse where he was killed. Mike and I are looking after him for a few days until he settles down and we can get him back in the system."

"Define looking after."

I sighed. This was the kind of thing Sampson had just been telling me I wouldn't be able to get away with if I was assigned to the Bureau. "Though he hasn't said so I'm afraid he might have been turning tricks to earn money. He was in Waikiki on Saturday night and recognized one of the men with Fields, so he called me. When we met up with him he said that if we turned him in he'd just run away from the next foster home. So we took him in."

Sampson sat up. "Tomorrow morning, I want you to take him back to the social worker who's handling his case. If he or she agrees, then I have no problem with Dakota staying with you. But if not, then you're putting him into the system, and I expect no arguments from you or from him."

"Yes, sir," I said.

Kitty knocked on the door then. "Dakota's stomach is rumbling louder than a 747 landing on the reef runway. I mentioned pizza and he nearly jumped out of his seat."

"Pizza sounds great," Sampson said, standing up. "Kimo, why don't you call Mike, and we'll meet up to share a couple of pies."

That wasn't a request; it was a command. I returned to my desk and called Mike's cell, as Dakota and Kitty high-fived. "Sampson found out Dakota's staying with us off the books and he's not happy," I said in a low voice. "He wants you, me and Dakota to join him and Kitty for pizza."

"As long as I get my Hawaiian, I'm happy," Mike said, referring to the ham and pineapple pizza he loved.

I chose to take the comment another way. "You've already got him," I said. "Sampson lives in Manoa. How about the Island Pies near UH?"

"I can be there in fifteen," he said. "Love you."

"Love you, too. Thanks."

I hung up to see Kitty and Dakota staring at me. "That's so sweet," Kitty said. "That you guys still say I love you all the time."

"It's like some kind of Hallmark card, living with them," Dakota said. "Honey this, sweetie that." He stuck his finger in his mouth and pretended to gag.

"You wait," Kitty said. "Soon enough you'll want someone to talk to you that way."

Kitty went with us in the Jeep, riding shotgun, with Dakota in the back. I wasn't sure if Sampson had sent her to ride with us to keep an eye on Dakota, or if they had just become new BFFs.

Over pizza, Sampson probed Dakota with the skill of a master interviewer. I don't think Dakota even realized he was giving up information about where he was from (the Newark suburbs), what his mom had done back home (waitress), and what he liked do for fun (he had enjoyed learning to swim with us, and wanted to learn to surf, too).

The sullen, frightened teenager disappeared for a while, replaced by a handsome, happy boy who was looking forward to a bright future. Mike and I shared a couple of looks across the table as we watched Dakota bloom.

When Kitty was eight, Sampson had married her mom and become her stepdad. From what I understood, her mom was a flake, and when the marriage ended and her mom moved to the mainland, Kitty opted to stay with Sampson. I could see why. He radiated a calm, generous stability. I'd reacted to that myself for four and a half years, and the biggest stumbling block in moving to the FBI was the thought that I'd lose the chance to work with him.

When we had demolished the pizzas and Sampson had concluded his interrogation of Dakota, he and Kitty stood under a street light for last goodbyes with Dakota. Mike and I walked over to where we both had parked. "Your boss is a great guy," Mike said. "I can see why you don't want to leave him. I wish I got that kind of support at work."

Mike wasn't officially out on the job, as far as I knew. A couple of his co-workers knew about me, and I was sure the news had spread through the department's coconut wireless—the informal gossip network on an island where we're all connected to each other by at least two or three degrees of separation.

"He says working for the Bureau will make me grow up," I grumbled.

"Well, then, I'm all for it."

I turned to look at him in the light of a gibbous moon. "What, you think I'm some overgrown kid? A loose cannon like Dakota?"

"Come on, K-man. You know as well as I do that you don't always act like you're a middle-aged guy with responsibilities."

"Middle-aged! I'm thirty-seven."

"Do the math, pal. If the days of our years are three score years and ten, and if by reason of strength they be four score years, then you've hit the middle." He smiled. "Psalm 90. I had to memorize it in Catholic school back on Long Island."

"You're starting to scare me," I said.

"Don't worry, I love you even when you act like a child." He leaned over and kissed me, though I didn't kiss him back. "Now go get Dakota and I'll meet you at home."

He turned toward his flame-painted truck. Because I believe in karma, and because I love him, I called, "Love you, too, sweetheart," to his back.

Dakota left Kitty and Sampson and joined me at my Jeep. As I backed out of the parking space I thought about what Mike had said—and Sampson before him. Was I just an overgrown kid? I didn't think so. I knew I had responsibilities and I met them to the best of my abilities. Sure, I didn't have the best impulse control in the world, but that was a function of character, not maturity.

I got onto the H1 toward home, and Dakota asked, "Do you think I could be a cop, Kimo?"

"I think you can be anything you want. But for now let's focus on getting you back in school." I looked over at him. "We're going to have to talk to your social worker tomorrow."

He nodded. "I figured. Will she let me stay with you?"

"I don't know. Mike and I aren't in the system as foster parents, at least not yet. Do you think you could stay with Terri and Levi for a few days until we got things settled?"

"But then I could come back?"

I already knew what Mike would say; his answer would be "of course." So it was just up to me.

I could have said, "We'll see." Or I could have made up some excuse—maybe even the same ones I'd used about a having a baby. Mike and I worked dangerous jobs and crazy hours. Neither of us had any business making a commitment to a kid.

But I'd been working with the gay teen group for a few years by then, and I knew kids like Dakota had instant bullshit detectors. So I took a deep breath and said, "If that's what you want, after you've had a chance to see what your options are, Mike and I would love to have you stay with us."

Wednesday morning I called Terri and she agreed to call Wilma Chow and make arrangements for us to meet at the end of the day. After a flurry of text messages back and forth everything was set. I'd drop Dakota at the offices of the Sandwich Islands Trust, the family non-profit that Terri ran, on my way to work. He'd spend the day with her, and then they would join Levi, Mike and me at Wilma's office at four.

"You're okay with this?" I asked him, as we walked out to my Jeep.

He shrugged. "I don't have much choice, do I?"

"Sure you do. I can drop you at Wilma's office right now and she'll place you in a foster home. Easier for me, Mike, Terri and Levi."

Dakota turned to look at me. "You wouldn't do that, would you?"

"Only if that's what you wanted."

"I want to stay with you and Mike."

"We're going to do our best to make that happen. But one of the things you learn as a grownup is that sometimes you have to play by the rules."

"That sucks."

"Yeah, sometimes it does."

Ironic, I thought, as I drove us toward downtown. Me lecturing Dakota about being a grown-up when it seemed like everybody around me thought I needed to hear the same words.

I couldn't find a place to park near the high-rise where Terri's office was, so I pulled up in front of the building and put my flashers on. "This is a two-way deal, Dakota," I said, before he got out. "I'm trusting you to go up to Terri's office and be cooperative. In return you trust all of us to look after you."

"I used to trust my mom for that."

I nodded. "And I'm sure that down somewhere, under the addiction, she loves you and wants the best for you. But just because one person lets you down doesn't mean you stop trusting."

"I know." He opened the car door and slid out. "See you later."

By the time I got to headquarters, Ray was already at his desk. "New homicide just came in," he said. "I looked it over and said that we'd take it."

"Why?" I asked, sliding into my desk.

"Because a witness saw two body-builder types leaving the scene in a black limousine," Ray said. "And the victim's an elderly woman."

I swiveled over to his desk to look at the report, which had been called in a few minutes before. The victim's name was Bernice Fong, with an address in the Kalihi Valley, in the hills above the Bishop Museum. Something about the name struck me as familiar, but I couldn't place it. That is, until I ran a quick background check on Bernice Fong, and discovered she was the widow of Judge Howard Fong—my father's mentor.

She was ninety years old, which struck me as pretty old to be out orchestrating murder. But you never know; I believe that as you get older you become a more and more concentrated version of yourself. If you're a jerk, you get meaner and nastier; if you're a nice person, you end up even sweeter. What would I be? Still acting on impulse when I reached that four score years Mike had mentioned the night before?

"She's got to be connected to Fields," Ray said. "Same two guys, same limo. But how?"

I thought back to my conversation with my father. "I know back in the fifties, Fields went to the Fongs' house, because my father remembers that."

It was my turn to drive, so we got in the Jeep and climbed up the Likelike Highway to Bernice Fong's house in Kalihi. It was a low ranch, backing up against a wooded slope of the Ko'olaus. A cruiser was parked in front of the house, its blue lights flashing, and a uniformed cop I knew, Lidia Portuondo, stood next to it, talking to a woman in a bright blue muumuu.

The Fong house was halfway down the street, and I drove past, made U turn, and parked behind the cruiser. It was a cool, breezy morning, the sun playing hide and seek with a bunch of fluffy clouds. The Ko'olaus loomed behind us in verdant green.

Lidia introduced us to the woman with her. "Mrs. Isabelle Gray lives across the street," she said. The woman was in her late sixties, a haole with pale skin and flyaway brown hair. She was slim and tall for a woman of her age, nearly six feet.

"It's just awful," Mrs. Gray said. "I've known Bernice for years. I'd never expect such a thing."

The Medical Examiner's van turned the corner up ahead, and Lidia walked over to direct it into place. "Can you tell us what happened?" Ray asked.

"I don't sleep well," Mrs. Gray said. "I have this pain in my left hip and it wakes me up every time I turn on it."

We smiled politely.

"I got up around two, and I was just sitting in my front window in the dark, waiting for the ibuprofen to kick in. I saw lights on at Bernice's and I thought that was strange; she usually goes to sleep so early."

She fiddled with the large diamond engagement ring on her right hand. "There was a big black limousine parked in her driveway and I assumed she had been at some charity event and come home late. Bernice and the Judge were always very social people, and even at her age the poor thing used to get herself made up like a little China doll and go out."

"But you didn't see her?" Ray asked.

Mrs. Gray shook her head. "I saw two men leave her house, get in the limousine, and drive away. At the time I didn't think anything of it. I just assumed they were her drivers. I've seen her take that kind of limousine before."

The van passed us and pulled into the driveway. I saw the Medical Examiner, Doc Takayama, get out. That was unusual; he didn't come to many crime scenes.

Ray was still focused on Isabelle Gray. "Can you describe the men you saw?"

"It was dark and I wasn't paying much attention. They looked young, and very muscular."

"Haole?" It was a mark of how long Ray had been in Hawai'i that he'd started talking like a real native.

"I just couldn't tell." She looked from Ray to me. "Should I have called the police then?"

"You had no reason to think anything was wrong, ma'am," I said. "But you did call this morning?"

She nodded. "Bernice is always an early riser. She gets up and brings in her paper and feeds her birds. When I saw she hadn't gotten the paper this morning I got nervous. So I took my key and went over there to check on her."

She began to cry. "The poor thing."

"Thank you for your time," Ray said. "If we have any more questions, will you be around today?"

"Yes. I don't think I can go out. I'd be too nervous."

She went back to her house and Ray and I walked up the driveway to Bernice Fong's open front door. We were greeted by the frantic chirping of a pair of small lovebirds in an elaborate bamboo cage near the entrance to the kitchen. The interior was done in the Chinese style, with black lacquer furniture, Oriental rugs, and pen and ink watercolors on the walls. It reminded me of the house where my father's best friend, Uncle Chin, had lived.

A diminutive woman in a black silk dressing gown sat on the carved wooden sofa, leaning back against the black cushions, her sightless eyes staring up. A single gunshot wound scarred her forehead. Bernice Fong looked enough like my petite, dark-haired mother that I felt a momentary shock.

Doc was standing to one side of the body, talking with one of his techs. "Single gunshot wound to the frontal bone. Most likely a hollow point."

"How come there's no blood?" Ray asked. "I thought head wounds were big bleeders."

"Position of the head meant the blood drained inside," Doc said.

"This look like the same kind of wound you found on Alexander Fields?" I asked.

"You think the cases are connected?"

I nodded. "Fields was seen getting out of black limousine with an elderly woman and two bodybuilders outside the warehouse where he died. The woman across the street saw two bodybuilders leave this house last night around two, driving a black limousine."

"I'd say the chances are very good," Doc said. "I'll see what kind of fragments I can dig out—if I can get enough for a ballistics comparison."

While Doc and his techs prepared the body for transport, Ray and I prowled around the house. There was no sign of forced entry. It appeared that Bernice Fong had already been in bed when her guests arrived; the sheets were tousled. There was little evidence that her guests had stayed long—no indentations in the sofa cushions, no empty beverage glasses.

The crime scene techs arrived and began their work. We looked through the papers in Bernice Fong's study, but couldn't find anything that looked relevant to the case.

It was after eleven by the time the body was gone and the techs had finished. Mrs. Fong had no immediate survivors and hadn't left instructions for her birds, so we had to call Animal Control to take them.

We took a quick walk around the outside of the house before we left. The back yard was immaculately manicured, the trees carefully trimmed, and I remembered that my father had worked in this very yard when he was a young man. It was good to see that his work was still maintained after all these years.

"We should find Pika Campbell," Ray said. "See if he has an alibi for last night."

"And last Tuesday night," I said.

We'd first run across Pika's stoner cousins, Leroy and Larry Campbell, when we were investigating a case two years before. I looked up their address on my netbook and we took the Likelike Highway downhill, past towering trees with vistas of the surrounding mountains. As we got closer to the H1 houses sprouted up around us under the lowering skies. "Going to rain," Ray said.

"We'll be long gone before it starts." I took the exit for the highway and headed Diamond Head, and as I predicted the skies cleared and the sun came out as we climbed back up into the hills on Puowaina Drive. The road was narrow and full of switchbacks, lined at first with expensive homes with valley and ocean views and a profusion of hibiscus and plumeria.

As we zigzagged into the Hawaiian homelands on the sides of Mount Tantalus though, the poverty in which many native Hawaiians lived became evident. Barefoot kids played in weedy yards, and decrepit cars littered driveways. Most of the houses could use a good coat of paint; some showed damage from long-gone tropical storms or hurricanes.

The Campbell brothers, two-bit dope dealers, lived in a beat-up shack with weeds growing around its foundation. The walls had once been white, but the tropical sun had faded them to the color of dried spit. One of the windows was broken and covered over with cardboard.

Ray rapped on the door and called out, "Mr. Campbell. Police. Open up."

We waited, and Ray was about to knock again when the door opened. Larry, a fat Hawaiian guy with dark dreadlocks, stuck his head out. "Hey, Leroy, it's da kine police," he said. "Long time no see, bruddas."

Larry yawned and stepped outside, and big, bald Leroy followed him. "How about your cousin Pika?" Ray asked. "He in there, too?"

"Nah, he wen bag two days ago."

"But he was living with you before he left?" I asked.

"Sometimes he moi moi wid us, sometimes wid his buddy," Leroy said.

To Ray's credit, he seemed to be following the conversation, which meant he was learning our island pidgin. Pika slept at their place sometimes, but had left two days before.

"Tacky?" I asked.

Larry nodded. "Yeah. Bodybuilder dude. Dumb as two rocks in a box."

That could describe the Campbell brothers, too. "You know where we can find him?" I asked.

"Try gym," Leroy said. "Ho brah, he alla time workin out."

"Which gym?" I asked. "Rascals?"

Larry shook his head, his dreadlocks, which were entwined with cowry shells, swinging like he was Stevie Wonder. "No, brah, he got fired from there." He turned to his bald brother. "You know what gym he go?"

Larry mimed thought, tilting his head to the side and putting a finger up to his chin. "No," he said, laughing.

"You know Tacky's last name?" Ray asked.

"Maybe Tiki," Larry said, his dreadlocks shaking. "Ha! Tacky Tiki!"

The brothers dissolved in pakalolo-induced laughter, grabbing their big bellies and throwing their heads back. I pulled out a card, though I knew it was probably useless. "You see Paki, you give us a call, all right?" I said, handing it to Larry.

"Yeah, brah, I make fo' call you," he said, making a shaka

and holding it up to his head, so his thumb was at his ear and his pinky at his mouth.

He and his brother started giggling again, and we walked back to my Jeep. As we drove away, I said, "I need to talk to my father."

"And those guys need a couple of slaps upside the head," Ray said.

I called the house, and I'd almost given up when my father finally answered. "Howzit, Dad," I said. "You on your own today?"

"I told your mother to leave me the phone before she left but she never listens."

"Uh-huh. How about I pick you up and buy you a plate lunch?"

"What's up?"

"I'll tell you when I see you. Ray and I are in Papakolea, so it'll take us a few minutes."

I could have made my way through the hills and narrow streets to St. Louis Heights; I had learned to drive in those mountains and knew the dead ends to avoid and the shortcuts to take. But it was easier to just go back down to the highway, passing those glimpsed vistas of the Ko'olaus and a rainbow rising over Kalihi, where Bernice Fong's house had become a crime scene.

I got off at University Avenue, which led up to the UH campus, and took Dole Street past block after block of student housing in the shelter of the mountains. "How's Julie's dissertation coming?" I asked Ray.

"She'd get more done if Vinnie let us sleep through the night," he grumbled. "But there's this mama-san down the hall, sweet little old Japanese lady, and Julie takes Vinnie down there for a couple of hours a day so she can concentrate. She's got the revisions back from her advisor and she's hoping the next run will be the last one and she can schedule her defense."

"So she might be graduating this May?"

He shrugged. "Probably not, because her committee will

undoubtedly want some changes, and then it's a bear to put the final manuscript together. So maybe she'll finish in August, maybe December."

I turned onto St. Louis Drive and began the climb up to my parents' house. "We've been up and down more mountains today than the last month," Ray said.

"You want flat, you go to Iowa," I said.

"Hey, Iowa's not flat, it's rolling," Ray said. "Or so I've been told."

"Never been," I said as I pulled up in my parents' driveway. My father appeared in the doorway, with a cane in his right hand. I jumped out of the Jeep and hurried over to him as he fumbled to lock the front door.

"What's with the cane, Dad?"

"Your mother insists. She says I'm having trouble with my balance."

Ray got out of the front seat and held the door open for my father. "Hey, Mr. K," he said. "Howzit?"

"This one gets more Hawaiian every time I see him," my father said. "You have a little keiki now, huh? A Hawaiian baby."

"Yup. He's gonna grow up speaking pidgin like a native."

That is, I thought, if Ray and Julie stayed in the islands.

I helped my father into the front seat, all the time worrying about how much older and more fragile he got every time I saw him. Ray climbed in the back, and we drove down the hill to one of my father's favorite lunch spots.

"So why does my son call me for lunch?" he asked, as we pulled into the parking lot. "You must need something."

"Dad, I'm offended," I said, smiling. "I can't take my old man out for lunch sometime?"

"Give it up, Kimo," Ray said, hopping out of the back and extending an arm to my father. "He's your dad. He knows you."

We walked into the restaurant, my father moving slower

than I'd seen before, and sat at a table by the window. We all ordered the plate lunch, an island tradition, developed to serve to plantation workers who needed to keep up their strength through long days. A main course, usually fish or chicken, two scoops of rice, a scoop of macaroni salad, and some shredded lettuce. My dad went for the fish; just to be contrary I got the chicken. Ray took chicken, too, but I don't know his motivation.

"I have some bad news, Dad," I said, after the elderly Chinese waitress had taken our order. I was pretty sure she'd been working there my whole life. Or else there was an interchangeable supply of old women with the same apron and the same faded lace handkerchief in her breast pocket. "We got called to a homicide this morning, and it's someone you knew. Bernice Fong."

"Homicide?" he asked. "You're sure she didn't just die? She was very old. Even older than me."

I was about to mouth off to him, mentioning the bullet hole in her forehead, but I controlled my tongue. "We're sure, Dad. And we're thinking it's connected to Alexander Fields' murder, too."

"I told you I knew him, didn't I?" he asked. "I used to see him around Judge Fong's when I was working on the landscaping. I always went by Al, you know, ever since I was a little kid. But one day Mr. Fields asked me what my full name was. I told him Alexander, and he said that was his name, too, and it was one I should be proud of. Remember Alexander the Great," he said.

He picked up a puffy roll and then tried to unwrap a pat of butter. I couldn't stand to watch him fumble with it so I opened one and handed it to him.

"Who killed Mrs. Fong?" he asked.

"That's what we're trying to figure out," I said. The waitress brought our platters and set them in front of us. "You know what might have connected her to Fields?"

"Wouldn't have been her," my father said. "Just him, old Judge Fong. They were very traditional people. The men used to meet in the Judge's living room, and Mrs. Fong would bring them coffee and tea and fried dumplings she made herself." He smiled. "They were so *ono*, those dumplings. Best I ever had."

Well, someone didn't kill Bernice Fong because of good dumplings, I thought. "When you say 'the men,' who do you mean?"

"Group of them," my father said, between bites of fish. "The Judge. Fields. Bennie Gomez, who owned a marina and a boat repair business. Matthew Clark, your friend Terri's grandfather. And Emile Gardiner, the real estate developer."

"That must be the same Gardiner Fields defended in that land-grab lawsuit," Ray said. "I remember that name Emile."

"His father was British and his mother was French," my father said. "Born in Tahiti, came to Hawai'i when he was a young man." As I ate, I couldn't help noticing how his hand shook as he tried to scoop some rice. Crap. My dad was a proud man, and I couldn't see him consenting to be spoon-fed.

While I was worrying about my dad's health, Ray was still focused on the case. "You ever listen in to what they talked about, Mr. K?"

"They used to argue about statehood, back then. But a lot of people did."

"They were all in favor of it?" Ray asked.

"All but Matthew Clark. Eventually he stopped going to the meetings. And then Mr. Gardiner offered me a job and I stopped working for the Judge."

"Gardiner?" I asked. "I thought you worked for Amfac?" Amfac was one of the "big five," the Hawaiian companies that had started out in sugarcane processing and came to control a lot of the territory before statehood.

"That was later. Mr. Gardiner had just bought a piece of land, and he was going to build houses for ordinary people. I was almost finished my degree in business at UH and he said I could work for him full-time and still go to school. When I graduated he gave me my first superintendent's job. Gardiner Properties went on to develop Aiea. Maybe even built that house where you and Mike live."

"Can you think of any reason why someone would want to kill Bernice Fong and Alexander Fields?" I asked, pushing my empty plate away from me.

My father shook his head. "Maybe something in the Judge's safe would tell you."

"He had a safe?" I looked at Ray. "Did we find that?"

He shook his head.

"Behind the picture of Chinatown on his office wall," my father said. "What kind of *maka'i* are you?"

Maka'i is the Hawaiian word for police. "Not the thorough kind, I guess," I said.

We dropped my dad off at home and I made sure he was settled in his recliner, with the TV remote, the phone and a glass of ice water. "The Judge and Mrs. Fong were always good to me," he said. "When Haoa was born I decided we would give him the Judge's English name. Howard."

"I'm glad I wasn't born second," I said. "You never told me. Who was I named after?"

"You'll have to ask your mother that one."

I shook my head and went back out to the Jeep.

Back at Bernice Fong's house, the safe was just where my father said it was. "Now all we need is the combination," Ray said. "You think she kept it around somewhere?"

"I wouldn't be surprised." We put our rubber gloves on again and started going through everything in the desk drawers, pulling out any papers that we thought might relate to Alexander Fields, Richard Clark, Bennie Gomez, Emile Gardiner, or whatever they were up to at the dawn of statehood.

"Bingo," Ray said, showing me an envelope from the safe's manufacturer. Apparently after Judge Fong died, Bernice had written to them for the safe's combination.

"You found it, you do the honors," I said.

Ray twirled the dials back and forth and the safe's door swung open. Mrs. Fong had kept her better jewelry in there: several strands of pearls, a diamond engagement ring and matching wedding band, as well as a tray of other pieces. A couple of gold coins rustled in fading paper bags below the deed to the house and her life insurance policy, as well as a lot of U.S. savings bonds.

And underneath it all was a manila folder with a couple of yellowed newspaper clippings. The headline on the first screamed, "Mainland Senator Found Dead in Chinatown Brothel."

"My father mentioned this," I said to Ray. We sat down next to each other at the Judge's desk and read the articles together. They spanned three days in January of 1959. Senator James LeJeune of Tennessee had been a vocal opponent of statehood for the islands, based on the racial mix of residents, who he said, "weren't real Americans because of their mixed blood." He had come to Honolulu on a fact-finding mission, invited by civic leaders who wanted to convince him of the benefits of statehood.

The night before he was scheduled to return to Washington on the Matson Line's Matsonia cruise ship, he was found dead in a Chinatown brothel. Both he and the Chinese prostitute he was with had been shot once in the forehead.

"Forehead," Ray said, pointing.

"Yeah," I said. "I'm seeing a pattern."

The Honolulu PD investigated, fingering a notorious pimp for the crimes. He protested his innocence, but was convicted anyway. He died in prison a few years later.

"Why would Judge Fong have kept these articles in his safe for all these years?" Ray asked.

I looked ahead, trying to think. But my eye kept going back to the painting of Chinatown that had covered the safe. "Come on, brah," I said. "Let's take a ride."

We locked up the safe, but I took the painting with us and drove down to Chinatown. I found the address of the brothel where Senator LeJeune had been killed and pulled up across from it. I held up the painting.

"This is freaky," Ray said. "It's like a perfect match."

A drunk woman in a red and white flowered muumuu sat on the curb in front of the building, talking on a cell phone. We couldn't help overhearing her as we sat there, the engine idling.

"The police pulled me over and they ran my name and discovered I had two outstanding warrants. So the motherfuckers took me into jail for two days."

I looked at Ray and we both smiled.

"Now? I'm back here on the street like always," the woman continued. "My daughter don't get off work until five. If she don't kick me out I'll stay with her."

A car pulled up behind us and I had to start moving again. I drove over to a Kope Bean and parked. We left the painting in the Jeep and went inside.

"Let's step back," I said, when we were both sitting in comfy chairs with our macadamia nut lattes. "We've got two murders in 1959 and the MO matches two murders today. We know that Fields, Fong, Clark, Yamato and Gardiner used to meet together around that time."

"Fields is dead, and so are the judge and his wife," Ray said. "What about the others?"

While my netbook was warming up, and then connecting to the free wi-fi, I said, "I remember Terri's grandfather was an opponent of statehood. He believed the islands should have been an independent nation. And my father said that he stopped coming to the meetings at Judge Fong's house."

"You think the rest of them came up with a plot to kill this senator? To eliminate opposition to statehood?"

"Seems like an idea," I said. "Let's see if any of the rest of these guys are still alive."

Bennie Gomez was long since dead, as was Terri's grandfather and Emile Gardiner. "Look at this," I said, pointing at a line in Gardiner's obituary. "Survived by his son Andre."

"Andy Gardiner," Ray said. "Friend of Shepard Fields."

"Not surprising, I guess," I said. "If their fathers were friends, they'd know each other, even though Gardiner has to be at least fifteen years older."

"But all these guys are dead," Ray said. "Fong, Yamato, and Gardiner. Matthew Clark, too, even if he pulled out of the group. Fields was the last man standing. Who would want to kill him now?"

"I don't know, brah." I looked at my watch. "But I've got to get over to the social worker's office at four."

"Drop me back at headquarters. I'll keep on looking for stuff on those dead guys."

"See if you can find anything on Tacky, too," I said.

"Tacky Tiki?" Ray asked, and we both laughed.

"Well, he's got to have a last name, though I doubt that's it."

I met Mike in the garage near Wilma Chow's office, and when we got up there we found Terri, Levi and Dakota waiting. After a flurry of hugs and handshakes, we all sat down. "How was your day, Dakota?" I asked.

"Okay. Terri took me over to see this school, Punahou. She said it's where you went."

I looked at Terri. "Punahou? Really?"

"It was good enough for you and me and Harry," she said.

"But it's so expensive," I said.

Levi laughed. "That's not a problem for either of us."

"Yeah, but it is for Mike and me. If Dakota eventually comes to live with us we can't afford Punahou tuition."

"Dakota took a placement test," Terri said. "He's smart enough to get in. And either he'll get a scholarship, or I'll take care of the tuition."

"But…"

"Kimo. Let it go." Terri nodded toward Dakota, who was watching us argue.

I took a deep breath and turned to him. "You see? This is what it's like having an ohana around you."

"Arguing?" he asked.

"Call it a difference of opinion," I said. "But in the end, we all want what's best for you. Did you like Punahou?"

He shrugged. "It's a school."

The door to Wilma's office opened and she stepped out to the waiting room. "I guess we should do this in the conference room," she said. "Follow me."

She led us down a hallway to a bland room with a rectangular table and chairs around it. "Dakota, why don't you sit across from me," she said. "Kimo, you and Mike can sit with me, and Terri and Levi, you sit with Dakota."

We followed her directions and sat down. "This is certainly an unusual case," she began. "I see that Mrs. Gonsalves has already satisfied all the requirements for becoming a foster parent. But that was two years ago—and you didn't follow up."

"After my husband passed away, I looked at a lot of different ways to rebuild my life. Becoming a foster parent was one of those. For a variety of reasons I chose not to follow that path at the time."

"But you'd like to do so now?" Wilma asked.

"Dakota wants to come and live with Mike and me," I said. "I'm confident that we'll qualify—but I know that's going to take some time. Dakota has agreed to live with Terri and Levi until Mike and I can take full responsibility for him."

Mike stepped in. "I own the house where Kimo and I live in Aiea, with a relatively small mortgage. The neighborhood is safe, and Dakota would have his own room. Each of us alone makes enough money to cover our basic expenses. We've both known Dakota for at least a year, and we're committed to providing him a safe, loving environment."

"We've both passed the FBI background clearance as part of our jobs," I added. "And I'm confident we can pass any other tests you have."

Wilma nodded. "I'm sure you can, Kimo. But I do have to consider what's in Dakota's best interest."

"Don't I have a say?" he asked.

She turned to him. "Legally? No, I'm afraid you don't. But I will talk to you and take what you say into my decision." She turned to us. "I think this would be a good time for the adults to head back to the waiting room so I can talk to Dakota."

We stood up. Mike put his hand on Dakota's shoulder, and I said, "I've worked with Mrs. Chow before, Dakota, and I know she's going to do what's best for you."

He slumped in his chair. "Whatever."

I reached under his shoulders and hoisted him upright. "Sit up straight and mind your manners. Everyone in this room wants to help you."

Terri laughed. "I guess we can see who the disciplinarian is going to be."

We walked back down the hall together. "Seriously, Terri," I said. "Punahou? You think that's the best place for him?"

"I was surprised at how well he did on the placement test," she said, as we all sat down again. "He's a lot smarter than he lets on. He'll get the kind of individual attention he needs to get back on track, and the school won't tolerate any bullying because of his sexual orientation."

"There's nothing wrong with the public school system," Mike said. "I graduated from Farrington, remember? But if Dakota can get into Punahou, and Terri can swing the tuition, I'm all for it."

"Levi?" I asked. "What do you think?"

He shook his head. "I don't have a horse in this race. I'm just here for moral support."

I gave up and turned to Terri. "You know anything about Alexander Fields?"

"The attorney? Just what I read in the paper. Why?"

"He used to go to meetings at Judge Fong's house in the fifties, with your grandfather and a bunch of other men, to talk about statehood."

Terri smoothed out her floral print skirt. I could tell she'd dressed for the part she was playing—the skirt, a white polo shirt and woven belt and a small white handbag made her look like a well-kept suburban mom. I'd seen her in other outfits—a chic black dress and pearls at society events; a well-tailored navy suit and expensive leather briefcase when she was attending board meetings of the Sandwich Trust.

"You already know my grandfather was against statehood," she said. "If he was going to meetings with those men it was because he wanted to convince them it was the wrong move. He said many times that if we didn't have a third option, then the vote shouldn't even go forward."

"A third option?" Mike asked.

Terri turned to him. "How much do you know about Hawaiian history?"

He shrugged. "Enough to get me a high school diploma."

"Well, for Levi's benefit, I'll give you a quick recap. After the U.S. overthrew the Hawaiian monarchy in 1898, the islands were governed under what was called an Organic Act, which made Hawai'i a territory, with a governor appointed by the president."

She shifted in her chair, crossing one leg over the other and straightening her skirt. "Everything changed after World War II. The U.N. came into being, and they adopted a resolution which called for self-governance of territories under colonial-style conditions."

"Did this relate to other countries? Or just the U.S.?" Mike asked.

"France, the United Kingdom, Australia and New Zealand are the countries I remember," Terri said. "According to the rules, there were supposed to be three choices on the statehood ballot: become a state, remain a territory, or return to being an independent nation."

"And the one to become independent never showed up on the ballot," I said. "That was the missing third option."

"Exactly," Terri said. "My grandfather always believed that someone rigged that election. But what's this all about? You think Alexander Fields was killed because of something that happened back then? Wouldn't the statute of limitations have kicked in?"

"Not for murder," I said.

Wilma Chow came back out then, followed by Dakota. "There's going to be some paperwork," she said. "But I'm confident that I can place Dakota with Mrs. Gonsalves for now. Kimo, you and Mike will have to go through our foster parent training course, but that'll take a couple of weeks to organize."

"Mrs. Chow says I can come stay with you guys sometimes," Dakota said. "Like visitation."

"Don't go putting words in my mouth," Wilma said, but she smiled. "I said you could sleep over in Aiea on a weekend night, if everyone agrees."

She handed me a pile of papers. "Fill all these out and return them to me." Then she turned to Terri. "If you come back to my office for a few minutes we'll get things going on your end. And then you can take Dakota home with you."

"I should go," Levi said. "Terri's mom picked up Danny after school. I'll swing by their house and pick him up, and then Terri can go up to Aiea with you guys and Dakota to get his stuff."

I turned to Terri. "Do you think your grandfather might have shared his suspicions more specifically with your dad?"

"Probably. They were very close," Terri said. "You want me to call him?"

"If it's all right, I'll follow Levi and talk to him face to face."

"I'll give him a call anyway," Terri said. "He's not so good with surprises."

"I'll wait here with Dakota until Terri's finished," Mike said. "Call me when you're on your way home so we can figure out dinner."

"Will do." I leaned over and kissed his cheek, then followed Levi to the elevator.

"Dakota seems like a good kid," he said as we waited.

"He's rough around the edges, but I think he's got a lot of potential."

"I can relate," Levi said. "I was rough myself."

"A nice Jewish boy like you?" I asked, only half joking, as we stepped into the elevator. "Rough for you was probably skipping Hebrew school now and then."

"You wouldn't say that if you saw my juvenile record," Levi said. "After my dad died I turned into a hell-raiser. Got into drugs and stole from my relatives and the neighbors to pay for my habit. Even went through one of those scared straight programs, which didn't do anything except introduce me to more guys like me."

"How'd you turn around?"

"Boarding school when I turned sixteen. I was so glad to get away from my stepfather that I was determined not to do anything that would get me tossed out of there and sent back home."

"I see that determination in Dakota," I said, as we walked through the garage. "He just needs to have that strong will focused in the right direction."

I followed Levi's Porsche out of the garage and I have to admit that part of me wanted to be in that sporty convertible, not in my utilitarian Jeep. Police work was never going to make me a millionaire. Mike and I were lucky to have secure jobs; we'd never have to face homelessness, as long as we survived any body blows life threw at us. But we'd never be rich enough to afford Punahou tuition, high-end sports cars, or luxury vacations. I rarely let money bother me—but thinking about having a kid, or even having Dakota live with us—was a sobering thought.

How had my parents managed, with three sons to support on a single income? My dad worked his butt off, that's how. As a kid, I resented that he was always working on weekends, instead of there to take me surfing or out hiking in the woods behind the house. Now I understood. I wanted things to be different for my own kid, but I wasn't sure how to manage it.

Terri's parents still lived in the oceanfront house where she'd grown up, just off Kalanaiana'ole Road in the shadow of Koko Head. Her family was descended from the original missionaries to the islands, and their money went back generations. Levi pulled up at the gated entrance and spoke through the intercom. Then he reached his hand out the window and waved me to follow him.

As I drove through the gate, my cell phone buzzed. I checked the display and saw that it was from Greg Oshiro. I figured he was just trying to get more details on our investigation into Alexander Fields' death, so I let the call go to voice mail.

I parked behind Levi in the cul-de-sac in front of the Clarks' house. It wasn't much bigger than the one where Alexander Fields had lived, but it was warmer and more welcoming. A hipped roof shaded the wood-railed lanai, which stretched around the house. It was a solid old building that had withstood many storms.

Mrs. Clark opened the carved wooden front door to us. "Hello, Levi. And Kimo, so nice to see you. How are your parents?"

"They're doing well, Mrs. Clark. My father's getting older, a little unsteady on his feet. But I hope they'll both be around for a long time."

"We're all getting older," she said. "You must send them my regards."

"I will. I was hoping to talk to Mr. Clark for a few minutes, if he's available."

She laughed. "I'll see if I can pry him away from his computer. Come in, please."

Danny sat on the living room floor, a game controller in his hands. He was growing more independent with every year. With his dark hair and round face, he looked like a miniature version of his father, a Honolulu cop who had been killed a few years before.

"Ever since his grandmother bought him an Xbox we have trouble getting him away from it," Levi said. "Hey, sport, what're you playing now?"

"Escape from the Death Star," he said, his eyes intent on the screen. "My Ninja robot warrior is on the run from a bounty hunter."

Levi walked over to join him, while Mrs. Clark led me down the hall to her husband's study. "Richard? Kimo Kanapa'aka is here."

Richard Clark's hair had turned white and his skin was wrinkled, but he still looked every inch of the corporate mogul he had once been, running a chain of home-grown department stores that rivaled Liberty House. He had sold the business to a mainland company and retired ten years before.

"Kimo! Come in, have a seat. I don't get many visitors over the age of nine these days."

"Thank you, sir," I said, reaching out to shake his hand. His grip was not as strong as it had once been, and his thin hand was spotted with bruises.

"Damn blood thinners," he said, noticing my gaze. "Makes it look like Evelyn beats me."

"Don't talk like that, dear," Mrs. Clark said. "Kimo's a police detective now, remember? He'll have me arrested on suspicion of elder abuse."

"Ha!" Mr. Clark barked.

I sat down across from him and he pushed the laptop aside on the polished koa wood desk. "I'm investigating the murder of Alexander Fields," I said. "I understand that he and your father were acquainted."

"My father knew every mover and shaker in the Territory," Mr. Clark said. "I remember he used to talk about Alex Fields. Sharp attorney, but too willing to cut corners for my father's taste."

"I'm afraid that something in his past might have led to his death," I said. "Did your father ever talk about meeting a group of men at Judge Fong's house?"

"The Cabal, he called them," Mr. Clark said. "My father didn't think statehood was the right path for the islands. But Fong's Cabal did, and my father spent a good deal of time trying to convince them otherwise. He finally gave up."

I opened my netbook and pulled up the first article about the death of Senator James LeJeune. Then I swiveled the computer around so that Mr. Clark could read. "Do you think this Cabal could have had anything to do with Senator LeJeune's death?"

He pulled on a pair of reading glasses and peered down at the screen. "I remember this," he said, when he had finished scanning the article. "Big scandal back then. Very titillating, too." He looked down over his glasses at me. "Don't tell Evelyn, but I patronized that establishment a few times myself, when I was a young man. Before I was married, of course."

"Did you know the woman who was killed, or the man who was convicted of the murders?"

He shook his head. "They didn't use pimps at that place. That's the first thing that looked fishy about the story. That man, the one they accused? He was a low-level drug dealer, peddling opium to old Chinese men. Nothing to do with prostitution at all."

"Why do think he was accused, then?" I asked.

"A cover-up, of course," Mr. Clark said. "This Senator was a very big deal back in Washington. HPD wanted to sweep this under the rug ASAP. Bad for business, you know."

I had been a cop long enough to realize that such things happened, though I hoped that the HPD I worked for wouldn't tolerate them. "What happened to the political opposition to statehood after LeJeune was murdered?" I asked.

"Evaporated," Mr. Clark said. "LeJeune was the big blowhard in Congress. Once he was gone the opposition faded away and the statehood bill sailed through." He pulled off his reading glasses and looked at me. "You think Fields and his Cabal were responsible for LeJeune's death?"

I nodded. "I don't know how it ties into Fields' death, but I'm going to find out."

I left a few minutes later, after looking over Danny's shoulder at the game Levi was having trouble prying him away from. On my way home to Aiea, I called Mike. "Terri and Dakota have already been here and gone. I'm making pasta carbonara for dinner."

When Mike wasn't happy, he relied on Italian food for comfort. "Sounds good. I'll be home in a few."

The house seemed strangely empty and quiet without Dakota, though Roby made a fuss when I walked in.

"I think this is the right thing," Mike said, as we sat down to eat a platter of pasta he'd prepared. "Bringing Dakota to live with us."

"Having him here will give us a head start on what it's like to take care of a kid. I know how much you want one."

"Don't put this all on me, Kimo. You've got to want it just as much as I do."

"Do I? I can't just agree because I love you and I know how much it means to you?"

"We're not talking about a movie choice." He pushed his chair back and stood up. "We're talking about our lives, and a new baby's life."

"Sit down, will you?" I waited until he was back in his chair before I continued. "I've been thinking about how I feel about Dakota. How I want to take care of him and show him the love he hasn't been getting from his mother." I took a deep breath. "And that's what I want to do with our baby."

"Really?"

I nodded. And then we were in each other's arms, kissing, and I wished for that moment that our biology hadn't predestined us, and that we could just go right up to our bedroom and get started on making that baby together.

Thursday morning I took Roby for a long walk around the neighborhood, trying to put together the pieces of the case. In January 1959, Senator James LeJeune had been shot and killed in a Honolulu brothel. I believed that the Cabal, as Richard Clark called them, had been involved somehow, in order to protect their pro-statehood interests.

The murder had been blamed on a pimp and the details swept under the rug. Alexander Fields was the last living member of the Cabal. Had he planned to clear the slate as he came to the end of his life? Was that why he was killed, to protect the secret?

I was sure that Bernice Fong was the woman who had accompanied Fields to his death, and that Pika Campbell, and probably his friend Tacky, had driven them to Lagoon Drive, killed Fields and burned the warehouse. Why not kill Bernice Fong with him? Why wait a week? And if what my father said was right, Bernice hadn't been a member of the Cabal at all; she had merely served them food.

Had she hired the men to kill Fields? Why? And why had she been shot?

My brain was fuzzy from too many details that didn't add up. I cleaned up after Roby, then led him back to the house. Mike was already dressed and he kissed my cheek on his way out the door. "Early meeting. See you later. Love you."

"Love you too," I said to his back. I fed the dog, showered and dressed, and drove in to work, no clearer on who had killed Alexander Fields or Bernice Fong.

"The techs picked up some fingerprints at the crime scene," Ray said, when I got in. "A couple of matches. Pika Campbell and another moke named Takvor Soralian, who goes by Taki." He swiveled his monitor so I could see the pictures from their booking. Both were hulking guys with angry faces.

"So that's him," I said. "What's his sheet look like?"

"He's only been in Honolulu for a couple of years. Before that he was in LA. And with an Armenian name like his, I thought he might have been into Armenian Power."

"Hold on. How'd you know his name was Armenian?"

Ray shrugged. "I grew up in Philly. Things there aren't as much of a melting pot as they are here. People have a certain kind of name, you know something about them. Where their family is from, what their religion is."

"Not from your name," I said. "Donne's not exactly Italian."

"Yeah, but Donatello is. My grandfather changed it to Donne so he could get a job back when companies didn't want to hire Italians."

"So you figured out Soralian was Armenian. What's this Armenian Power?"

"Been reading up on FBI stuff. It's a gang based in LA, into drugs, murder, fraud, gambling—you name it, they've got a tentacle in it. I got Francisco Salinas to check on him, and sure enough, he had some dealings with AP. A couple of arsons, a kidnapping. Not sure whether he's working for them here, though."

"Arson? I wonder if he was the one who set the fire in the warehouse." I dug out my cell phone and called Mike. "Can you run something for me?" I asked. I gave him Takvor Soralian's name and the information we had. "See if his name ever came up in an arson in LA, and if the same MO was used—the matchbook thing."

"Like I told you, it's a pretty common thing. But I'll give it a check. Love you—bye."

"Love you too." I turned back to Ray. "We have an address on Soralian?"

"Interesting," Ray said. "He's definitely bunking with Pika."

"Don't tell me. The Iolani Palace."

Ray nodded. "How come nobody caught this before?"

I shrugged. "They were only pulled in on minor beefs. Nothing ever went to trial." I sat back in my chair. "So we've still got zip."

"Well, maybe not," Ray said. "One more set of fingerprints found at Bernice's Fong matched a guy who was picked up two years ago for a DUI."

"Someone we know?"

"Andre Gardiner."

I whistled. "Now that's interesting. So Gardiner was with Pika and Taki."

Ray shook his head. "Can't say for sure. Gardiner could have been there a day before or a month before. We don't know what kind of housekeeper Bernice was."

"Still, worth paying Andy Gardiner a visit. We know where he works?"

"Gardiner Properties has an office downtown."

I called Gardiner's office and identified myself to the receptionist. "I'd like to stop over and speak to Mr. Gardiner. What would be a good time?"

She put me on hold, and when she came back she said, "I'm sorry, but Mr. Gardiner is booked up all day today and tomorrow. I can fit you in on Monday."

"Monday doesn't work for me," I said. "How's this. I'll show up at your office in about fifteen minutes and wait there until he has time to speak to me. I'll bring a couple of uniformed officers with me and we'll hang out in your reception area."

"Hold on."

The next voice on the phone was Andy Gardiner's. "Where the fuck do you get off threatening my secretary?"

"Not a threat, Mr. Gardiner. We need to speak with you and we're willing to work with your schedule."

"Twelve-thirty. I can give you ten minutes." Then he hung up.

"You have such a way with people," Ray said. "I always admire that about you."

"Admire this." I gave him the finger, and he laughed.

We spent the next couple of hours learning everything we could about Andre Gardiner. Like me, Terri and Harry, he had graduated from Punahou, though at sixty-eight he was thirty years older than we were. He had gone to Reed College in Oregon, a popular destination for Hawaiian students, and graduated with a degree in business. Then he had returned to Honolulu and joined his father's company.

He married and had a couple of kids. In 1992 he divorced his wife and moved to a condo in Kahala. His father died in 1995 and Gardiner took over the family business, and soon after that he'd been picked up driving his Jaguar convertible at nearly a hundred miles an hour down the H1 in the middle of the night.

I did a quick search and found that while Gardiner Properties still owned a substantial range of properties around the island, the company hadn't built anything new in fifteen years. A search of property sales showed that every year or so the company sold another shopping center or office park. If things went along as they were, Andre Gardiner would soon be scraping the bottom of the barrel his father had left him.

"So Gardiner could be in financial trouble in a few years," Ray said. "But how do we make that into a motive for murder?"

"Beats me. But something tells me we're on the right trail. And I like the fact that Gardiner had a DUI a couple of years ago."

"Why?"

"Because he may have to hire a limo when he wants to go out drinking."

Ray nodded. "Which puts him in contact with Royal Rides. You want to call that dispatcher again?"

I did a quick search through the files on my netbook and dug up the phone number for Royal Rides. The helpful guy I'd spoken with the other day had been replaced by a woman with a heavy Chinese accent. I identified myself once again and asked if she had any record of a client named Andre Gardiner.

"You have subpoena?" she asked, though she mangled the word. "No records without subpoena. Company porricy."

"I spoke to a guy the other day named Chris. Can I talk to him?"

"He my son. Stupid. Not here."

"When does he come on duty?"

"He no give you information without subpoena." She hung up.

"I'm looking forward to delivering a subpoena to her in person," I grumbled.

"Speaking of in-person, time to get over to Gardiner's office." Ray led the way to the garage, where it was his turn to drive.

The first thing we saw when we opened the door to the reception area of Gardiner Properties was a nearly life-sized oil painting of Emile, hawk-nosed and distinguished. There was something very French about him—like an older Louis Jourdan. I couldn't judge the likeness, but the figure in the painting looked stern, sharp and prosperous.

We identified ourselves to the receptionist, a very pretty young haole with dark brown hair in a girlish ponytail, and she carried on a hushed conversation with someone on the other end of the phone line as we sat down in comfortable leather armchairs.

A few minutes later, an older woman with her hair in a bouffant dyed a false shade of blonde came out to get us. "You handle this one," Ray said to me. "I'm good out here."

I was surprised but didn't show it. I followed the cloud of blonde hair down the hall to a large office with picture windows overlooking the Ko'olau mountains.

Andy Gardiner had none of his father's good looks or commanding personality. His face was rounder, his bulbous nose spidered with red. Like his father, there was something French about him, but it was more an air of dissoluteness, combined with a louche sort of Tahitian lassitude. He wore a dark suit that had hung limply on his pear-shaped body, with a wrinkled white shirt and a green tie the color of old dollar bills.

"Thanks for fitting me in, Mr. Gardiner," I said, as I sat down across from his broad, empty desk. "I just have a couple of questions for you."

"If you're nosing around Shep for his father's murder you're on the wrong trail," he said.

"Actually, I'm here on another matter. Do you know a woman named Bernice Fong?"

"Aunt Bernice? Of course. I've known her all my life. What about her?"

"I'm afraid she was murdered on Tuesday night."

"Murdered? Don't be ridiculous. She had to be nearly ninety years old. Probably just gave up the ghost."

"Not with a bullet hole in her forehead," I said.

Andy Gardiner paled. "Really?"

"Really. When was the last time you saw her?"

"I'd have to check my calendar. A few months ago."

I leaned back in my chair. "What kind of housekeeper was Mrs. Fong?" I asked.

Gardiner cocked his head and looked at me. "What the fuck does that have to do with her death?"

"We found your fingerprints at her house. Unless she hadn't dusted in a few months, that means you're lying."

"Like I said, I'll have to check my calendar." He reached into his desk drawer and pulled out a leather datebook.

He flipped it open. "Oh, of course. Aunt Bernice made some of her famous dumplings last week, and I went over to have some. She even gave me a package for my kids." He looked up at me. "You can check with them, if you want."

"When was that?"

"Last Sunday. The sixth."

"I noticed that you have a police record for DUI. You ever hire a limousine company called Royal Rides to drive you around?"

"You're an asshole, you know that, detective?" he asked. "You barge into my office and you challenge me about Aunt Bernice, then you bring up my arrest record. I have powerful friends in this town. You don't want to fuck with me."

"Friends like Shepard Fields? You and he go in together on killing his father?"

He stood up. "We're done here. Get out before I get the Chief of Police on the phone."

I stood up, too. He looked like he was about to blow a gasket. "Have a nice day," I said, and walked out of his office.

He was still yelling when I got back to the lobby, where Ray was leaning on the desk laughing with the beautiful receptionist. "You watch those pink mai-tais," he said to her as he stood up. "They can be killer for haoles like us."

"I can hold my liquor," she said. "You take care now."

We got into the elevator and Ray pulled his wedding ring out of his pocket and slipped it back on his finger. "What are you up to?" I asked.

"Brittany has only been in a limo once in her life," he said. "When she went out with the boss."

"Royal Rides?"

He put on a Valley Girl voice. "And the driver was such a sweetheart! He told us his name was Pika, which means rock. I felt his muscles and they were as hard as rocks!"

I laughed. "Excellent work, detective. So now we can put Gardiner together with Pika Campbell. Now all we have to do is find Campbell and his bromance buddy."

Greg Oshiro called again as we were driving back to headquarters. "Sorry I missed your call yesterday," I said. "Trying to juggle two cases at once."

"Bernice Fong?" he asked.

"Yeah. You know her?"

"I spoke to her Tuesday morning," he said. "She was frightened."

"We need to talk, brah. Where can we meet?"

"I'm just getting ready to go to lunch. I have to do an interview over at the Aloha Tower Marketplace afterwards. Want to meet at the Hi Town Café?"

"We can be there in about ten minutes."

After Diamond Head, the Aloha Tower is Honolulu's most recognized landmark, built in the 1920s to welcome cruise ship passengers. Now it's the control tower for the port, and also houses a cluster of shops. I parked in the garage and got to the café a few minutes before Greg, giving Ray and me the chance to order our paninis and sodas, then stake out a table outside.

Greg arrived just as we were settling down. He looked like he might be losing some weight—probably all that chasing around after his two little girls. Or maybe Anna was controlling his diet better than he ever did.

He went inside and ordered his own food. When he brought his tray out to us, I gave him a couple of minutes to eat before I asked, "So. You spoke to Bernice Fong yesterday?"

He nodded. "She called me at the paper Tuesday morning. Said that Alexander Fields had told her I was working on a book with him, and she wanted me to come out to her house and talk to her."

"She give you any reason?"

"Not at the time. But I figured she might be good for a human interest story so I drove over there. She was nervous about something, but she wouldn't say what at first."

He took another bite of his panini. When he finished chewing, he said, "She kept asking me if Fields had told me anything about the 1950s."

"What did you say?" Ray asked.

"I told her Fields had told me he had done some things in the past that he wanted to atone for, but that he'd never been specific. Which was the truth."

"How did you leave it with her?" I asked.

"She would never tell me exactly what she was worried about. I asked if I could interview her for the paper and she put me off. I was irritated about the waste of time but what could I do? She was ninety years old or something. Not like I could pressure her." He looked from me to Ray. "Her death is connected to Fields' murder, isn't it?"

I nodded. "We're just not sure how."

"By something that happened back in the fifties?"

"Off the record until we give you the go-ahead?" I asked.

"If it has to be."

"Go back through the archives and look for articles about the death of a Senator from the mainland named James LeJeune," I said. "He was killed in a brothel in Chinatown and I think Fields was involved somehow, along with Bernice Fong and her husband."

"You think that's the thing Fields wanted to atone for?"

"Makes sense, doesn't it?" Ray asked. "He never talked about it?"

Greg shook his head. "I'd have to go back through my notes, but I don't remember anything. And I think I'd recall the murder of a big-time politician."

Greg left a few minutes later for his interview, and Ray and I stayed on in the sun, sipping our lemonade. "Let's see if we can put a timeline together," I said. "Fields is writing his memoir, and he wants to come clean about Senator LeJeune's death. He tells Bernice Fong."

"Why?" Ray asked.

"Either she was involved, and he wants to warn her. Or the Judge was, and he wants to let her know before he goes public."

"I'll give you that," Ray said. "You think Fields told Gardiner, too?"

I opened the netbook and checked the dates. "Gardiner said he went to see Bernice Fong on Sunday the sixth. So even if Fields didn't tell him, Bernice must have." I started taking notes. "Pika and Taki picked him up the next day in the limo. Bernice Fong was with them. They went to the warehouse, where Fields was shot and the building was torched."

"Bernice Fong was worried," Ray continued. "She called Greg Oshiro to ask what he knew. You think she called Gardiner again?"

"Has to be. He must have decided she was a liability, and he sent Pika and Taki to kill her."

"Or went with them and killed her himself," Ray said. "Gardiner could have been at the warehouse, too."

"Dakota only saw the two bodybuilders and the old man and old woman," I said, typing away. "But that doesn't mean that Gardiner wasn't with them. Just that Dakota didn't see him."

"Motive, means and opportunity," Ray said. He held up his index finger. "What's Gardiner's motive? He didn't commit the murder. He was like, what, sixteen years old?"

"Protecting his father's name?" I asked.

"Really? Kill two elderly people you've known all your life, just to protect the reputation of your dead father?"

I shrugged. "I've heard of worse motives. And you saw that huge portrait of Emile Gardiner in the reception area. Andy Gardiner's a loser."

"Let's say you've got motive, though I'm not sure about it. How about means?"

"Taki and Pika," I said. "They're thugs with minor beefs. According to the receptionist, Gardiner knew Pika, because he was their driver when they went out."

Ray frowned. "I give you that he knew them. But it's a big jump from having a guy drive you around to bars to hiring him to kill for you."

"We don't know that he had Pika or Taki kill for him. He could have done the killing himself."

"Again, you're stretching credibility here. He's a seventy-year-old guy who has nothing more on his record than a DUI. Suddenly he's turned into a stone cold killer?"

"You're harshing my mellow," I said.

"Somebody's got to keep you on track. If I give you motive and means, we've still got opportunity."

"That's the easy one," I said. "Bernice made him some dumplings to get him over to her house. Then she told him that Fields was going to spill the beans."

"Speculation. We don't know that."

"Fine. You call the shots, then. What do we do next?"

"We find Pika Campbell and Takvor Soralian." Ray picked up his cell and asked me for the number for Royal Rides. I gave it to him, and he dialed. "Yo, how ya doin?" he said, in what sounded like almost a parody of a Philadelphia accent, though I had a feeling it was close to his native language. "I'm looking to hire a limo to take me around the island and my buddy told me youse guys are great."

He listened for a minute. "Yeah, my buddy told me to ask for a guy named Peeky?" More listening. "Yeah, tomorrow works. My hotel? The Moana Surfrider. You just have him ask for Vinnie. They know me there."

He ended the call. "Nine o'clock tomorrow morning."

"You do that well," I said.

"If my father heard me talking like that he'd knock me one. He worked hard to lose his accent and he wouldn't let any of us use bad grammar."

When we got back to headquarters Lieutenant Sampson motioned us to his office. "Sit," he said, and pointed at the chairs. I was tempted to put my paws up like Roby, but Ray caught my eye.

"You've been out exercising your usual tact and diplomacy, I understand."

Great. Andy Gardiner had made good on his threat to call the chief of police, and the shit had rolled downhill, first to Sampson, and now to us. I was about to argue when he shook his head and said, "She saw you pocket your wedding band, you know."

"Huh?" I said.

"Not you, Kanapaka'aka. Your partner. The one who's supposed to play by the rules and keep you in line."

"Harmless flirtation," Ray said. "And she told us what Gardiner wouldn't."

"And then she told the boss, who is encouraging her to file a sexual harassment complaint." He crossed his arms over his chest, encased in a light blue polo shirt without any adornment. "I'm assuming the information you got was necessary?"

"Dakota identified one of the guys who drove Alexander Fields to the warehouse where he was killed," I said. "A body-builder named Pika Campbell. Brittany confirmed to Ray that Pika had driven her and Andre Gardiner in his limousine in the past."

"Did Dakota ID Gardiner as well?"

I shook my head. "He only saw two bodybuilders, Alexander Fields, and an elderly woman we believe was Bernice Fong."

"So what kind of case are you trying to make?" Sampson asked.

Ray stepped in. It was his ass on the line, for a change. "We believe that Gardiner hired Pika Campbell and his friend Takvor Soralian to drive Fields and Mrs. Fong to the warehouse. We needed to make sure Gardiner had contact with the limo company and with Campbell as a driver. Because he knew both the victim and the man who drove the victim to his death, we have reason to suspect that Gardiner is connected to the case."

Sampson nodded. "Andre Gardiner has powerful friends, as I'm sure he told you when you visited him. You'd better know what you're doing if you're going to accuse him of anything."

He nodded toward the door. "Go."

We went. "That was a refreshing change," I said, when we were back at our desks. "For once I'm not the one in trouble. Maybe I'm maturing after all."

"Doubtful," Ray said. "Gardiner's smart. He knew that if he complained about the way you treated him he'd be putting himself on the line. So he shifted the complaint to Brittany."

"Sampson's right, though. If we're going after Gardiner we'd better have a fourteen-carat case."

We went back to Andre Gardiner's file. Without a subpoena we couldn't access his bank or phone records, and we didn't have enough evidence to convince a judge to grant one. "Look at this," I said. "Gardiner has a concealed weapons permit for a nine-millimeter handgun. That matches the kind of gun used to kill both Fields and Bernice Fong."

"He's too smart to use his own gun," Ray said.

"Could have been unplanned," I said. "Maybe he was just taking Fields to the warehouse, and then Fields started arguing and Gardiner shot him."

"This trip to the warehouse," Ray said. "What do you think Fields had there?"

"Something that tied Gardiner's father to the murder?" I asked.

"But what?"

"I have no idea." I looked at the clock. "We've put enough overtime into this case. I'm going to cut out early and stop by Punahou. I want to talk to someone about Dakota."

"All right. I'll hang here with my thinking cap on."

As I drove up to Punahou, I tried to shift my thoughts away from murder and on to Dakota. The school was founded in 1841 to educate the children of Congregational missionaries, and had been teaching the movers and shakers of Honolulu—as well as members of the hoi polloi like me—ever since. It was one of the oldest and largest private schools in the country, with an endowment that matched many colleges, and a board of trustees that included alumni and community leaders, including my good friend Terri Clark Gonsalves.

I couldn't shift my thoughts away from Andy Gardiner, though. When I got to Punahou I identified myself to the security guard and found my way to the library, where I pulled down the yearbooks for the years Gardiner had been there. He had been a popular, academically gifted kid and played multiple sports. He was the president of his junior class. But by the end of his senior year, he had dropped most of his activities, and he no longer made the Dean's List.

That was curious, I thought. Senator LeJeune had been killed in January of 1959, just as Andy Gardiner had been in the middle of his senior year. Had something his father did knocked him off the tracks? Suppose he had found out about his father's role in the Senator's death, and that caused him to rebel?

When I finished with the yearbooks, I went down to the guidance counselor's office. She was a haole woman in her late fifties, with frizzy black hair and red-rimmed glasses.

"Mrs. Matluck?" I asked, through the open doorway of her office.

"It's Ms. Matluck, but you can call me Eileen. You are?"

"Kimo Kanapa'aka. I'm hoping to become Dakota Gianelli's foster father."

"Oh, Dakota. Yes, I met him yesterday. Come in and sit down." She spoke with the flat accent of the midwest. "I understand right now he's living with Mrs. Gonsalves?"

I nodded. "Just until my partner and I get the paperwork complete to be foster parents."

"How can I help you?"

"I wanted to talk to you about Dakota. He's a good kid but he's been through a lot lately." I sketched out his background to her, and she made a few notes.

"Punahou will be a good environment for him," she said, when I was finished. "I hope he'll thrive here."

"So do I. I graduated from here, as did my brothers, so we have a strong connection to Punahou. Terri Gonsalves is one of my best friends, and has been since we were at school here."

"I'll keep an eye on Dakota for a while, just to make sure he's settling in well. If I have questions who should I call?"

I gave her my card, and thanked her for her time, then walked back outside. Classes had just let out and there were swarms of kids everywhere. Most of them were wearing green, and it took me a minute to remember it was St. Patrick's Day.

I didn't even notice Dakota until he was right next to me. "Are you here to pick me up? Can I come back to you and Mike yet?"

"Dakota, it's only been a day," I said. "You know what Mrs. Chow said. It could take a couple of months."

"As long as you're here, can I come to your house for dinner? I want to see Roby."

"Let me call Terri."

Terri had some work she wanted to finish, so she was glad I could pick up Dakota. "I'll bring him back to your house after dinner," I said.

That brought up the question of what we were all going to eat. There wasn't much food in the house, so I called Mike and he agreed to pick up a bucket of fried chicken on his way home.

"Terri says you and Mike are going to have a baby," Dakota said as I drove through the downtown streets toward the highway.

"Not exactly," I said, looking at him out of the corner of my eye. He was facing away from me, out the window. "Our friends Sandra and Cathy want to have a baby, and we're donating sperm."

He turned toward me. "So the baby won't live with you?"

"God, no," I said. "Oops, I shouldn't have been so eager about that."

Dakota laughed.

"I'm hoping that the baby will live with them, and come over to us for a visit now and then. At least until he or she gets out of diapers."

"Babies are a pain," Dakota said. "My cousin back home had a baby. He cried all the time, and it drove her crazy."

"Babies can do that."

"No, I mean, really crazy. She drowned him in the bathtub."

"Jeez, Dakota. That's terrible. What happened to her?"

"She went to jail. Everybody in the town where we lived knew about it and my mom got mad at some lady at a bar when she was talking trash, and punched her. My uncle paid off the lady and said my mom should take me and get out of town for a while.

That's why we came to Hawai'i."

No wonder Dakota was screwed up, coming from the family he did. I hoped that being around Terri and Levi, and me and Mike, would help him see that there could be better things in his future.

We got home and let Roby out for a quick pee in the yard. He was so excited to see Dakota that he had a hard time concentrating on his business. I had to send Dakota inside to clean up before dinner in order to get Roby to pee.

We ate around the kitchen table, Roby sprawled on the floor next to Dakota, hoping for cleanup patrol. I had a vision of the next couple of years—me, Mike, Roby and Dakota together. Expanding our table to add Sandra and Cathy and a baby. It was going to be like our family events when I was growing up, adults and kids and dogs, everybody laughing and talking story, even a tipsy aunt or uncle doing the hula.

"Can I take Roby for his walk?" Dakota asked when we were finished eating. "Please?"

"Don't go too far from the house," I said. "And be sure to pick up his poop. I don't want any neighbors yelling."

He grabbed Roby's leash from the counter, and the dog went through his usual jumping and twirling as Dakota tried to hook him up. I cleared the table as Mike began washing the dishes. I brushed past him on my way to the refrigerator, bumping my butt against his, and he turned around and smiled.

I leaned up and kissed his cheek, grizzled with five o'clock shadow. "How long do you think he'll be?" Mike asked.

"Not long enough for what I want to do to you." I wrapped my arms around him and nuzzled his neck, our bodies pressed against each other.

Then I heard the gunshot.

Immediately we disengaged and I ran for the front door. I hadn't taken my gun out of my hip holster when we came in, so it was right there when I needed it. I burst through the front door as another shot rang out in the still evening, followed by Roby's frantic barking.

A dark car accelerated and sped off down the street, too fast for me to get a glimpse of the license plate, or even to tell a make. Dakota was lying on the side of the road half a block from our house, holding his thigh and crying. Blood pooled around his leg. He'd let go of Roby's leash and the dog was chasing the car down the street.

"Roby! Get back here!" I called as I ran toward Dakota.

In the background I heard Mike banging something. Where was he when I needed him? Did I run after Roby or stop to check Dakota?

Fortunately the dog turned back toward us when I called him. I leaned down next to Dakota. "What happened?"

"We were just walking and somebody from that car shot at me," he said, between gulps.

"What do we have here?"

I looked up to see Dominic Riccardi. He was a doctor at the VA hospital, where his Korean-born wife, Soon-O, was a nurse. He got down to the ground and looked at Dakota's leg. I realized Mike must have been banging on his father's door.

A moment later Soon-O appeared with Dominic's medical bag. "Not too bad," Dominic said, speaking in a reassuring voice. "I'll stop the bleeding and get you bandaged and then we'll head over to the emergency room for a proper cleanup."

Mike and I stepped back and let Dominic and Soon-O take over. They worked so smoothly together, and I envied them that. Mike and I alternated between love and anger so often I couldn't imagine us ever working together.

Looking at him, I saw his mouth was set in a grim line. I was sure he was going to blame me for what had happened to Dakota.

Maybe I'd hit a nerve with Andy Gardiner, and he had sent Pika and Taki—or come himself—to take me out. Dakota was almost as tall as I was, with the same dark hair, though his was longer, and I could imagine someone might have mistaken him for me.

But it was also possible that Dakota had been the target. Perhaps Pika and Taki knew that Dakota had seen them outside the warehouse, and they were trying to wipe out a witness. Or one of Angelina's drug-dealing associates was trying to kill him because of something we knew nothing about.

There were an awful lot of possibilities why someone would want to kill a fourteen-year-old boy. Too many.

Dominic stood up. "I'll drive," he said. "Soon-O will sit in the back seat with Dakota. You boys can follow us."

He helped Dakota stand up and put his arm around the boy as they hobbled across the yard to the driveway on the Riccardis' side of the house. Mike grabbed Roby's leash, and took him to the house while I started my Jeep.

Dominic and Soon-O were already gone by the time Mike jumped in. "What hospital?" I asked him.

"Tripler, of course."

Tripler was the Army Medical Center where Dominic and Soon-O worked. Though Dakota didn't have any armed forces connection, so technically wasn't eligible for care there, I knew that wouldn't stop Dominic.

I backed down the driveway. "Who was it?" Mike asked.

"I don't know. I just saw a dark car speeding away."

"But it had to be someone from one of your cases." He turned to face me. "This is what it's going to be like if we have kids, isn't it? We'll always be afraid that someone will come after us, or our kid?"

I tried not to respond to the anger in his voice. That would escalate the problem and we'd be at each other's throats before we got to the hospital. "Dakota witnessed a man being led to his murder," I said carefully. "And his mother's in prison, and we don't know what he's been doing between the time she went away and the time we took him in. So there are way too many variables right now to make any conclusions."

He didn't answer, just turned forward. I parked in a visitor's spot a few hundred feet from the emergency room entrance. "I understand what you meant now," Mike said as we jumped out of the Jeep. "About the danger from both our jobs. I thought you just meant you and me. But now I see you meant a kid, too."

"We can't let fear run our lives," I said.

We caught up to Dominic, Soon-O and Dakota at the check-in desk. The triage nurse knew Soon-O and found Dakota a treatment room. "You boys wait out here," Dominic said as he and Soon-O led Dakota through a pair of swinging doors.

Mike and I sat down across from each other on hard plastic chairs and I dialed Terri's number.

"We're on our way," she said, as soon as I explained where we were.

I ended the call and looked at Mike. "I need to call Ray and let him know what happened."

"You can go outside," he said. "I'll wait here."

I recognized the tone of his voice and wanted to rise to it, but instead I took a deep breath and walked back out to the parking lot.

"You and Julie and Vinnie all right?" I asked Ray, as soon as he answered his cell.

"Yeah. What's wrong?"

I told him about the shooting.

"Jesus! How is he?"

"I think he's okay. Dominic took care of him right away. We're at the ER at Tripler now."

"What can I do to help?"

"Just be careful," I said. "We don't know who shot at Dakota or why. If they were after me, they could come for you next."

Ray and Julie had been saving for a house, but for now they were still in an apartment in a Waikiki high-rise, with a doorman and a key-coded elevator. "Don't go out tonight," I said. "I'll let you know if anything else happens."

"How's Mike taking this?"

"He's freaked. I am, too, but I'm trying to hold it together."

"Call if you need anything."

I started walking around the parking lot. I wanted to get in the Jeep and drive over to Andy Gardiner's house and confront him—but that was a bad idea. Instead I called Harry Ho. I hadn't been able to dig up any dirt on Gardiner legitimately, but Harry had excellent hacking skills, which he loved to practice in legitimate ways whenever he could.

"Hey, brah, I've got a job for you," I said, when he answered. "I need anything you can find on a guy named Andre Gardiner."

"Hold on, let me get a pen. You sound really pissed off. What did this guy do to you?"

"Did Terri tell you Mike and I are taking in a foster kid?" I asked.

"Yeah, we talked yesterday. He's staying with her now, right?"

"Uh-huh. Except he was over our house tonight walking Roby, and somebody took a couple of shots at them."

"Are they okay?"

"Yeah. Dakota took a bullet in the leg, but we're here at Tripler so Dominic can make sure he gets taken care of."

"And you think this guy was responsible? Why?"

"It's just a gut feeling now." I explained quickly about the death of Senator LeJeune, and the involvement of Gardiner's father.

"Spell the names."

I did.

"I'll get right on it. I'll call you when I have something."

"Thanks, brah. You're the best." I hesitated for a minute, before hanging up. "You and Brandon," I said. "I mean, I know you care about him. How did you know? I mean, did you just wake up one day and…"

"I thought he was a cute kid when I met him," Harry said. "And then Arleen and I started dating, and she made sure that I spent time with him so I would know for sure that they were a package deal."

I stepped onto the curb to let a speeding SUV barrel past me, toward the ER door.

"I pretty much knew as soon as I met Arleen that she was the one. I had already bought her the ring, and I was getting ready to propose, and suddenly I realized that I wasn't just marrying her, but that I was taking Brandon on, too."

The doors to the SUV opened and a man and woman spilled out, the woman carrying a baby in her arms.

"And I was so happy about that," Harry said. "I realized that I loved Brandon just as much as I did Arleen, and I wanted both of them in my life. For their own selves, not just because he came with her. He's a great little guy, you know. Sometimes he's a brat and sometimes he's just annoying, but he's mine now."

The woman carrying the baby rushed into the ER as the man stood there watching, then got back into the car and pulled slowly forward toward the parking lot.

"Thanks, brah," I said. Then I went back into the ER myself to see what I could do.

Terri, Levi and Danny arrived as Dakota was being discharged. He'd left his backpack in the Jeep when we got home for dinner, so I handed it over to Terri. The air had cooled down, and the skies were so clear I could see constellations I'd learned about when I was Dakota's age.

"Can I still go to school tomorrow?" he asked Dominic as we all stood together in the parking lot.

"I never want to keep a smart young man like you out of school," Dominic said. "As long as you take it easy you should be fine."

We stood there awkwardly for a moment. Then I walked over to Dakota and hugged him. "I'm sorry this happened to you."

He hugged me back. "It's okay. I have something cool to talk about in school tomorrow."

Mike hugged him, too, and then Dominic and Soon-O had to get in on the action. It was a few minutes later before Mike and I were in the Jeep heading navigating the curving exit from the Tripler complex.

"I've changed my mind," Mike said. "About having a kid with Sandra and Cathy."

"Let me ask you something," I said, as I stopped at the traffic light. "Your father was a soldier in Korea, and he got shot, right?"

"So? He was an adult. He made his own decision about enlisting."

"I understand that. And your mom was his nurse, so she saw a lot of people get hurt. Young kids, even."

"What's your point?"

I looked over at him. "My point is that they still went ahead and had you. Even after everything they'd seen. You think they didn't know the risks they were taking?"

"Nobody shot at either of them once they were out of Korea."

"What if I take the job with the FBI?" I asked. "You know how those Feds are. They never get their hands dirty. I'd be safe, and nobody would come after you or Dakota or the baby."

"I don't want you to change your whole life for me," he said. "I love you and I want you to be happy. I'll be just fine if all we ever do is be good dads to Dakota."

"I'm tired of getting shot at," I said. "I never thought I'd say that, but maybe it means I'm growing up after all. I think it'll be fine over at the Bureau, as long as I'm still working with Ray. Like Sampson says, it'll be good for me."

Mike reached toward me, and I grasped his left hand with my right. I squeezed, and he squeezed back. Then my stomach grumbled.

We both laughed. "I hope you put that fried chicken somewhere Roby couldn't get it," I said.

"I don't remember. I might have left it on the counter."

"Oh, shit." I pulled up in the driveway and we jumped out. "If he's already gotten at the chicken running isn't going to help," I said, even though we both kept on running up to the front door.

Roby met us at the door, yelping and jumping around. We pushed past him toward the kitchen.

The bucket of fried chicken was still on the counter, but lying on its side, a couple of biscuits spilling out the front. The kitchen floor was littered with chicken bones and crumbs of fried skin. "Roby!" I said. "Bad dog!"

He lowered his head and slunk away to the living room.

"There's still a couple of pieces left in the bucket," Mike said as he righted it. "I'll warm it up in the microwave while you clean up the debris."

We sat down to eat a few minutes later. Roby came back in and plopped on the floor by our feet. "If you think you're getting any more of this, you're sadly mistaken," I said to him.

"He's a good boy," Mike said, reaching down to ruffle the dog behind his ears. "You saw the way he went after that car."

"Fat lot of good it did," I grumbled. It was almost eleven by the time we finished eating, so we took Roby out together for a quick pee. We were about a block away when something flew out of the darkness right at us.

My adrenaline flared and I turned toward the motion. But it was only a bat, out in search of some tasty moths for dinner. A predator, but not one that could prey on me or the people I cared about.

Mike went into the bedroom while I closed up the house, and when I got there he was lying naked on the bed, his hands behind his head, and his stiff dick looking very happy to see me. I stripped down in record time and joined him in bed.

After we had given each other as much pleasure as we could, we spooned together, Mike's arm around my shoulder, and drifted off to sleep.

The next morning I left Mike to walk Roby and scrambled out of the house fast, grabbing the paper on my way to the Jeep. I had to meet Ray at seven to arrange our rendezvous with Pika and his limo at the Moana Surfrider and I didn't want to be late.

We stationed a patrol car near the far end of the drive, which curved beneath a three-story columned portico. Two of the other plain clothes detectives on our shift covered the entrance to the driveway, while another two were stationed under a couple of palm trees on the other side of Kalakaua.

At nine, Ray stood at the hotel entrance, wearing his loudest Hawaiian shirt—which was saying something—one with a garish print of hula dancers and surfboards. He had aviator-style sunglasses and a dollop of white zinc oxide on his nose. All he was missing was the word "tourist" tattooed on his forehead.

I sat on a rocking chair on the colonnaded porch with a radio transmitter in my ear, scanning the steady flow of oncoming traffic, as cabs and limos and airport vans disgorged and accepted passengers. The bellhops kept busy moving luggage in and out of the hotel.

"You're not waiting here for us, are you, detective?"

I looked up to see Stephanie Cornell, wearing a sundress splattered with abstract flowers in bright green, yellow and orange. Her green sandals and matching purse coordinated the outfit, and she wore big designer sunglasses that reminded me of Jacqueline Onassis.

Lee Poe was right behind her, sporting a vintage Reyn Spooner aloha shirt and khaki shorts, with a puka shell necklace of the kind I used to wear when I was a teenager. It was incongruous on a fifty-something man.

"No, something different," I said, turning my gaze back to Ray and the driveway.

"Have you made any progress at all on finding out who killed Stephanie's father?" Lee demanded.

"It's an open investigation." Out of the corner of my eye I saw a black limo rolling up the driveway. I stood up. "Excuse me, I have to go."

"You can't just walk away from us," Lee said.

The limo pulled to a stop and a man I recognized from his mug shot as Pika Campbell jumped out. Ray walked over to him. I tried to follow, but Lee blocked me.

"You're getting in the way of a police action," I said to him. "Move away now."

I tried to sidestep him but he wouldn't give up, and he raised his voice. "I want to know what you're doing, detective."

Pika looked up. I don't know if he overheard Lee, or his instincts warned him of a trap, but he jumped back into the limo and tried to get away. I pushed around Lee and dashed down the steps. "Attention all units. Stop the limo."

The patrol car backed up and blocked the driveway exit, and the shuttle van in front of Pika blew his horn. Pika was blocked in front and back, and he jumped out of the limo and took off on foot. He saw the uniforms ahead of him and turned left, then must have realized that the two men coming at him were cops, too.

I caught up with Ray at the curb as Pika darted into traffic on Kalakaua, to the accompaniment of horns and screeching brakes. He pivoted off the hood of a cab and swung sideways. Right into the path of an oncoming bus full of Japanese tourists.

The driver hit his brakes, but not fast enough, and Pika Campbell smashed full-face into the front of the bus, his hands splayed out to try and block the oncoming tons of metal. As we, the driver, and the busful of tourists watched in horror, he slid backwards down the front of the bus's big glass window, to the street. His head hit the pavement with the sound of a melon smashing, and within seconds there was a growing pool of blood around his head.

Ray and I stood there, neither of us saying anything.

One of the officers from the patrol car called traffic homicide, and the other began directing traffic around the accident.

Lee Poe came up to me looking shame-faced. "I'm sorry I got in your way."

I shrugged. "Things happen. We make decisions all day long. Sometimes they're the right ones." I looked over at Campbell's body. "Sometimes the wrong ones."

Stephanie came up to join us. "I recognize that name—Royal Rides," she said, pointing to the license plate frame on the limo. "My father used to use them."

"We think the driver over there was the one who took your father to the warehouse where he was killed. We were planning to interrogate him."

"Did he kill my father?"

"We have a witness who saw Mr. Campbell lead your father into the warehouse. We still don't know what went on inside."

Stephanie and Lee were on their way to Fields' house, where she and her brother were going to divide up Alexander Fields' physical assets. "Don't worry, we won't need the police,"

Stephanie said. "Shepard and I had a long talk yesterday. Neither of us have kids, and with both of our parents gone all we have is each other."

"Not quite all," Lee said. "There's me, and there's Tim."

Stephanie squeezed his hand. "I know. But we're the last of our blood, and we decided we need to get along. Neither of us is particularly attached to stuff so we should be able to get this done quickly, and get the house on the market."

Pika had left the keys to the limo in the ignition, and one of the plainclothes guys drove it to the impound yard, where we would have the evidence techs go over it for anything that might connect the limousine and Pika to the murders of Fields and Mrs. Fong.

Stephanie and Lee hailed one of the cabs that had been backed up, waiting to discharge passengers, and Ray and I went back to headquarters. Our best lead had just become road pizza, and we didn't know where to go next.

"What are we missing?" I asked, as we sat in Waikiki traffic on our way downtown. "There must be some loose thread we can pull that will unravel this case."

"Let's start back in the fifties," Ray said. "Your father said there were five members of this Cabal, right?"

"Eventually four, after Matthew Clark backed out. Judge Fong, Emile Gardiner, Alexander Fields, and Bennie Gomez."

Something was percolating in the back of my brain and it took me a minute. "Gomez. Was he Eliseo Gomez's father? The guy we met at Fields' funeral?"

"Let's check." Ray used his cell phone to pull up the newspaper obituary on Bennie Gomez, and sure enough, he was survived by his son Eliseo.

"You think he might know something about what his father was up to?" I asked.

"Only one way to find out."

I called Gomez's office. I figured I'd get another runaround, but instead he came on the line himself. "I'm glad you called, Detective. I was going to call you. Can you come over to my office?"

"I'm on the road right now. How does that work for you?"

"I'll see you when you get here."

Gomez's office was in a single-story stucco building a few blocks from Honolulu Hale, our city hall. A large billboard rested on the roof, with Gomez's face and an ad for his personal injury practice.

The receptionist led us into his office. "Do you know what a tontine is?" Gomez asked, as we sat down.

"Some kind of investment scheme, isn't it?" I said.

"In general, yes. A group of investors get together, and when the last one dies, the investments are liquidated."

"This have anything to do with your father, Alexander Fields, Emile Gardiner, Harold Fong, and Matthew Clark?"

He nodded. "All except Clark, though." He opened his desk drawer and pulled out a sealed envelope. "My father left this in his safe. I found it when he passed away, but I've been obeying the instructions not to open it until now."

Ray and I leaned forward. "Not to be opened until after the death of Alexander Fields, Bennie Gomez, and Emile and Andre Gardiner."

"You have any idea what's inside?" I asked.

He shook his head. "My father was a good man. His grandfather was brought here from the Azores to work in the fields, and his father became a subsistence fisherman. My dad worked his way up from a single fishing boat to owning a marina. He sweated so I would be able to go to college and law school."

"Any idea why Andy Gardiner's name would be on this envelope, too?"

Gomez looked at it. "You know, I never noticed that. I just assumed they were all men of that generation." He went to pull the letter back. "I guess we'll have to wait a few more years, then."

I leaned forward. "Mr. Gomez, we have reason to believe that Andre Gardiner is behind the murders of Alexander Fields and Bernice Fong. If that letter might give us clarification, we need to look at it."

"My father must have had a reason to keep it secret."

I nodded. "And if Andy Gardiner discovers you have it, you could be as much at risk as Mr. Fields and Mrs. Fong."

"I won't tell him, then."

"Ah, but now that we know the letter exists…"

Ray said, "Kimo."

"You wouldn't tell him. That would be against…" I could tell Gomez was racking his brain for some argument.

"It might be against a personal moral code," I said. "Putting an innocent citizen at risk of being killed. Of course we'd do our best to protect you, but…"

"You're a bastard, detective."

I shook my head. "Nope. Just trying to do my job and find out who killed two people." Out of the corner of my eye I saw Ray shaking his head.

Gomez pushed the letter across the table. "Here."

The envelope was sealed, so I reached for a glass-topped letter opener on Gomez's desk, and slit it open. Inside was a single piece of white lined paper, hand-written. "God forgive my soul," it began. "I have helped to conceal a murder."

The letter outlined how Senator LeJeune had been visiting Emile Gardiner at his home, and the two of them had argued. The Senator had been shot in the middle of his forehead, and Gardiner had called Gomez, Fields and Fong there to figure out how to dispose of the body. Bernice Fong had a distant cousin who was the madam of a brothel in Chinatown, so they decided to take the Senator there. They figured they could discredit him at the same time as they got rid of him.

We continued to read. Gomez, Fong and Fields had helped Emile Gardiner transport the Senator's body to the brothel in Chinatown. "Emile insisted that a prostitute had to die too, to make the story more believable," Gomez wrote. "I argued with him, but the others supported him. I left after we carried the Senator's body into the room. But the next day when I read the paper I saw that a girl had been killed as well. I know I should have spoken up but I was too afraid of losing everything I had. I would have gone to jail, and my son would not have been able to go to college. But this has been heavy on my heart for many years. I confessed my sin to my priest, and he assigned me many devotions, and instructed me to provide this confession as well."

"Can you testify that this is your father's handwriting?" I asked Gomez.

He nodded. "But you won't be able to use it in court because the opposing counsel won't have the opportunity to cross-examine."

"The letter doesn't mention Andre Gardiner," Ray said. "Why was his name on the envelope?"

"Because it concerned his father?" Gomez suggested.

Ray leaned forward. "But Shepard and Stephanie Fields aren't mentioned. And why did your father leave the letter for you, and not to be opened after you were dead, too?"

"I don't know," Gomez said.

I looked at the letter again, reading carefully. "How good was your father's grammar?" I asked Gomez, after I'd finished.

"He was a stickler for proper speech," Gomez said. "Used to yell at me if I spoke pidgin."

"So he understood the difference between the active voice and the passive voice in writing?" I asked.

"He's been dead for a dozen years, detective. I can't testify as to his command of English grammar."

"Look here." I pointed at the letter. "He says 'the Senator had been shot in the middle of his forehead.' If I'm remembering my Punahou education, that's the passive voice. The active voice would be something like 'Gardiner had shot the Senator in the middle of his forehead.'"

"I still don't understand what you're getting at," Gomez said.

Ray stepped in to interpret. "Your father is being careful not to say who shot Senator LeJeune."

"Look at the letter," I said. "Gardiner called your father, Judge Fong, and Mr. Fields to the house after LeJeune was dead. So none of them were the killer. They're just accessories after the fact."

"But what if Andre Gardiner was at the house with his father," Ray said, and I nodded. "Suppose he was involved in the murder somehow. That would explain why his name is on the envelope, but the rest of your names aren't."

"And that would give him a motive to kill Fields and Mrs. Fong—if they could place him at the scene of the Senator's murder." I folded the letter up and slipped it back into the envelope. "I'm going to use this to convince a judge to issue a subpoena for Andre Gardiner's personal records. We may never be able to find anything to convict him of murdering Senator LeJeune, but I believe we can lock him up for Fields and Mrs. Fong."

As Ray and I were driving back to headquarters, Harry called my cell phone. "I couldn't find much on Gardiner," he said. "Mostly medical stuff. He had a nervous breakdown during his first year at Reed College and had to be hospitalized. He's been in and out of Alcoholics Anonymous for years. Does any of that help you?"

"It's good, Harry," I said. "Proves that he's damaged, and with what we've just learned it only makes our case stronger. Thanks, brah."

It was already after noon by then, so we picked up take-out burgers and ate at our desks. When we finished, we sat down with Lieutenant Sampson. "Do you have enough to pull Gardiner in for questioning?" he asked.

"I think so," I said. "But I'm afraid to tip our hand too quickly. I'd rather collect all the evidence and make a clear connection between him and murders."

We went back to our desks. There was an email from Wilma Chow, with a link to the parenting classes Mike and I had to take to qualify as foster parents for Dakota. I clicked through and signed us both up—every Saturday for a month. There went my surfing time. But I hoped that whatever we learned there would come in handy once Sandra had the baby and we had to help out.

We spent the afternoon preparing our subpoena. We wanted phone records for Gardiner's home and business as well as anything connecting him to Royal Rides, Pika Campbell, and Takvor Soralian. We were looking for a nine-millimeter handgun as well.

We tried to cast our net wide enough to encompass things we didn't know we needed, but we were constrained by the rules of evidence. Finally we had the paperwork together and took it to Judge Yamanaka's office for a signature.

While we waited in the judge's outer office, I finally had a chance to pick up the morning paper. I skimmed through the national and international news and then handed that section to Ray as I moved on to the local section.

"Holy shit!" I said. The judge's secretary looked up at me and frowned.

"What?" Ray asked.

Greg Oshiro had written a follow-up story to the murder of Alexander Fields. It was mostly a long retrospective of his career, but buried in the middle of the article Greg mentioned that he had been working with Fields on his autobiography, and that Fields had passed on copies of many documents to him relating to the push for statehood, and that Greg would be reviewing them and publishing the results.

"Stupid, stupid, stupid," I said, shaking my head as I handed the section to Ray. "What if Gardiner reads this and thinks Greg has the same kind of letter that Bennie Gomez left?"

"Gardiner doesn't know about Gomez's letter," Ray said. "But you're right, he could think all kinds of things. You'd better call Greg and warn him."

I called the *Star-Advertiser's* office and asked to be put through to Greg. The man who answered the phone at the city desk said Greg was out on assignment but he could put me through to voice mail. I declined and called Greg's cell.

"Where are you?" I asked. "We need to talk."

"Home. Anna had some minor surgery yesterday, and she's still in the hospital recovering. I'm playing stay-at-home dad and watching the girls." He turned away from the phone. "Sarah! Get down from there!"

He came back to me. "I had an interview scheduled for today and luckily the guy was willing to come over to the house. You don't get many sources so cooperative."

"Source?" I asked. "Who?"

"Guy named Andre Gardiner. Old friend of Alexander Fields. He's going to fill me in on some background."

"Jesus, Greg. He's our suspect in Fields' murder. You've got to get out of the house. Fast. Take the girls and go. Ray and I are on our way."

In the background I heard the sound of a doorbell. "Too late," Greg said. "Sounds like he's here."

Ray and I jumped up. He told the judge's secretary we'd be back for the subpoena, and we took off at a run. "Can you get out the back door?" I asked Greg as we went.

"The back yard is fenced and the only way out leads past the front door."

I thought fast. I didn't think Gardiner would go into Greg's house with a gun in hand; he'd sound Greg out first, try to discover what Greg had. "You have a neighbor you can call to come take the girls?" I said. "At least get them out of there."

The bell rang again in the background, as Ray and I left the court building and ran toward the Jeep. "Yeah, there's a stay-at-home mom next door. I'll try and leave Gardiner here and take the girls over to her house."

"Smart thinking. Ray and I will be there as soon as we can."

Ray was already on his phone calling dispatch to request a SWAT team. "What's his address?" he asked me as we got to the Jeep.

"Call me back if you can and leave your phone on," I said to Greg. I hung up and handed the cell to Ray so he could read the contact information, and I gunned the Jeep out of the parking lot and onto the street. I made it to the Likelike Highway pretty easily, and Ray put the flashing light up on the roof. I began darting and weaving around slower traffic on the broad, four-lane divided highway, blowing my horn at clueless tourists and making tight swings of the steering wheel to get around them.

The mountains rose up to our left, and the land dropped off steeply to the right. It was a dangerous place to have an accident, but fortunately the traffic was light enough so that we made good progress. We passed a broken-down station wagon on the right shoulder, boxes, garbage bags and suitcases lined up behind it as a young woman in a high-waisted baby doll dress and rubber slippers stood beside two chickens, all of them watching a man work on the engine.

We curved into the entrance of the Wilson Tunnel and the darkness closed around us. Ray grabbed the door handle as I swerved yet again with too little maneuvering room. "Why hasn't Greg called me back?" I asked. "I want to know what's going on up there."

"Focus on getting us there in one piece," Ray said, as light blossomed ahead of us and we came to the tunnel exit. A broad vista of the Windward Shore opened up to our right, and Ray's cell rang.

"SWAT's on their way," he told me after he finished the call.

It was a gorgeous, picture-postcard kind of day. The sky was clear and light blue, and the mountains to our left were verdant green, with bits of gray rock showing the island's spine. The land leveled out around us, and we passed Kaneohe District Park and a line of cars waiting to turn in at Windward Community College.

I slowed as we approached Haiku Road, and Ray took down the flashing light. The SWAT team wasn't there yet, but as we cruised past Greg's house I saw a black Mercedes sedan parked in front. I drove to the end of the street, turned around, and parked. "What do you think?" I asked. "We call Greg? Or we do some recon?"

"Recon," Ray said. "Let's wait to make the call until we know what's going on."

Both Ray and I kept a pair of bullet-proof vests in our vehicles: one HPD issued, one we'd each bought just to be safe. We strapped ourselves in and began walking toward the house. Adrenaline was rushing through my veins as I worried about Greg and the two little girls. I didn't want to add them to the statistics for this case.

The houses were close together and there wasn't enough room to get around the side of the house without someone noticing. The house to the right had a lot of kiddie debris in the front yard—a Big Wheels, plastic bucket and shovel, and a couple of headless Barbie dolls. "That must be the stay-at-home mom," I said. "I'll go in there and look through her windows."

"I'll go around the other way." Ray held out his hand in a shaka to me. "Be safe."

I returned the gesture. "You too."

I walked up to the front door and knocked. A harried-looking young woman with lank blonde hair answered, holding a drooling girl on her hip. "Yes?"

I showed her my ID. "I'm worried about something going on next door," I said. "May I come inside and take a look through your windows?"

"Going on?" she said. "What?"

"I don't want to worry you," I said. "Could be nothing at all. May I?"

She stepped aside. A slightly older boy sat on the carpet in the middle of the living room, taking apart a plastic dump truck. "Who are you?" he asked me.

"Just a friend of your next-door neighbor." I walked through the living room to the kitchen, which looked out toward Greg's house.

The homes were mirror images of each other, so I found myself looking through the window at Greg's kitchen. By leaning forward I could see through the kitchen to part of Greg's living room. I couldn't see him or Andre Gardiner, because a big body-builder with his back to me blocked the view. That had to be Takvor Soralian.

My phone buzzed with an incoming text. *GO in chair, AG stand,* Ray wrote.

I texted back, *Taki back 2 me. U C a gun?*

*No bt sure there is 1.*

I turned to the mother. "Take your kids and go into a back bedroom. Stay there until I tell you it's all right to come out."

"What's going on?"

"Just do it, please."

I went out the front door. The SWAT van pulled up at the end of the street and I ran down to talk to the commander, a gruff Nisei named Yamashita. I briefed him on the situation as Ray came up behind us. "The big Japanese guy, Greg Oshiro, is a newspaper reporter. He's in there with his two little girls," I said. "The older haole is a business executive named Andre Gardiner; we think the bodybuilder is his muscle, a guy named Takvor Soralian."

"Who's in charge?" Yamashita asked. "Gardiner?"

I nodded. "Either Gardiner or his late father committed a murder about fifty years ago, and Gardiner's been trying to cover it up, killing everyone who knew about it."

"But you don't know what he wants in this situation?"

"Nope."

"Then that's the first thing we need to identify. In most hostage situations, the captor doesn't want the hostages per se. There's a target, who can provide what the captor wants, whether it's money, a safe exit, or performance of a specific task. The hostages are bargaining chips. We can't negotiate until we know what this guy wants."

"We don't actually know that Greg and his daughters are hostages," I said.

"Then why did you call us out?"

I didn't know what to say. It had been a knee-jerk reaction to call in the SWAT team, but perhaps we had overplayed our hand, and all it would take was somebody talking to Gardiner.

I looked at Ray. "I guess it's time to call Greg and see how things are going inside."

Yamashita and his men stayed out of direct sight of the house, and I called Greg's cell. "Come on, Greg, pick up," I said, tapping my foot nervously.

He caught the call after five rings, just as I was thinking it was going to voice mail. "Hello?"

"Greg, it's Kimo. Are you and the girls all right?" I turned the phone so that Ray and Yamashita could hear.

"Sorry, I can't talk right now. I'm in the middle of an interview. Let me have one of my girls get back to you."

"Are the girls in the back bedroom?"

"That's correct. But I'm on deadline here—I've got a gun to my head to get this story finished."

"Literally?"

"Listen, my interviewee is getting nervous so…"

I heard a man's voice say, "Give me that phone." And then he was addressing me. "Who is this?"

"Mr. Gardiner? This is Detective Kanapa'aka from HPD. What brings you to Mr. Oshiro's house today?"

Yamashita started making stretching motions to me, then turned to his team.

"Do you think I'm stupid, detective?"

"No, sir. I think you're very upset about something. I'd like to help you if I can."

He barked a harsh laugh. "It's too late for that." He ended the call.

The SWAT team fanned out. Two guys ran up to the stay-at-home mom's door, while another two circled around the other side of the house.

"I'm going up there," I said. "I think I can get him to talk to me."

"I wouldn't advise it," Yamashita said. "I'm getting my men in place. As soon as we have a clear shot we'll end this."

"There's a civilian and two little girls in there. If I can short circuit a problem I need to try."

"Kimo…" Ray began, but I was already walking toward the house.

I went right up to the front door and tried the knob. It was unlocked, and I turned it slowly and quietly. But as soon as the door opened, Takvor Soralian pivoted and trained his handgun on me.

I put my hands up. "I just want to talk to Mr. Gardiner." I took a step into the living room. "Mr. Gardiner? You're worried about your father, aren't you? His reputation?"

Andre Gardiner turned to face me, though he kept his own handgun pointed at Greg, who was sitting on his sofa. The girls were nowhere in sight.

"My father? My father was a prick. And he's been dead for years. I couldn't care less about him."

"Why bring this all up now?" I asked. "Did Alexander Fields threaten you? Was he going to expose your father for what he did?"

Gardiner sneered. "He wanted to purify his soul. Fucking asshole. His soul was so dark it'd frighten Satan. He was going to tell everyone what I'd done. And even though it was fifty years ago, there's no statute of limitations on murder."

I looked at him. "You killed Senator LeJeune?"

"I thought I was doing what my father wanted," Gardiner said. "He got so angry when he talked about this mainland asshole who was screwing up all his plans. He said things would be so much easier if something would just happen to the guy."

"You were only what, sixteen?" I asked. "You didn't know what you were doing."

"Oh, I knew all right. I'd been going out hunting with my father and some of his friends for years. I was a better shot than he was. He arranged a meeting with the Senator at our house, one last try to convince him to change his mind. I heard them arguing, and I knew the Senator was never going to agree."

It was hot in the house, and sweat was dripping down Greg's face. I felt it beginning to pool under my arms and drip down my back. "What did you do?"

"I got my gun from my room and I walked out into the living room. I kept it behind my back, and my father said, 'Son, let me introduce you to Senator LeJeune.' He was sitting in an easy chair by the door to our lanai, and I walked up, put the gun to his forehead, and fired."

I couldn't imagine doing something like that when I was sixteen. There had to be something seriously wrong with Andre Gardiner's wiring.

"Wow. What did your father do?"

"He started yelling at me! Do you believe that? I had just done him a massive favor, and all he wanted to do was yell at me for making a mess. 'Just like always, I'm cleaning up after you,' he said. Then he locked me in my room. It wasn't until I saw the papers the next day that I figured out what he had done."

I wiped my forehead with the back of my hand. Takvor Soralian did the same thing. He still had his gun pointed at me, but he was watching Gardiner.

"That's why you had problems at Punahou your senior year," I said. "You were upset. I can understand that. I killed a man a couple of years ago, so I know what that's like."

"That didn't bother me. It was the way my asshole father treated me that made me crazy. Like I was some kind of criminal. Made me go to see psychiatrists, sent me to fucking Oregon to go to college instead of UH with my friends."

Fathers and sons, I thought. We never seem to get that part right. On the whole, I thought my own father had done a good job of raising us, but I had my own resentments, and I know my brothers did, too.

"Even so, Mr. Gardiner. There's no physical evidence any more. It would have been his word against yours."

He shrugged. "Well, I've confessed now. So that means I'm going down. Might as well take a couple of you bastards with me."

He took his gun off Greg Oshiro and aimed at me. I heard

the deafening blast reverberate in the small house and took a deep breath.

When I let my breath out I realized I was still standing, and it was Andre Gardiner who was lying on the floor. Soralian dropped the gun he had fired at Gardiner and put his hands up. I ran over to him and grabbed it, then picked up the one that Gardiner had dropped. Then I yelled, "All clear in the house!"

Ray was at the door a moment later. "What happened?"

"Mr. Soralian made a calculated decision to change sides," I said, as I pulled a pair of handcuffs from my belt.

Greg jumped up from his chair and hustled toward the back bedroom.

"I didn't kill anyone," Soralian said. "Gardiner shot them all."

"Hold that thought until we read you your rights," I said.

I checked Gardiner for a pulse, but Taki must have been a hell of a shot, and Gardiner was dead. Yamashita grumbled about us calling the SWAT team out when they weren't necessary, but I ignored him, and he left to tell his team to stand down. Ray called the Medical Examiner's office to come take away Gardiner's body, and a patrol car to take Soralian down to headquarters for booking.

I found Greg in the back bedroom, sitting on the bed with Emily under one arm and Sarah under the other. "You all right?" I asked.

"My blood pressure's through the roof, but I'll be all right, as long as these little ones are okay."

"That was a pretty stupid thing you did," I said. "Inviting a murder suspect to your house. By all logic you ought to be dead by now."

"I didn't know he was a murder suspect. You didn't tell me."

"Greg. It was an open investigation. You should know enough not to mess with one."

"I thought he was just going to fill in some details about the islands at statehood. I didn't think he'd say anything connected to your investigation." He clutched the two girls close to him, leaning down to kiss first one, then the other.

"The past is always present," I said. "We're going to need a statement from you. As soon as Anna comes back to look after the girls, call me."

He nodded, and I walked back out to the living room, stripping off the hot vest. A couple of uniforms took Takvor Soralian away, and while Ray and I waited for the ME, I filled him in on my conversation with Gardiner. "How did you know he did it, not his father?"

"When he said that there was no statute of limitations on murder. If his father had killed LeJeune, that wouldn't have mattered. You can't prosecute a dead man."

"But you can still charge one who's living," Ray said, nodding. "Did he say who killed the prostitute?"

I shook my head. "He said his father locked him in his room after he shot the Senator. And in his letter, Bennie Gomez said he didn't do it, and he wasn't sure which man had. But it was probably Gardiner senior, wouldn't you think? He was the one who needed to protect his son."

I looked at Ray. "Would you kill someone to protect Vinnie?"

"To keep him from harm? Of course. But if he did something wrong... I'm not sure. You never know how things are going to play out in life, you know? You try and raise a kid right, but sometimes..."

We had seen enough cases together of well-brought-up kids who had done something wrong. I'd seen it in my own family, and Ray had seen it in his, too. No matter what you do, it seemed, you couldn't always protect everyone, not even from their own impulses.

We drove downtown. Ray got started on the paperwork while I went downstairs to the holding cells. I had Rory Yang bring Taki to an interview room, where I was set up with a tape recorder.

Ray poured him a cup of the sludge that passes for coffee at the station and we got started.

Taki was a big, muscular guy, but he looked sad and kind of sheepish. I turned on the recorder and read him his rights for the record. He agreed to be taped and to answer questions.

"I knew Pika from the gym. We used to hang out together. One day he calls me up and says that one of his clients needs some muscle, could I come along? I said sure."

"When was this?"

"Last week. Tuesday."

He described riding with Pika to pick up Gardiner, then to Bernice Fong's home. "Pika and me, we waited in the limo while Andy went into the house. When he came out with the old lady, she was talking all the time. How he needed to calm down and all. She said she would only go with him if he promised to behave."

He laughed. "He kept saying 'Yes, Aunt Bernice,' but you could tell he wasn't really listening to her or going to do what she said. He gave Pika this address in Kahala, and when we stopped at the gate Andy said to tell the man it was just Mrs. Bernice Fong to visit."

He picked up his coffee and took a sip, then made a face.

"Yeah, it's not Kope Bean," I said. "Sorry."

Pika shrugged. "Andy had me get out and open the door for Mrs. Fong, and he stayed in the car until the old man had already come out on the porch. The old man was kind of surprised to see him, not happy, you know? He said something like 'I don't have anything to say to you.' Then Andy goes, 'Well, I have something to say to you,' and he pulls out the gun and motions everybody into the house."

"What did you and Pika do?" I asked.

"We kind of looked at each other like, what kind of shit is this? But we both been around guns enough to know you don't mess with them. We followed the three of them into the house. And then Andy starts in with, 'Where's the gun?' It was kind of freaky, because, like dude, you've got the gun in your hand. But turns out there was this other gun he was asking about."

"What gun was that?" I asked.

"They both went back and forth for a while, like what gun? And shit like that. And finally Andy says 'I know my father gave you the gun I shot the sheriff with.'"

Ray and I looked at each other. "The sheriff?" I asked.

"Oh, sorry, I was getting confused with that song, you know?" He started to sing in a bad falsetto. "I shot the sheriff, but I didn't shoot the deputy."

"Back up, Taki," I said. "What did Andy actually say?"

"It was the gun he shot the senator with," Taki said.

"You ever hear him mention the name James LeJeune?"

"That's the one. Didn't recognize the name but I don't get into politics too much. The old man said everything he had was at this warehouse, so Andy had us all go back to the limo. In the driveway the old man started arguing, said he had this gizmo around his neck that would track wherever Andy took him, and he'd better watch his steps."

Taki laughed again. "Andy just grabbed the chain around the old man's neck and broke it, and tossed the gizmo into the bushes. Mrs. Fong told the old man he was really stupid. When we were back in the limo she tried to whisper something to the old man but Andy shut them up."

"What happened when you got to the warehouse?"

"Andy told me and Pika to take Mrs. Fong and the old man into the warehouse. He stayed in the car for a minute to make a phone call. Then when he came in he sent me back out to the car to keep a lookout. I heard a gunshot from inside the building and I was ready to take off, but Pika came out then. Andy was right behind him, dragging Mrs. Fong by the arm. She was crying and he was yelling at her." He looked up at us. "I get something for all this, right? You make things go away for me?"

"The DA is the one who makes the deals," I said. "He's going to need the whole story in order to know what he can do."

Taki looked down at the table. "I hung out with some bad people in LA. I left there so I could come clean and start over again. But Pika knew that I could start a fire, and he must have told Andy. Andy offered me ten grand to light up the warehouse."

"With Fields' body inside," I said.

"Taki said the old man was already dead. And Andy had a gun. I was afraid he'd shoot me if I didn't cooperate." He looked over at us. "That's coercion, right? I had to do what he wanted or he'd shoot me."

"That'll be in the record. I'm sure the DA will take that into account. What happened after that?"

"Pika drove the limo down the block and we waited to make sure the building caught. Then Andy had us go back to Mrs. Fong's house. Pika and me waited in the limo while he walked her up to her door. I couldn't hear what he said but he was waving the gun at her like a crazy man. She turned and scurried into her house like a scared little rat, and he came back to the limo and said to take him home."

Taki drank some more coffee, making a face again. "Andy had us come in with him and wait in the living room." He shook his head. "I didn't like it, man. I wanted to get the hell out of there, but Pika wanted the money. Andy came back a few minutes later with ten grand for each of us. He told us that if we said anything about what happened that night he'd hunt us down."

He put his hands flat on the table. "You see, I didn't have any choice, right?"

"What happened next?"

"Me and Pika went out and got drunk. I stashed most of the money and tried to forget about that night. Then everything was cool for a while. Pika called me up Wednesday and said he needed me to go with him again. I didn't want to, but he told me Andy would come after me if I didn't go."

He shuddered. "He just shot poor old Mrs. Fong right there

on her sofa," he said.

"Who?"

"Andy, man. The old lady opened the door and the three of us walked in. I felt bad, 'cause it looked like we dragged her out of bed. But she was really nice. She even offered to make us tea. Andy just told her to sit down. He said, 'Sorry, Aunt Bernice, but I've been thinking about it and I can't take the chance you'll tell anyone what you know.' Then he shot her, and we left."

"Just like that?"

He nodded. "Yeah. He wanted to go out drinking with us but I was freaking out, and I guess Pika was, too. We dropped him at his house. He never even paid us for driving him."

"How come none of the witnesses we have put Gardiner at the scene, either of the warehouse fire or Bernice Fong's murder?" I asked. "All anyone saw was two bodybuilders."

Taki laughed. "Andy thought he was some kind of ninja. He was all dressed in black, and he kept sneaking around behind either me or Pika."

"Let's talk about last night," I said, thinking of Dakota's shooting. "Where were you?"

Taki looked down at the table.

"Get it all out," I said. "It's like pulling off a bandage. It only hurts if you do it too slowly."

"Quilting."

"Excuse me?"

He looked up. "I belong to this quilting circle, all right? We meet on Thursday nights at the Kope Bean in Mililani. It's not just women, you know. There's a couple of other dudes."

"Hold on. You're telling me that last night you were at a coffee shop making a quilt?"

He nodded. "It's this very cool Hawaiian group. We work from these old patterns and we make quilts that we donate to charity. I don't like to tell people about it because it doesn't go with the, you know, rest of the package."

"I'm assuming you can give me names of people who will testify that you were there?"

"Yeah. But why? Nothing happened last night."

"There's this teenage boy who's going to come live with me and my partner as our foster son," I said. "He was at our house last night, walking the dog, when somebody in a dark car cruised past and shot at him."

"Had to be Pika or Andy," Taki said. "Not me. I'd never shoot at some kid, no matter how much somebody was paying me."

I nodded. "How about this morning?" I asked. "How did Gardiner get in touch with you?"

"Pika must have given him my number. He called and told me he needed a bodyguard, and Pika wasn't answering his phone. I wanted to say no. But I was scared of the dude."

"Where'd you get the gun?"

"He gave it to me before we got out of the car. I didn't want to take it. But he promised me another ten grand if I'd just cooperate." He looked at me. "I didn't know who was in the house. I didn't know about those girls."

"One last question. Why'd you shoot Gardiner?"

"He was crazy, man. I knew if he killed you, the cops were coming down hard on the house, and if Gardiner didn't shoot me a cop probably would. So I shot him." He shuddered again. "That's the first time I ever killed anybody, for real. First time I ever shot a gun not at the range."

The DA and the public defender showed up, and I left the three of them to negotiate and went back upstairs. It was the end of our shift and I was exhausted. I sat down for a few minutes to recap with Ray and Sampson.

"You rush in where angels fear to tread," Sampson said. "Why didn't you let SWAT handle this?"

"Because it wasn't really a hostage situation," I said. "Gardiner had nothing to negotiate for, and Greg had nothing to give him. I didn't know that Taki was going to turn on Gardiner—and he might not have if I wasn't in there."

"I'm with Kimo on this one," Ray said. "We couldn't take a risk with those two little girls in the house."

"The papers are going to have a field day with this case," Sampson said. "They're going to dredge up the past, and a lot of people are going to be unhappy. I'm just waiting for the first call from the chief."

"Tell him about snakes," I said, and both Ray and Sampson looked at me. "Why are we so freaked about snakes landing in Hawai'i? Because they have no natural predators. There's nothing to keep them from reproducing and destroying the native wildlife."

"Your point is?"

"We're the natural predators for slime like Andre Gardiner," I said. "Us, and every other one of the policing agencies here. We're just doing what God and Mother Nature intended us to do."

Sampson shook his head. "I think I'll hold off with the analogies."

"Speaking of the other policing agencies," Ray said. "Any word about our transfer to the FBI?"

"You want to go through with that?" Sampson asked.

"I do."

I looked over at Ray. "I do, too. As long as there's still a place for us back here at some point."

"I can't guarantee anything," Sampson said. "You know as well as I do that assignments are based on qualifications and need. But I'll fight to get you back, if I can."

"That sounds like as good as we're going to get," I said.

Sampson looked at me. "What made you change your mind?"

"Dakota getting shot," I said. "I'm tired of putting the people

I care about in danger. I want a nice safe desk job for a while."

Sampson laughed. "You think you'll get that at the Bureau? And you really think you'd be happy if you did?"

"Worth a shot." I looked down at the floor. "Mike and I, well, we've agreed to father a baby with a lesbian couple we know. If I'm going to be a dad, then I want to do whatever I can to take care of my family."

"I'll hate to lose you both. But I've had my eye on a couple of patrol officers who just passed the sergeant's exam and I like the idea of training some new detectives."

At the HPD, detective is an assignment, not a rank; you have to become a sergeant before you can move into homicide.

"But you're not off my roster yet. Go home, get some rest, and come back here tomorrow ready for a new case."

"Thanks, Lieutenant," Ray said, and stood up. I echoed his thanks and we walked back to our desks.

"So," Ray said. "Something new on the horizon."

"It's like Woody Allen said in *Annie Hall*," I said. "If you're a shark, you've got to keep moving or die."

"I don't think that's exactly the way he put it," Ray said. "But it works for me." He steepled his hands above his head and began swaying back and forth as he sang. "Can't you feel 'em swimmin' around. You got fins to the left, fins to the right. And you're the only bait in town."

"We're sure a mixed bag of cultural references," I said, laughing. "I guess that's why we work so well together."

"Guess so," Ray said.

I didn't realize how tired I was until I was in my Jeep trying to fight rush hour traffic toward home. I kept yawning, and gripping the steering wheel for support, and because I hoped the cramping in my fingers would keep me awake.

My cell phone rang as I was passing the Aloha Stadium, which loomed dark and empty to my left. "Oh, God, what is it now?" I said out loud. But I grabbed the phone and saw it was Gunter calling.

"Hey," he said.

"Hey yourself."

"I was thinking…" he said, then paused. "Um, maybe you, you and Mike…"

I yawned. "Sorry, it's not you, Gunter. It's been a long day."

"I want you to meet Cinco," he said in a rush. "Like go out together. Sunday brunch?"

"I have to ask Mike. But probably. So you're coming out of the closet with him?"

"It's not like I was hiding him or anything."

The sun came out from behind a bank of clouds and I had to raise my hand to shade my eyes. "Sure it is, Gunter. You've been bitching at me for years about settling down with Mike and you were afraid I'd give you the same shit back."

"We don't have to do it," he said.

"Beachside Broiler, Sunday at eleven," I said. The BB was a sprawling buffet in a Waikiki hotel, with tables right on the beach. Gunter and I had often eaten there when I lived in Waikiki. "I'm hanging up. See you Sunday."

I kept on yawning as I climbed Aiea Heights Drive, and I was so relieved to pull into our driveway I closed my eyes for a minute. I woke to hear Roby barking from inside the house, irritated that I was home but not with him. I dragged myself out of the Jeep and up to the front door. The dog was so delighted to see me you'd think I'd been away for weeks, not just a long day. Mike wasn't home yet, so I hooked Roby's leash and walked him down to the corner and back. Then I stripped down, took a quick shower, and fell into bed.

I woke to see Mike looming above me, and smelled the distinctive charcoal, sugar and onions that meant *bulgogi*, Korean barbecue. "You didn't answer your phone," he said. "So I went ahead and got us dinner."

Roby was dancing around him, eager for his taste of beef. I sat up and yawned. "Sorry. Took a power nap."

Over dinner I told him about the day, including Gardiner's death and Taki's arrest. "So who shot at Dakota?" he asked.

"Not clear. Most likely Gardiner. But we'll see if we can get a ballistics match."

Mike pushed aside his plate. "About last night," he said.

"Uh-huh."

"I mean, what we talked about on the way home from the hospital."

"I think we have a great life," I said. "I love you and Roby and I'm looking forward to having Dakota here. That's enough for me. But I want you to be happy."

"It's just such a big commitment," Mike said. "And seeing what happened to Dakota last night scared me. What if we have a kid, and something happens?"

"Your parents managed with you, and mine with me," I said. "And their parents with them, and so on all the way back in time. Just because we don't have the right plumbing to have a kid without some outside assistance doesn't mean we won't be able to manage." I paused. "But if you're not ready now, then we just have to tell Sandra and Cathy."

"What if they find someone else and we lose this chance?"

"It's not like buying an airline ticket," I said. "If the universe means for us to become dads, the opportunity will be there. When we're ready for it."

"I like it when you hang around with Terri," he said. "You get all philosophical."

I stood up and began clearing the table. Roby realized there was no more food coming, and he rose and lumbered over to his bed, where he turned around twice and then settled down, his head on his paws, looking at us.

When the kitchen was clean, we moved to the living room, lounging on the sofa facing each other with our legs entwined. "I'm a big wimp, aren't I?" Mike asked.

"In many ways," I said, and he kicked me.

I laughed. "It's a big step, having kids. I think I'm ready for it, and I think you are, too." I looked over at him. "This afternoon I told Sampson I want to move over to the Bureau."

"What did he say?"

"That he was sorry to lose us, but he already had some baby sergeants on tap to replace us. Very heart-warming."

"Pragmatic." Mike sat up and pushed my legs to the floor so he could come sit next to me. "So we're in this thing?"

"Baby-making? Guess so."

He leaned over and kissed me. "Cool."

I kissed him back, and pretty quickly he was on top of me on the sofa and we were losing clothes and making Roby nervous.

Eventually we moved to the bed and then fell asleep cuddled together. The next morning, Saturday, we met up with Terri, Levi, Dakota and Danny at the farmer's market at Kapiolani Community College. We nibbled on barbecued abalone, shrimp fried rice and wedges of mushroom and spinach omelettes made with farm-fresh eggs. Dakota had never had kalua pork, and he became an instant convert. It was funny to see Danny walk him around, showing off his knowledge of local foods.

Dakota's leg had been bandaged, and kids from school had

signed it as if it was a cast. It sounded like he was settling in there, and he was already talking about different clubs he might join. "They have a gay straight alliance," he said. "This kid already invited me to come to the next meeting."

I looked at Mike and couldn't help wondering how different our lives would have been if we had been able to be so open about who we were back in adolescence. Would we even have met? What if we'd both been able to fall in love in high school, or college? How differently our lives might have turned out.

Terri made us sit through a lecture by a master gardener, and then we heard some local students playing slack key guitar. There were so many different flavors of coffee, chocolate, shave ice and breads and cakes that we were all in a constant state of taste bud arousal.

When we were done, Dakota came home with Mike and me, and we downloaded an old surfing movie and the four of us sprawled around the living room watching. At least I think Roby was watching; he might have been looking at us rather than the TV.

Sunday morning we all slept in, scrambling to get Roby fed and walked, then the three humans showered and dressed for our brunch with Gunter and Cinco. "I wish we didn't have to do this," I grumbled, as I drove along the H1 toward Waikiki.

"You're jealous," Mike said.

"That's dumb. How can I be jealous when I have you?" I said. "I want Gunter to be happy. I just don't know that this Cinco guy is the right one for him."

"You don't want him to settle down. He's your id, remember? You want him to be that swinging single you used to be."

"And I'm not even a dad yet," I said. "So much for that happy life."

I was cruising slowly along Kuhio Avenue in Waikiki past a long row of high-rise hotels, on my way to the parking garage, when my cell rang. From the custom tone, the theme from *L.A. Law*, I knew it was Sandra, and I put it on speaker. "Howzit," I said.

"I'm already feeling nauseous, but Cathy says I'm exaggerating," she said.

I looked over at Mike but spoke to the phone. "What do you mean?"

"I got the eggs on Friday," she said. "I can feel it. There's something growing inside me."

"You can't know that so soon, can you?" Mike asked.

"My mom told me she knew exactly when she was pregnant with me. Like within hours."

"We're going to be parents," I said, speaking to the phone but looking at Mike. "Holy shit."

"My feelings exactly," Sandra said. "Oh, crap, I've gotta pee. Talk to you later."

"A whole new world," Dakota sang from the back seat. "A new fantastic point of view."

"He must have been hanging out with Ray," Mike said, and we both laughed. "But he's right. It's a whole new world."

I reached over and took his hand. "And it starts today, with the three of us."

"And Roby, too," Dakota chimed in.

"And Roby, too," I said. "Now let's go meet Gunter and welcome the newest member of our ohana."

Which is exactly what we did.

# ALPHA AND OMEGA
*A Mahu Investigation Bonus Short*

"These babies are squashing my kidneys, Kimo," Sandra grumbled, as she struggled up the walkway to the front door of my parents' house in St. Louis Heights, overlooking downtown Honolulu and the Pacific Ocean beyond. She was a stocky fireplug of a woman, with truck-driver shoulders and close-cropped hair, and as her belly swelled with the growing twins she looked more and more like a beach ball with a head.

Her diminutive partner, Cathy, followed behind her. She was half-Japanese, but that half was clearly dominant; she had a sheer fall of waist-length black hair and the fine hands of an artist—though her art was poetry. Over a year before, Sandra and Cathy had asked me and my partner, Mike, if one or both of us would join them in making a baby. Cathy was the more maternal one, but she had some problem that prevented her from carrying a child. After a long discussion, Mike and I had both given sperm, and Cathy had donated eggs. Several of them had been fertilized and implanted into Sandra's womb.

The first ultrasound showed us what Sandra was already feeling: she was carrying twins. The boy and girl, nicknamed Alpha and Omega for the time being—as the first and the last babies Sandra would ever carry—had taken over her life since then. She was a high-powered attorney with a Rolodex of every lesbian in the Aloha State as well as the political and legal clout to gain, and win, high-profile cases. But after six months her obstetrician had confined her to bed rest to ensure she could carry the twins to term. She had not reacted well to having her activities curtailed.

This early December luau, sandwiched between Thanksgiving and Christmas, as if we needed another opportunity to overeat, was her last outing before popping the babies out. All four of us knew our lives were about to change in a drastic way. Mike's and my golden retriever, Roby, romped around us, even as our teenage foster son, Dakota, tried to corral him without success. As he scrambled after the dog, his board shorts slipped down, showing the waistband of his boxers, and his T-shirt rode up.

If only I had known myself at his age as well as he did, how different my life might have been. It sometimes astonished me how much my world had changed in the five years since I'd been dragged out of the closet.

"Here you are!" My mother appeared at the front door, all five-foot-nothing of her in a bright blue muumuu, her coal-black hair pulled into a bun on her head. "I was worried you wouldn't be able to come."

My mother is a tiny dynamo, even into her seventies. She ruled my big, blustery father, my two brothers and me with an iron fist in a velvet glove, and though she doted on every one of her grandchildren she was eager to see Sandra add to that number.

My parents had organized this massive luau to welcome Sandra and Cathy into our extended family and provide an opportunity for everyone to shower the soon-to-be-born twins with baby gifts.

My mother took Sandra by the arm and led her inside, settling her in a comfy chair in the living room with an ottoman for her feet. Mike and I walked into the kitchen, where my aunts and my sisters-in-law jockeyed to get food out for the hungry masses. Dakota joined my nieces and nephews, who were swarming from the downstairs den through the kitchen and out to the back yard.

Mike and I detoured around the food prep and walked outside with Roby, then let him loose to speed over to a pack of family dogs hovering near the kalua pig roasting in a pit dug in the back yard. Family and friends were all around us, and quickly we were all chowing down as if we'd never eat again: Hawaiian specialties like my mom's chicken long rice, my sister-in-law Liliha's shark-fin soup, my godmother's sweet and sour spareribs and my aunt Pua's Portuguese sausage and beans. Mike's mother had brought *bulgogi*, a spicy Korean barbeque, and my mother and my sister-in-law Tatiana had been baking cakes and pies and cookies all week, which shared space with platters of fruit, tubs of mango sherbet and chocolate ice cream in coolers, and about ten different types of salted, dried and preserved fruits called crack seed. I don't know where the name came from originally, but it's almost as addictive as the cocaine derivative.

Keola Beamer was playing on the stereo, singing about his family rocking in a wooden boat, but I could barely hear the music under the laughter and chatter of too many family members in one place. Fortunately my parents' yard backs up on Waahila Ridge State Park, and the kids made their own campground under the trees.

Sandra and Cathy were the center of attention. Everyone had either a gift or a piece of advice for the new moms. As the dads, Mike and I got our share—everything from jokes about our ability to change diapers to confidential suggestions to handle teething (a little brandy on the gums) and diarrhea.

After we finished eating, Mike and I sprawled on the ground next to the pair of lawn chairs where Sandra and Cathy sat. My mother brought a stepladder out of the house and set it up, then stepped up on it. Tatiana hurried over to steady her. "Quiet down, everybody!" she boomed, and we all turned our attention to my mom.

"Al and I have an announcement to make," she said.

My father got up from his chair and tottered over to her, leaning on his cane. I hope I am as handsome as he is when I reach my eighties. His black hair has gone gray and there are lines on his forehead that weren't there ten years ago, but his half-Hawaiian, *hapa–haole* genetic mix has served him well.

With the boost from the stepladder, and my father's shrinking over the last few years, she was almost eye-to-eye with him. She took his hand. "You all know that we love this house, and we love being so close to our two oldest sons and their families. But it's time for a change."

"After nearly fifty years with this woman, she's finally letting me have my way," my father said. "We are going to sell this house and move into a condo by the water."

My father, both my brothers and I all had the native Hawaiian love for the ocean. Lui, Haoa and I had grown up surfing with our dad, and I think all of us were happiest when we were either on the water or at its edge.

"Where are you going, Tutu?" Haoa's eldest, Ashley, asked. She had inherited her mother's luxurious ash-blonde hair and father's height and love of surfing. At nineteen, she was already a star on the women's circuit.

"We're looking around Diamond Head," my mother said. "No plans yet. But it's time for us to start cleaning out this old house. And my boys know what that means. If you want something, you take it, or it goes for sale or to charity."

"There goes the Kimo shrine," Mike whispered to me, and I elbowed him. It was true; my room remained as I had left it when I went to college in California—my surfing trophies and posters on the walls, my childhood books on the shelves.

I hated the thought of parting with those old memories—but Mike and I lived in a three-bedroom duplex which was already overflowing. We had converted our junk room into a bedroom for Dakota when we got the official approval as foster parents. The third bedroom was an office Mike and I shared, which would also serve as makeshift nursery when the twins were with us.

"That's all," my mother said, taking my father's hand as she stepped down from the ladder. "Now eat some more!"

Once the adults were groaning from eating too much, my mother organized her grandkids into a cleanup brigade. Dakota tried to slink away but she caught him. "Dakota! You are just as much my *keiki* as everybody else. So you work too!"

He slumped his shoulders and pushed back his shoulder-length black hair, but I could see he was happy to be accepted as another grandson. Around us the kids carried the platters into the kitchen, emptied the trash and folded up the tables, and Mike and I tried to help Sandra stand up. "I'm as big as a house," she cried. "Your parents don't need a condo. They can just live in me."

We each stood to one side and lifted, with Cathy pushing from the rear. "Please, God, take these children out of me!" Sandra said.

Mike and I helped her totter out to the car while my mother loaded Cathy up with leftovers. "I want a Caesarian," Sandra said. "Now!"

"Buck up," Mike said. "Where's that butch little lesbian we all know and love?"

"She's gone. All that's left is a baby machine."

We shoveled her into the front seat of the car as Cathy came out of the house, surrounded by an army of keikis carrying plastic containers of leftovers and shopping bags full of unwrapped gifts.

"How are you going to manage all this at your house?" I asked. Cathy looked almost as tired as Sandra, with dark circles under her eyes. And the babies weren't even born yet.

"We have a nosy neighbor across the street. She'll come over and help us unload everything," Cathy said, as she shoved all the packages into the trunk. "We go to the doctor on Wednesday. If Sandy hasn't gone into labor by then he's going to induce."

"You want one of us to come with you?" I asked. Mike and I had gone to a couple of visits with Sandra and seen the ultrasound.

"Bring a forklift." She leaned up and kissed both of us. "Thanks. I'll confirm soon."

Mike and I stood in front of my parents' house and watched them drive away. "Every time I remember we're going to be dads, it scares the shit out of me," I said.

"If my dad and yours could manage, then so can you and I," Mike said. "Now come on, let's clean out some of your junk while we're here."

We trudged up the stairs to what had been my room. When I opened the door, though, I was surprised. "What happened to the Kimo shrine?"

All my stuff was still there—but instead of the immaculate neatness my mother had always maintained, the room was a mess. My single bed was piled with old clothes. The floor was stacked with boxes.

"This can't all be yours," Mike said.

"It sure can't. Mom!" I felt like a teenager again, stretching the word out to multiple syllables.

She came up the stairs behind us. "Oh," she said. "I didn't realize you would start taking away so soon. I've been using your room as a staging ground. You wouldn't believe all the stuff we've had stuck away in this house. Even things from my mother-in-law."

"Really?" I asked. My granny had always been a bit of an enigma. She was a very proper white Mormon woman from Idaho who had come to Hawai'i as a schoolteacher, married a native Hawaiian man, and given birth to six children, four of whom lived to adulthood. Granny died when I was eleven, so I didn't know her well, and I found her imperious and scary. She had always lived in the same small bungalow in the McCully neighborhood just inland from Waikiki.

My dad's oldest sister, my aunt Elizabeth, had married a serviceman and moved to Kansas. His younger brother, Uncle Philip, was a non-conformist who didn't believe in marriage or having kids. He and his long-time girlfriend lived near their second sister, Aunt Margaret, and her family in Hilo. After Granny died my father was the only one left to claim anything, and he moved a few boxes of her stuff to our house.

"You want any of this?" my mom asked. "I don't and I know it will be terrible to convince your father to throw any of it away."

I opened the closest box and found a photo album of my father and his siblings when they were little. "Look at Dad!" I said. "How cute was he?"

Three boys and two girls sat in a wooden cart hitched up to a white goat with a long beard. I could tell my dad easily; he was the biggest and the cutest, holding the goat's reins like he was in charge.

I looked up at my mom. "I'll take these and sort through them."

Mike sighed. "I'll start carrying them downstairs."

We recruited Dakota to drag six boxes of family memorabilia out to my Jeep and stow them in the back. We said our goodbyes reluctantly, rounded up Roby, and then headed downhill to the highway that would take us home.

Dakota was quiet in the back seat, with Roby's head in his lap. I first met him when he began coming to a gay and lesbian youth group I helped out with, and when his mother when to prison he had been homeless. Mike and I registered with the state as foster parents in order to bring him into our home legally.

"You have a good time today, Dakota?" I asked over my shoulder.

"It was okay."

"Just okay? Don't let Tutu Lokelani hear you say that. When she makes a luau she expects rave reviews."

"She's not my grandmother."

I looked in the rear view mirror and saw him slumped against the seat.

"Does that mean Mike and I aren't your dads?"

"Not for real. Not like the babies."

Mike twisted around to look at Dakota as I got onto the H1 highway, a broad strip of concrete that cuts through the heart of O'ahu. Except for the occasional palm trees by the side of the road, it could be anywhere in the United States.

"Kimo and I went through a lot of shit so you could come and live with us," he said. "Hours of parenting classes. Piles of paperwork. If you think we're giving up on you just because our family is growing, you're wrong as can be."

"What does ohana mean, Dakota?" I asked.

We had a running joke in our household, a line from the animated movie *Lilo and Stitch*, about an alien who lands in Hawai'i and pretends to be a dog in order to fit in.

Dakota slumped farther down in his seat, his head down.

"Say it, Dakota," Mike said.

"Ohana means nobody gets left behind," he mumbled.

Mike reached back to grab Dakota's hand. "And it means you're always going to be part of our family, our ohana. Forever. You understand that?"

"Uh-huh."

Roby sat up and licked Dakota's face, then tried to climb around behind him. "Get out of my hair, you goofy dog," he said, and all of us laughed.

By the time we got home, Dakota had gotten over his pout, and he carried all the boxes inside without prompting, stacking them in the office.

Monday afternoon Mike had to go up to the North Shore to pick up some evidence for a case he was investigating, and he picked Dakota up from school and took him along. I got home around four and after I walked Roby we went out to the back yard together. I relaxed in a big Adirondack chair and he sprawled at my feet as I began looking through the albums of my dad's childhood.

The sun was sinking behind the Ko'olaus, but the temperature was in the mid-seventies and a gentle breeze ruffled the leaves of the kuhio tree at the back corner of the yard. Someone was barbecuing, and the tangy scent of meat and charcoal floated by.

It was freaky the way my father looked so much like I did when I was a kid. When you looked at me and my brothers together, you could tell we were family—but each of us had taken a different dip in the gene pool. Lui looked the most Asian of us, Haoa the most Hawaiian. I'd always looked the most haole—and I realized, seeing my dad as a kid, that he had, too. The brother who was a year younger was almost his twin; he was the one who had died of pneumonia as a boy. How weird must that have been for my dad, losing a brother? I couldn't imagine life without Lui and Haoa around.

Under the albums were some failed attempts at quilting that my grandmother must have abandoned. The quilt on the bed Mike and I shared was the first one she completed, back when she was a newlywed. My parents had another, better quality one.

I was sifting through the fabric scraps when an old-time sepia photograph spilled out. My grandmother, looking impossibly young, wore a white wedding gown with a lacy veil over her forehead. To her right stood an older couple I assumed were her parents.

I peered closer, looking for evidence of my genetic makeup. My great-grandfather was a stern-faced man with light-colored hair cut short. He had big ears and a broad nose, and didn't look like anyone I'd ever claimed kin to.

My great-grandmother was an older version of my granny. I remembered that Granny wore her salt-and-pepper hair in a tight bun, and I saw she'd copied her own mother on that. They had the same widely-spaced eyes, the same tight smile.

Why was the picture sliced in half, cutting out my grandfather and his parents? I flipped it over and saw the photographer's mark—from Helena, Montana.

That was interesting. I'd always thought my grandmother never returned home after coming to Hawai'i to teach. But if she was married in Helena, she and my grandfather must have gone back there.

I skimmed through the rest of the boxes. The only thing of interest was an old leather-bound book with *My Diary* in script across the front. When I opened it I found Granny's name, Sarah Carhartt, written in neat penmanship on the front page.

The sun had sunk below the horizon by then, and it was too dark to read, so I carried the diary into the bedroom, followed eagerly by the dog, who must have thought we were going in to dinner, and sat up in bed to read the old-fashioned handwriting.

> *I am about to embark on the adventure of my life. I will turn eighteen on May 15, 1933. The next day, I*

> *will marry George Harmon and I will accompany him*
> *on his mission to the Hawaiian Islands.*

Huh? George Harmon? What about my grandfather, Keali'i Kanapa'aka?

Roby began barking, and I heard the front door open. "Loo-cie, we're home," Mike called, in his Ricky Ricardo imitation. I put the diary aside and went out to the kitchen, where Mike laid out a bucket of fried chicken. The three of us sat around the table and talked about Mike's investigation, Dakota's day at school, and the diary I had found.

Mike fed Roby a piece of chicken and said, "Your grandmother was married before? What happened to him?"

"I haven't gotten that far," I said.

Between cleaning up after dinner and helping Dakota with his homework, I didn't get back to the diary that night. I was curious enough, though, that I took it with me to work, on the off chance I'd get some time to read at lunch.

No such luck. My partner Ray and I were roped into helping with the intake for a group of youth gang members, and I was swamped with that until just after two, when Cathy texted: *Sandy labor. QMC now.*

QMC was The Queen's Medical Center. I ditched the last of the paperwork on Ray and took off. My office at Honolulu police headquarters was close by, so I was there before Mike. I found Cathy at the nurse's desk in the delivery ward. "The doctor says she's only a few centimeters dilated, so it's going to be a while," she said. "But you know Sandy. She wants the babies out now."

"She's due for a major attitude adjustment," I said. "We all are. Babies live at their own timetable, not ours."

"Believe me, I know."

Cathy went back into the room to help Sandra with her breathing exercises, and I called my mom, and then Mike's, to give them the latest news. Then I paced around the waiting room until I remembered my grandmother's diary, on the front seat of my Jeep. I retrieved it and sat on a hard plastic chair to continue reading.

I started again with that first sentence. I had never heard that Granny had been married before my grandfather and I was eager to see if she got out of the upcoming ceremony. But she didn't; she described her wedding in mind-numbing detail, from the simple white satin gown with a "very stylish" matching cap, to everyone who attended the reception.

Granny was born in Utah and moved to Idaho Falls with her parents when she was ten. The stake, or Mormon congregation, had been there since 1895. The way she described the town reminded me of black-and-white Westerns I had seen—the old-fashioned buildings in the downtown, the prevalence of horses and cows. She loved to go out to the falls and sit there by the water contemplating the raw power.

Well, that was something she and I had in common, I thought. The love of water ran deep in our family.

I had never known that she had been brought up a Mormon; neither of my parents were religious, and they had raised my brothers and me with a general appreciation of all beliefs— we attended Christmas Eve mass at the Kawaia'aho Church downtown; honored the Kami—the nature spirits—of the four directions at the Shinto New Year's Festival; and studied the ancient gods of the islands at Hawaiian school one afternoon a week.

Reading between the lines, I discovered that Granny's family was quite wealthy, while George's was not. After hearing a returned missionary speak in Idaho Falls, George felt the call, but his family could not afford the cost of sending him to Hawai'i. It looked like theirs was a marriage of convenience; her father footed the cost of the mission, and Granny had the chance to escape Idaho Falls and see the world.

I skimmed past the details of her first night as a married woman until she was ready to leave home. There are some things we just don't need to know about our grandparents.

*My adventure begins! My first time on a train. As we
leave Idaho Falls my parents stand at the station beside
George's. Will we ever see them again?*

I put the book aside. That must have been so tough—to be
an eighteen-year-old girl leaving everything behind for a new life
somewhere else. How long did it take letters to travel from Idaho
to Honolulu back then? The first trans-Pacific telephone cable
was laid from Japan to the US via Hawai'i in 1934, but it must
have been extraordinarily expensive to make calls.

I remembered my grandmother as a woman of few words,
but you wouldn't know it from her diary. She described the train
compartment and everything she saw out the windows from
Idaho Falls to Ogden, Utah. Then they transferred to the Union
Pacific for the trip to San Francisco.

I scanned along, looking for information on the mysterious
George Hammond—but there was very little. Occasionally she'd
mention him in passing.

*Every meal on the Streamliner is an event! George and
I had the Nebraska Corn-Fed Charcoal Broiled Steak
for dinner tonight, with baked potatoes and fresh corn,
and a delicious lemon cake for dessert.*

So I knew what George was eating—but who was he? How
did he feel about the marriage? None of that was there.

The swinging door to the visiting area bounced open and
Mike strode in. "Where is she? Did she have the babies already?"

"Are you kidding? Cathy said she's only a few centimeters
dilated, so it could be hours."

Mike shuddered as he sat down next to me. "I don't want to
hear the clinical details. Just thinking of Sandra's vagina gives me
the creeps."

"I can pull up some pictures online to show you," I said. "I know you've never seen one in person yourself."

"And you've seen way too many," Mike said. We had both been conflicted about our sexuality when we were younger. I slept with as many girls as I could, hoping to find the one who could erase my uncomfortable desires. Mike had never experimented that way, confining his sexual experimentation to a series of random encounters with men.

We heard a deep, throaty scream come from behind the closed door to the delivery room. "Let me just say I am so glad women have babies and not men," I said.

"I hear you."

Mike had some phone calls to make, so he stepped outside. I promised to get him if anything happened, and went back to my grandmother's diary.

A true small-town girl, she was awed by San Francisco. She and George attended a worship service with a congregation in Oakland, founded by Mormons who had traveled to California around Cape Horn. While George met with the church elders, she spoke with a woman who visited the islands and learned about the louche customs of the people there.

> *The native women wear skirts made of grass! The*
> *Hawaiians are a simple people, content to live from the*
> *plenty of their land. But the church at Laie has made*
> *many converts.*

She described in great detail the cruise terminal where she and George boarded the Lurline for their trip to Honolulu. Then her diary stopped for several days.

I looked at the clock and realized that Dakota would be getting out of school soon. Most days, he took a bus from Punahou that dropped him at the base of Aiea Heights Drive, and he walked the last blocks uphill. He was responsible for taking Roby out, and then working on his homework until either Mike or I returned to fix dinner.

It didn't look like we'd be home by then. I called my best friend, Harry Ho, who lived down the hill from us with his wife and son. "Yo, brah," I said, when he answered. "Can Dakota have dinner with you guys tonight?"

"Sure. What's up? You both working?"

"Nah, Sandra's the only one doing the work today."

"For real? She's in labor?"

"Yeah."

"Good luck. Arleen says she was in labor with Brandon for nineteen hours."

I groaned. "So maybe Dakota and Roby could stay over with you tonight?"

"No problem."

"*Mahalo*, brah. I'll call him."

Life had been so much less complicated when I was single and living in Waikiki. If I worked late, all I had to worry about was where I would grab some fast food for dinner. But now with a partner, a foster son and a dog, there were always complicated arrangements to figure out.

Dakota was already on the bus home when I got hold of him and explained the situation. "Sure. I'll go up home and get Roby and then go down to Harry and Arleen's. I owe Brandon a rematch on Fluorescent Fighters anyway."

He was only four years older than Brandon, and the two of them got along pretty well. "Cool. I'll call you later."

I hung up and went back to Granny's diary.

> *I have been severely ill since we left the harbor. George attained his sea legs immediately, and he has been very kind, bringing me broth and plain toast whenever I have the stomach for it. I cannot help but consider, lying*

*feverish in my bed, whether this is God's punishment.*
*I must confess I do not possess the determination*
*George has for spreading the Book of Mormon to the*
*Hawaiian people. I just wanted to get out of Idaho*
*Falls. But I promise, if I recover, to be the best wife I*
*can be and devote myself to the Lord.*

Poor Granny, I thought. To love water the way she did—but find that being at sea made her sick. That had to be awful. And her doubts were touching. But I couldn't imagine a God who would punish someone who was trying to do good. At least let the poor woman get to Hawai'i!

Mike came back inside and we sat together for a while, both of us fidgeting. "What's going on in there?" he asked. Then his stomach grumbled. When I looked at the clock I realized it was almost six.

"You want me to ask the nurse?"

"Yeah."

I got up and walked down the hall to the nurses' station. "I wanted to check on Sandra Guarino," I said. "How's she doing?"

"Are you the dad?"

I nodded. "One of them."

To the nurse's credit she didn't even raise an eyebrow. "She's in the transition phase from active labor to delivery right now. She should be achieving maximum dilation within the next hour or so. She's carrying twins, right?"

I nodded. "Alpha and Omega."

"Interesting names."

"Oh, not their permanent ones. That's just what Sandra has been calling them."

"Well, you should be able to speak to them directly within the next two hours or so. Maybe sooner. But the doctor is monitoring her now to make sure there aren't any complications."

Cathy had briefed Mike and me about the possible problems with twin births, like twisted cords or breech births. Most twin pregnancies lasted only an average of thirty-five weeks. If the twins popped out too early, their lungs, brain and other organs might not be completely ready for the outside world, and they would be more vulnerable to all kinds of infections and developmental problems.

We were lucky that Sandra had been able to keep them inside as long as she had; the babies should be just a week or two short of full-term when they popped.

My stomach grumbled and the nurse smiled. "There's a vending machine down the hall if you want."

I thanked her and checked out the machine. I thought the turkey sandwiches would be safe. I got one each for Mike and me, a couple of bags of chips, and a couple of cans of soda. "Thank you, Lord," Mike said, when he saw what I was carrying. "I didn't get to eat lunch and I'm starving."

"Here you go," I said, handing him his food. "But you don't have to call me Lord. Kimo will do."

"How about numb nuts?" he said, around a mouthful of turkey sandwich.

We gobbled our sandwiches and then Mike yawned. "I'm going to catch some Zs. Wake me if anything happens."

I looked at him. "You can sleep?"

He shrugged and closed his eyes.

I got up and paced around for a while, imagining all the complications. I just wanted Alpha and Omega to be healthy. I sent up a couple of prayers, to the various gods of my childhood, promising to be the best dad I possibly could.

Then I sat down with Granny's journal again.

> *My seasickness has passed at last. George tells me he*
> *prayed for me, so maybe his prayers, and mine, were*
> *answered. I was finally able to go outside today, and the*

*ocean was so beautiful—a bright blue, sparkling in the
sunshine, stretching on for miles and miles.*

Good for Granny. I was glad she could enjoy a bit of the trip.

*This morning we docked at Honolulu. What a
sight! The tall, stately Aloha Tower, and the Royal
Hawaiian Band welcoming us with native music,
streamers, and the flower necklaces called leis. Mine is
just beautiful, a string of white and purple orchids that
smell heavenly. It is awfully hot here, though! One of
the elders from the stake in Laie met us and drove us
to our new home in a Ford just like my father's. The
simple cottage a few blocks from downtown is charming,
with large windows and a broad, overhanging roof.*

I skipped ahead. Granny was unhappy in Laie. George was
engaged in his mission every day, proselytizing and teaching.
Granny was bored by the other Mormon women and their focus
on home and family, and found them just as provincial as the
women of Idaho Falls. Laie was worse than Idaho Falls, though,
because at least there she had family and friends. And Idaho
was not so infernally hot. Their house was not even close to the
ocean. She complained about the strange place names and found
the few native Hawaiians she met frightening.

Suddenly the door to the delivery room burst open, and two
nurses and a doctor pushed Sandra out on a gurney. As they
sped down the hallway, Cathy stepped out carrying a tiny baby
wrapped in a blanket. She was wearing a hospital gown over her
clothes and had a mask on a string around her neck.

"What's the matter with Sandra?" I asked her.

At the same moment, Mike asked, "Did she have the babies?
Where's the second one?"

Cathy's face was streaked with tears. "The doctor called it

abruption," she said. "The first baby came out, and then Sandy started losing a lot of blood."

Another nurse followed Cathy out of the room. "It's a separation of the placenta from the uterus," she said. "It's a common complication with twins, but it is serious. Are you the donor?"

She looked at me and I was about to say that Mike and I were both the fathers, but Cathy stepped in first. "I told her you and Sandy have the same blood type."

"That's true," I said. "We're both AB and Rh negative."

"That's the rarest type," the nurse said. She was a Filipina in her fifties, with a kind face and dark hair in a bun. "I'm not sure we'll have enough on hand for what she needs. Can you donate?"

"Absolutely."

"Good. Come with me."

I left Mike with Cathy and the first baby. I didn't even know if it was the boy or the girl. The nurse motioned me into an examining room and said, "I'll be right back."

I couldn't sit down. I was so worried about Sandra and the other baby. Would it be all right? I had no idea what the medical condition entailed, but from the way they rushed Sandra out of the delivery room it couldn't be good.

The nurse returned with an armful of stuff. "Have a seat," she said. "Read this form and fill it out while I get ready for you."

I took the form from her and sat on the examining table. I skipped through the first part easily; I was healthy, and hadn't been in contact with anyone who wasn't. The second section was more complicated. I had to recall the details of the times I had been hospitalized, and remember the name of the pill I was taking for high cholesterol. I thought I was out of the wood when I finished that—until I came to the blood donation statement.

I had forgotten the bias blood banks had against gay men. When I came out of the closet I stopped giving blood as my own private protest against what I felt were archaic standards. I also stopped lying about my sexuality. I didn't walk around with a sign that read "I'm here, I'm queer, get used to it," but I answered questions honestly.

But if I answered yes to number seven on the form, that I'd had male to male sex within the past seven years (hell, within the past seven days) the nurse was going to tell me I wasn't qualified to give Sandra the blood she needed.

Fuck that. I checked "no" and completed the rest of the form and handed it to the nurse. She scanned it quickly, and I waited for her to catch me in my lie. After all, she knew that Mike and I were both the fathers of Sandra's baby, and she'd have to be clueless not to figure out what was going on.

But all she said was, "Give me your right arm."

I must have been fidgeting, because she said, "Please, sit still. Try to calm down. Sandra's going to be fine, and so are both the babies."

She didn't know that. But I closed my eyes and visualized my happy place, that deserted beach where I go with my surfboard, ready to catch the best wave I can. I felt the needle but I didn't flinch. I kept my eyes shut and focused on the waves rolling in.

"All done," she said. "You can go back to your partner and your baby."

So she knew. I got up and thanked her and walked back down the hall to the delivery room. No one was in the hallway.

I peeked in the door. Mike and Cathy were sitting in armchairs next to each other. Cathy was holding the baby and Mike, wearing a gown like Cathy's only much larger, was already playing peek-a-boo.

I stepped inside. "Get a gown," Mike said, pointing to a pile on a table.

"Any news on Sandra?" I asked, as I pulled on the gown.

"Not yet," Mike said. "This is the boy. Our son." He held the newborn out to me, wrapped in a blanket. His little eyes opened and he stared at me.

"Oh my God," I said, and my heart did a flip-flop. "He's amazing!"

The door opened behind me and I had to jump aside as the Filipina nurse stepped in. "Sandra's out of surgery and she's in recovery now. If you all want to come with me you can meet your new daughter."

Mike handed the baby back to Cathy, and we followed the nurse down the hall to another room. She pulled aside a curtain to reveal Sandra lying on a gurney. She looked like crap—her flyaway light brown hair was plastered to her scalp, and her eyes were red with tears. But she held the second twin clasped in her hands.

Mike stepped close to Sandra, and she handed the baby girl to him. I looked at the perfect little girl, and then at him, and when our eyes met, I began to cry. Mike followed me a moment later. Then Cathy and Sandra joined in.

"Look at us," Sandra said, wiping away her tears. "A bunch of crying fools."

"Very happy crying fools," I said.

Mike handed the girl back to Sandra. Cathy was slumped into a chair next to the gurney. I've seen victims of violent crimes who looked in better shape.

"So. Names?" I asked. We had discussed a bunch of options but never settled on any.

"This little one came out first," Cathy said, cradling the baby girl in her arms. "So we were thinking of calling her Amy. And then Owen for the boy."

"Alpha and Omega," I said. I popped out my cell phone and started taking pictures of the babies, which I emailed to all the grandparents along with the relevant details of time and weight. Each of us called our parents then, and the room was so noisy the babies began to cry. "Get used to this," I said to them. "You've come into a big, boisterous family."

A pair of nurses, drawn by all the noise, came in. "Time for both moms to get some rest," the first one said. "We'll take the little ones to the nursery. Are you breast feeding?"

"I'm going to try," Sandra said. "But I'm not sure this cow will have enough milk."

"We'll work things out," the nurse said. "Now you get some rest. Your babies will be hungry soon, and you need to recover from the C-section."

After a round of kisses between adults and babies, Mike and I walked out. It was close to eight o'clock. "Should we pick up Dakota and Roby?" I asked.

"You want to?"

"Actually, I was thinking we might have one last night without parental responsibility," I said. "What do you think about that?"

He grinned at me. "Does that involve the two of us getting naked?"

"You bet."

"Then I'm all for it. Meet you at home."

He leaned in and kissed me. "We're dads," he said. "I can't believe it."

"We've been dads since Roby came to live with us," I said. "We're just expanding the ohana."

I got home first; I always drive faster than Mike. Though he was only a couple of minutes behind me, I was already lying in bed naked, waiting for him. "That's something I'll never get tired of coming home to," he said, stripping his own clothes in record time and hopping into bed with me.

I turned toward him and we kissed. We both had five o'clock shadow and vending machine breath but it didn't matter. Both of us were hard and I felt the need pulsing through me. I slipped back against the pillows and raised my ass to him.

He scooted down and nuzzled his face against my ass cheeks. The bristly sensation made me crazy, even more so when he stuck his tongue up my chute and began flicking it back and forth.

My dick was already leaking precum but I didn't want to touch it. I reached down to run my fingers through his dark, wavy hair. He mumbled something.

"What? I can't understand you with your tongue up my ass," I said.

He pulled his face away. "I said, get the lube."

I reached over to the bedside table and struggled to open the drawer. We kept our sex stuff hidden away now that we had Dakota in the house with us. Even though he was gay, too, he was only fifteen, and what we did in the privacy of our bedroom was none of his business.

"Oh, give it a rest," Mike said, after I kept fumbling. He stood up and opened the drawer, then pulled out the bottle of lube. He stood beside me as he squirted some in his hand, then began stroking his dick lasciviously.

"Don't play with me," I said. "I need your dick in me ASAP."

"You're a bossy bottom, you know that?" he said. "Fortunately I find that kind of thing sexy."

He straddled me, holding my legs over his shoulders. I felt the muscles strain and wondered how long we'd be able to keep up such positions as we both neared forty. But what the hell, it worked now.

He fingered my hole with one, then two gooey digits, then carefully positioned his dick at the entrance. Then, ever so slowly, he slid into me.

We had long since stopped using condoms. We were both healthy and monogamous, so there was no reason for protection. Feeling his warmth inside me, skin to skin, was an awesome sensation. It got even better when he began moving back and forth, plowing farther and deeper into me. I moaned with pleasure as he hit my prostate and my dick jumped.

I reached for it but Mike batted my hand away. "This is my show." He wrapped his slippery fist around my dick and started jerking me in time to his motions. It reminded me for a minute of that old party trick, where you rub your stomach and pat your head at the same time, and I laughed.

"You think this is funny, bud?" He picked up the pace and all I could do was roll my head back against the pillow and give myself up to the sensations.

When I was twenty, all somebody had to do was touch my dick and I'd be ready to spout off. As I got older I was able to control myself better—or maybe the body just didn't respond so quickly. Either way, I struggled to hold out as long as I could, relishing the double feeling of Mike's hand on my dick and his cock up my ass.

Experience also led us to recognize each other's signals. As his breaths got faster and shallower, I knew that meant he was close to coming, and I allowed myself to let go, to welcome our orgasms. He slammed into my ass with one last massive thrust and I felt the heat of his sperm surge against my channel, and then I yelped with pain and pleasure and let go a stream of semen against my chest.

He let my legs down and rolled up next to me, with his arm around my shoulders and my head on his hairy chest. "Love you, babe," he said, then yawned. "Nobody's going to change that. Not even a pair of brand-new keikis."

"I love you too, sweetheart," I said.

He was snoring a moment later. I extricated myself from his arms and went into the bathroom, where I washed up. I couldn't sleep. I was too excited at the thought that our babies were in the world. So I sat at the kitchen table with my grandmother's diary.

I was eager to see how far the entries took her—would I see my grandfather there? The births of my father and his siblings? I skimmed through a couple of weeks of boring entries, Granny growing more and more disenchanted and unhappy.

*Today George came home early because he was running a fever. I put him to bed with a cold compress and tried to provide the same care for him he gave to me when I was sick on the boat.*

There were no entries for a couple of days.

*George continues to fade away and I feel powerless
to do anything to help him. A doctor came up from
Honolulu and said that he had never seen such a bad
fever. The more time I spend by his bedside, mopping
his brow, holding his hand, the more I realize how
much I care for him. He is such a good man, and does
not deserve such an illness. He loves this island and its
people, and I have come to see things through his eyes.
When one of the Mormon ladies comes to sit with him
for a few minutes, I walk to the ocean's shore and pray
to our God, and the gods of the Hawaiians, to heal
him. Those few moments by the water's edge are my
own salvation.*

Another gap of a few days.

*I have not been able to write for some time because my
heart has been too heavy. Just as I saw how much I
cared for my beloved George, he was taken from me.
He was buried two days ago in the cemetery on the hill.
Since then I have been in bed myself, prostrate with
grief. Today for the first time I am able to sit up, take
some broth, and pen a few words.*

*I do not want to go back to Idaho. There is nothing
for me there. Here, though, I may be able to make a
difference, and keep George's memory alive. And I have
come to love this island as George did, from the rough
surf to the tempestuous winds to the endless sunshine.
The elders have suggested that I go to Honolulu, where
a Mormon family has a spare bedroom, and I can find
some work as a teacher to support myself.*

I sat back. So that explained the story I had been told growing up, that Granny had come to Hawai'i as a teacher. Not exactly the truth—but then, I had learned from years as a homicide detective that the truth is rarely simple.

There was just a single page left in the diary.

> *Leaving Laie was harder than I expected. We had so few possessions and yet everything reminded me of George. A very nice young native man named Keali'i drove up from Honolulu to pick me up, and he helped me sort through everything and load up his truck. He was so very kind, and made this difficult process so much easier.*

That was it—at least for this volume. I would have to search through the rest of the boxes to see if Granny had started another diary of her life in Honolulu. I was pretty sure that the nice young native man named Keali'i was my grandfather. I wanted to read more, to see how their love affair developed and how their family had grown.

I yawned, and looked at the clock. It was after one in the morning, and I'd had a very long day. Time to go to sleep and rest up for the new day—and for dealing with the new life ahead of me.

# About the Author

NEIL PLAKCY is the author of *Mahu, Mahu Surfer, Mahu Fire, Mahu Vice, Mahu Men, Mahu Blood,* and *Zero Break* about openly gay Honolulu homicide detective Kimo Kanapa'aka. His other books include the *Have Body, Will Guard* series, the *Golden Retriever Mysteries,* and numerous stand-alone works of romance and mystery. His website is www.mahubooks.com.

# TRADEMARKS ACKNOWLEDGMENT

The author acknowledges the trademark status and trademark owners of the following wordmarks mentioned in this work of fiction:

ABC Store: ABC Stores

Ala Moana Center: General Growth Properties, Inc.

Ala Wai Marina: None

Alcoholics Anonymous: Alcoholics Anonymous World Services, Inc.

Aloha Tower Marketplace: None

Amazon: Amazon.com, Inc.

Barbie: Mattel Inc.

Big Wheels: None

Bluetooth: Bluetooth® SIG

Boston Style Pizza: Boston Style Pizza

Boy Scouts: Boy Scouts of America

Craig's List: craigslist

Facebook: Facebook

Hallmark: Hallmark Cards, Inc.

Hawaii Five-O: CBS

Honolulu Community College: University of Hawaii Community Colleges

Jaguar: Jaguar Land Rover Limited

Jeep Grand Cherokee: Chrysler Group LLC

Jell-O: Kraft Foods Global

Johnnie Walker: John Walker & Sons

Kia: Kia Motors America

KINE 105: Cox Media Group

Liberty House: Macy's Inc.

Lilo and Stich: Disney

Matson Line: Matson

Mercedes: Daimler AG

Moana Surfrider: Starwood Hotels & Resorts Worldwide, Inc.

Porsche: Dr. Ing. h.c. F. Porsche AG ("PAG")
Punahou: Punahou School
Reyn Spooner: Reyn Spooner, Inc.
Rolodex: Sanford, A Newell Rubbermaid Company
Salvation Army: The Salvation Army
Stanford University: Stanford University
Star-Advertiser: Star Advertiser
Starbucks and Frappuccino: Starbucks Corporation
The Mary Tyler Moore Show: None
Toyota and Highlander: Toyota Motor Sales USA
University of Hawaii: The University of Hawaii
Valium: Roche Products Inc., Hoffmann-La Roche Inc.
Vicks Vapo-Rub: Trademark Expired
Walmart: Walmart Stores, Inc.
Wheel of Fortune: Califon Products Inc.
Xbox: Microsoft Corp.
Youtube: YouTube, LLC
Zippy's: Zippy's Restaurants

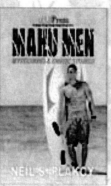

CPSIA information can be obtained at www.ICGtesting.com
Printed in the USA
LVOW12s0827050813

346296LV00001B/17/P